The Secrets Sisters Keep

By Abby Drake

THE SECRETS SISTERS KEEP
PERFECT LITTLE LADIES
GOOD LITTLE WIVES

The Secrets Sisters Keep

Abby Drake

AVON

An Imprint of HarperCollins*Publishers*

HarperCollins books may be purchased for educational, business, or sales promotional use. For information please write: Special Markets Department, HarperCollins Publishers, 10 East 53rd Street, New York, NY 10022.

FIRST AVON PAPERBACK EDITION PUBLISHED 2010.

Designed by Diahann Sturge

Library of Congress Cataloging-in-Publication Data
Drake, Abby.
   The secrets sisters keep / by Abby Drake.
      p. cm.
   ISBN 978-0-06-187832-9 (pbk.)
   1. Sisters—Fiction. 2. Family secrets—Fiction. I. Title.
PS3604.R345S43 2010
813'.6—dc22

2010015008

10 11 12 13 14 OV/RRD 10 9 8 7 6 5 4 3 2 1

For Lucky

The Secrets Sisters Keep

Chapter One

Uncle Edward had wandered off.

Ordinarily, it would have been little cause for alarm, as he often enjoyed an adventurous romp. But a grand celebration for his seventy-fifth birthday was scheduled this weekend, and the whole family was coming, maybe even Carleen, though no one knew that but Ellie, and Uncle Edward had sworn her to secrecy.

"I'll try the boathouse," Ellie shouted to Henry, Edward's man-friend, whom she wanted to blame for the disappearance. After all, Henry and Edward were lovers, and Ellie suspected Henry had been pressuring him to commemorate the birthday by crossing the border into Connecticut and getting married, which no doubt would affect Edward's will.

But that wasn't the problem right now.

Dashing from the terrace past the caterers, who were erect-
ing a white-and-gold tent in the south garden, power-waddling
down the embankment that led to the water at Lake Kasteel,
Ellie prayed nothing had happened, that Uncle Edward hadn't
slipped on the rocks and fallen and broken his damn neck. He
claimed to know every obstacle on his land, every tree root
and stone, every hollow and hill, but five acres was a lot of
ground, and sometimes he could be forgetful.

Besides, wouldn't tree roots and stones (unlike some ornery
people) shift and change over time?

Edward had bought the place during his years as a producer,
when all of Broadway had jostled and jockeyed for invitations
to his Gatsbyish parties at this lavish summer playground
north of New York City. Back then, Ellie, Amanda, Carleen,
and Naomi (whom everyone simply called Babe) had hidden
beneath the wide staircase in the mansion's big foyer or in the
fat, blue-blossomed hydrangea that cupped the slate terrace,
and muted their giggles and gasps while they'd observed the
comings and goings and in-betweens of this one and that, that
one and this.

It had been an exhilarating atmosphere (complete with
high drama and carnival acts), an education of a most notable,
inappropriate kind for four young sisters who summered with
their uncle while their parents were doing whatever they did
when they were *sans kids*.

Ellie had no idea if the voyeurism had harmed them.

Amanda had gone on to become a Park Avenue social-
ite, having married an architect who, Amanda hinted, often
worked with The Donald. They had three children who were
pretty but spoiled in a prep-school, lacrosse-playing way.

They'd honored Edward with their presence last Christmas: it was clear they had come for the gifts.

Babe had become a star in her own right, a strawberry blonde, voluptuous leading lady, now wed to yesterday's top-box-office, action-flick man who was much older but looked a lot younger thanks to a face-lift, maybe two. Ellie hadn't seen her youngest sister since Babe had left home, but she kept up on her life via e-mails and phone calls and *People* and *Us*, though the media attention had dwindled proportionately with each passing year.

Carleen, well, Uncle Edward had insisted on inviting her, and perhaps he was right, perhaps it was time.

As for Ellie, she'd had a quick marriage and a quicker divorce, thanks to Carleen. She'd moved from Manhattan back to Lake Kasteel, relinquishing her job as an Egyptologist at the Metropolitan Museum of Art and settling into cloistered recuperation far from public view.

Edward had decided, by then, to live in the mansion year round. So Ellie had become a kind of caretaker and, over time, had morphed into a beleaguering (she supposed) caregiver for him. The truth was, she was happier at home than out in the big world. After all they'd been through, who wouldn't have been?

But now it was many years later and guests had been invited, including her sisters, because Edward was seventy-five.

Seventy-five, but missing. It just wouldn't do.

"Uncle Edward!" Ellie cried as she reached the creaky old boathouse. "Where on earth are you?" She opened the slatted wooden door to the cottagelike structure and peered into the small, dark room. Mute wicker chairs stood wearing faded sheets; the air smelled like dampness and mildew and charcoal embers reminiscent of days when the cozy fireplace brought welcome relief from an unexpected storm.

But it had been forever since those summers of boating and sunbathing and toasting marshmallows at the end of the day. Back then they'd all gotten along; they'd loved one another in spite of themselves.

"Uncle Edward, are you here?" Her tone escalated to exasperation. She opened the door to where the boats were. Water lap-lapped the sides of the canoe as it tipped back and forth, back and forth. But in the next bay, where the rowboat should have been harbored, there was nothing. The rowboat was gone. Just like Uncle Edward.

Chapter Two

Amanda Dalton Delaney gathered the suit-
cases and duffels of her knotty clan—two ungrateful sons,
one princess of a daughter, and one besmirched husband, who,
she'd recently learned, was having an affair with a Brazilian
slut who waxed backs for a living.

She blotted the dampness from her brow. The last thing she
wanted was to go to this god-awful party.

She was, however, bound by guilt. After all, her kids had
Uncle Edward to thank for their educations, and she and Jonathan had Edward to thank for, well, a lot: Jonathan's job at
one of the top commercial architectural firms in Manhattan;
the brownstone at Park Avenue and East Eighty-first Street
that Amanda had required so her children could be raised in
the city, not the country; the major gift Edward donated most

years to the opera, rewarding Amanda and Jonathan with the finest seating at performances and special events. Edward had once commented that while he did not understand Amanda's penchant for opera over Broadway, at least it was real art, not like film, and New York was a real city, not like Hollywood.

Babe might have taken exception, but she'd been long gone by then. Besides, Amanda had always assumed Edward was the one who'd ponied up the funding for Babe's first starring role, which had ended up a commercial success, lucky Babe.

Tucking her crocheted handkerchief into her small purse, Amanda smoothed her white linen dress (which, with its touch of rayon, was guaranteed not to wrinkle) and toyed with the black Tahitian pearls at her throat. She mused at how unfortunate it was that Edward's generosity was limited to occasional outbursts, though she'd never known if providing a roof over her sister Ellie's head included an ongoing allowance.

Ellie, of course, was the most stable one of the bunch. If Amanda could arrange a few moments with her, she might reveal Jonathan's indiscretion. Trying to handle this alone was like needing a root canal: one second all was quiet, you thought you could forget it; the next second it flared, white-hot, as if shot by a needle straight into a nerve.

Rock-solid Ellie-the-eldest was a good choice to confide in. She would know how to respond; she was the compassionate sister, the nonjudgmental aunt. It did not matter that Amanda's children—while adoring Ellie in person—snickered off-camera at her organic cotton wardrobe of crop pants and shapeless cardigans that concealed a slightly round frame; at the fact that she used only scentless, all-natural lotions and soaps that hadn't been tested on animals, at least not on the kind one petted and named.

Still, Amanda might regret airing her dirty laundry even to Ellie, because it was distasteful and might open herself up for later persecution, especially if Uncle Edward found out about Jonathan. When Amanda first met Jonathan, Edward hadn't really liked him, had said he was *pusillanimous* (a word Amanda had needed to look up) in spite of having been raised in salt-of-the-earth Burlington, Vermont, in spite of having gone to Princeton. Of course, Edward was lactose intolerant and had never cared about the dairy products that once drove Vermont's economy. Nor did he appreciate anything Ivy League, having graduated from the *School of Hard Knocks, Magna Cum Laude.*

Amanda had never been sure if Edward had changed his mind about her husband. God forbid they should discuss anything that might conjure emotion.

Peering out the side window of the foyer now, she looked for the private car that would drive her with the luggage to Mount Kasteel and its coveted lake. Jonathan and the boys—"Huey and Dewey" Uncle Edward called them, claiming difficulty remembering their real names, Chandler and Chase—would take the train up that night. Heather would drive in with her *boyfriend du jour,* whom Amanda hadn't met but whose family had a home on Nantucket, where the couple had been sailing for most of the month.

So her kids would be there along with her husband and her long-lost celebrity-sister, Babe, with whom, for some reason, Amanda's contact over the years had been limited to happy holiday greetings. Ellie was the one who'd stayed in touch with their youngest sister and often passed on the news to Amanda, which was fine. Amanda was far too busy for inane correspondence.

But now Babe would be at Uncle Edward's, plus a couple of hundred other guests, according to Ellie.

Yes, it would be an interesting weekend. Secretly (only because Amanda dared not say it out loud and risk jinxing the possibility), she prayed Uncle Edward would choose this celebration to make a long-awaited announcement—a division of property, remuneration to his clan—now that he surely was nearing the end of his life.

And, God, she needed money, even more than she needed advice about Jonathan's back-waxer.

Amanda had no idea how large her uncle's fortune was, how much would come her way. Or if—after dutiful gifts to his servants and the man that he slept with—the bulk would be divided four ways or three, depending on whether Carleen was omitted, which of course she would be.

Wouldn't she?

Tipping back her head, Amanda let out a short laugh, surprised she'd entertained an absurd notion otherwise.

She quickly dismissed thoughts of Carleen and reeled her focus back to the prize.

The timing, of course, could not have been better. In addition to erasing her mounting debt (which would give new meaning to the word *bailout*), the inheritance would give her power. Power over the current adulterous situation. Power to finally show her pusillanimous husband a thing or two about the importance of money and status and being faithful.

She twiddled her pearls again and wondered if, instead of

all the nonsense, she should use that new power to step off her treadmill-of-a-life and just run away.

"Maybe he ran away," Henry said as he darted around the tent people and scampered ahead of Ellie down toward the boat-house. She'd gone up to the mansion and recruited his help: paddling a canoe was never easy for one person, especially when she was that person—a forty-seven-year-old, unath-letic, twenty-pounds-overweight recluse. At least Henry was lean ("as thin as a campaign promise," Edward often described him) and still nimble at age fifty-nine, which he credited to having developed an addiction to Ping-Pong in college.

"Why on earth would Edward run away?" Ellie barked. "He's been looking forward to this weekend."

"Maybe he realized he's too old for a comeback."

Henry tried to be funny whenever he spoke. Edward called it endearing; right now, Ellie found it irritating.

"The party was his idea," she retorted.

Henry opened the door without further comment, plod-ding into the darkness in his lime green Crocs, his boney knees nearly knocking beneath the hem of his madras Ber-mudas. He moved into the room, then into the bays where one boat sat, one did not. Ellie followed; her heart was beating quickly. She brushed back a few cobwebs, selected two paddles from the half-dozen that dangled from rusty wall hooks, and handed one to Henry. "You get in first," she said, "and steady the canoe."

Henry obeyed. Ellie, after all, was the keeper of the house. Edward often deferred to her, his eldest niece, as if she were the one who owned the big place, as if she had a sizable booty in her own name. Henry had been "with" Edward a couple of decades, yet despite the things he and Edward might or might not do behind Edward's closed bedroom door, Ellie knew she had more clout. Quite probably, Henry knew that, too.

He stabilized the canoe while Ellie stepped in and sat down facing the lake. The narrow seat was damp and probably dirty. She smoothed her beige cotton pants and palest-pink shirt, then adjusted the chinstrap of her straw gardening hat. She hoped she'd remember to change her clothes before the others arrived, especially Amanda, who tended to have a stroke when she saw her sister un-ironed.

Sliding the paddle into the water, she swiped it toward the back.

Henry responded with swift, wordless motion, as if they one-two paddled every afternoon.

The boat glided from its garage without argument.

"Let's try the island," Ellie yelled back, though there was no need to shout: neither powerboats nor spray-spritzing Jet Skis were allowed on Lake Kasteel, much to the dismay of un-suspecting vacationers who paid a New York fortune to rent four bedrooms on the waterfront and wound up with nothing noisy to do with the kids. "Maybe he decided to read." When the girls had been young and there was too much commo-tion, Edward frequently escaped to the uninhabited island ("Squirrels only," he'd remark) with a flask full of schnapps and a decent book. Dickens. Hemingway. Someone like that.

"He should know better than to go boating alone," Henry said, his jaw clearly clenched.

"If his intention was to go to the island to read, he wouldn't have considered it boating."

The reply sounded like *harrumph*.

"Besides, the boat has a life preserver," Ellie added, because she didn't want Henry to worry about that. He did, she supposed, really care about Edward. Why else would he have stayed long after the lights had gone out on Edward's career?

Extinguished, Edward had once called it matter-of-factly. *Like a last gasp before death.*

Ellie shivered a little and pushed on the paddle again.

Chapter Three

"*I've changed my mind,*" *Babe said as the plane* taxied toward the gate at JFK International.

"What?" Beside her, Wes adjusted his sunglasses and raked his fingers through his thinning, yet highlighted, hair.

"I can't do this." Though she heard from Ellie once in a while and politely hello-ed Amanda on an annual basis, there were reasons why Babe hadn't returned home in spite of her success at becoming a "star." Why had she let Wes talk her into it now?

Wes laughed. "Of course you can do this. It's all arranged."

"This is different. It's my family. Not a bash in the hills." The "hills" were the Hollywood Hills, where Babe hadn't been invited to a single party since she'd turned thirty-five

two years ago. She'd thought marrying Wes might have re-
ignited her career, but it turned out he was in worse career
shape than she was—his last four films had bombed, and the
once-famous six-pack of his abs now drooped from too many
decades on earth. At least he'd made up for what he'd lost in
appeal by having invested wisely when the going had been
good.

"Not to worry, darling," Wes repeated. He leaned over and
kissed her cheek, which, Babe knew, was smoother since she'd
secretly snatched eighteen thousand dollars from her husband's checkbook and had a few well-placed nips and tucks.
Thank God, the surgeon was discreet. "I've been trying to tell
you. Families are more important than you think."

She examined her manicure. An unpleasant tag of skin
scuffed her cuticle. "And I've been trying to tell you, you don't
know mine."

Since notice of the party had arrived (along with instructions to pack a white outfit for a special family photograph
Edward wanted snapped), Wes had talked a lot about his es-
trangement from his two sons. His ex-trophy-wife had moved
in with a talk show host who included her on his show every
day. The boys now went, too, taking the stage next to the host's
two Paris-Hilton-look-alike daughters. *Today's ideal blended
family*, the ratings acclaimed. Ouch.

Babe had never had kids, only an abortion, courtesy of Carleen, who'd been only too glad to arrange it. Even so, Babe
sensed her husband's sorrow. Which, she supposed, was one
reason she'd agreed to return to New York.

"Edward is no different from us," Wes had bellyached. "He
once savored the bright lights. He now knows the dark side.

Believe me, the man would give anything to have the good stuff back."

Babe wasn't sure about that, but she had decided to let Wes think he and Edward had something in common other than hailing from a similar generation. She'd learned from her previous unions that sometimes it was better to keep your mouth shut and let your man have his own opinion, especially when the topic didn't really matter. *Choose your battles,* her mother had advised one day when fourteen-year-old Babe had asked why Daddy had a mistress in midtown. She had thought that would have been a fair-sized battle in the marital arena, but Mother had shrugged and left Babe in the room, staring at the photo Babe had taken of her father and his lady-friend dining at the Algonquin. Mother had not given the picture a side-glance.

Still, Babe *chose her battle* whenever Wes babbled on like a male jerk. She reminded herself that his blah-blah didn't matter. What mattered was today and tomorrow. Which was why she'd already talked to her agent about launching a fragrance collection while some fans still remembered her name. Maybe she'd even add a line of signature jewelry. Moving forward made more sense than waiting around until she could be slotted for mature female roles, the kind Sarandon and Streep had made viable and fun. Besides, starting a business made more sense than continuing to peck at Wes's accounts just because hers were nearly depleted. Needing a man for financial support had never been in Babe's comfort zone. She'd watched her mother do that for too long.

The plane curved toward the gate and came to a stop. The seat-belt sign dinged, and Babe let out a sigh. Tugging at the hemline of her skirt, she supposed she shouldn't have worn spandex. Uncle Edward would dismiss her as too California; Amanda would say thirty-seven was too old to parade that kind of attire; Ellie would smile and keep any critical thoughts to herself. Thank God Carleen wouldn't be there.

"Smile," Wes said as he unclicked his seat belt and stood up. "You never know who might be in an airport."

They waited for the attendant to unseal the door, then stepped out of first class as if they still belonged there. They moved up the gangway and into the concourse. That's when, amid the clutter of gift shops and the reek of fast foods, cameras started flashing and someone boisterously shouted, "Wes! Babe! Wes and Babe! Over here!"

Oh, God, Babe thought. *What's happening?* But because she was a star and knew how to do this, she tossed a wide, automatic smile, glad Wes had paid for a recent whitening.

"See, darling?" Wes said with a naughty wink. "I still have a few friends here and there."

She laughed a sweet-sexy Babe-laugh, then surrendered again to the flash of the cameras, wondering what on earth her husband was up to, and if it was the real reason he had insisted that they come.

He wasn't on the island. Ellie and Henry had scoured the perimeter like cable TV reporters stalking the Red Carpet. But there was no sign of the rowboat, not even tucked in an inlet or a wooded hideaway, so there was no point in going ashore.

"Where now?" Henry asked.

Ellie scanned the lake from the castle at the south end to the hills to the north. The slate-colored water was as calm and flat as a nineteenth-century Hudson River Valley painting—

all that was missing was the morning mist, but it was no longer morning, it was after four, and the others would arrive soon.

Damn. Where was Edward?

She lowered the paddle into a huddle of lily pads and watched them part as if in a ballet. Edward liked being mischievous, that was true. In his younger years he'd enjoyed a reputation as an imp, a lively producer who, during rehearsals, would switch the prop water with gin just to watch the actor's reaction, who would hide a whoopee cushion inside a sofa just as the leading lady sat mid-monologue. His antics had not been harmful or hurtful, embarrassing, sometimes, but they'd always elicited laughter and an "Oh, Edward," with a swat or two to his cheek or his arm or, if he were lucky, a hearty grasp of his backside by a favored star.

To Ellie's knowledge, he had never disappeared.

"Maybe he's back at the house by now," she said, hoping she sounded optimistic. However, the truth was, Lake Kasteel was fairly large. They might not have seen him if he'd gone overboard; his rickety boat might have sunk. But though Edward had squandered most of his youth as a blue-eyed, roly-poly, quick-witted Irishman, a few years into his relationship with Henry, Henry had goaded him into fitness, beginning with T'ai Chi in a chair. Since then Edward was almost athletic, not knob-kneed like Henry, but fit enough to swim if a need arose.

So if he'd gone overboard, he still might be safe.

"If we circle the shoreline around the lake, we can check all the docks," Henry said. "Maybe he tied up the boat and went socializing."

But Ellie knew that Edward had never become friendly with the lake neighbors. Most of them, after all, were only there for the summer. Many of them had, at one time or another, no doubt peered through binoculars at the parties at Edward's, or rowed their own boats close to his section of shore. Nothing invasive, really. Just for a peek. Edward often said it was more fun to stimulate his neighbors' imaginations than to invite them over and have them see what bores his friends and he really were. *Haha.*

"I can't imagine whom he would visit," Ellie said. Then again, she couldn't imagine why he had left before the party. And why he hadn't told anyone. Especially her.

"Does he have any old acquaintances around here? A boyfriend, maybe?"

He did not mention a *girlfriend,* though Ellie supposed, like many, that Henry had heard the story long ago of Edward's heated affair with a woman—the purported *true love* of his life—whose identity remained a mystery. *She broke his heart,* the gossip had buzzed throughout Times Square, *so he turned back to men.* Ellie sighed and reminded herself that was ancient, unimportant history. "No, Henry," she said. "Edward has no old boyfriends around here."

"Let's go back, then," he said. "Maybe you're right. Maybe he's home."

She stroked once, twice, three times, turning the canoe. She waited until Henry caught up with her rhythm, then started paddling back toward the house.

Chapter Four

"*Pick me up Sunday evening at six*," *Amanda* instructed the driver as he pulled into the circular driveway inside the gates at *Kamp Kasteel*, the name the girls had once playfully christened Edward's lake mansion. She drained her champagne glass, set it in the holder, and opened the door as soon as the car stopped. There was no need to wait for help. She was home, after all. Well, sort of. "Leave the bags on the walk," she added, then took a deep breath and got out.

The place looked better in summer than in winter. Twisted arborvitae stood like sentries at the double front door, burgundy roses clawed their way up the stone walls, softballs of peonies tossed pinks and whites all over the lawn.

Once, Amanda had loved coming here. She'd loved watching the elegant women in their jewels and their hairdos, in their 1980s glitz. She had intended to become one of them: a wife of a renowned Broadway investor, perhaps, a man worth so much he could give it away. How could she have known Jonathan would not measure up?

"Ivy League, schmivy league," Uncle Edward had commented the night before she and Jonathan married. "I'm not sure he has spirit. You need a man with spirit, Amanda. You have so little of your own."

She hadn't been sure what Edward had meant. Ellie had told her to pay him no mind, that Edward was trying to be a competent parent, because by then their mother and father had been killed in the fire and there had been no insurance and Edward had assumed the role of their guardian and sole means of support, though Babe had been the only one not yet of age.

The truth was, Jonathan did not have spirit. But he'd loved Amanda, he really had. And he'd stood by her through the whole scandal, saying he would still marry her, and, by God, he had. She wondered if he'd be as loyal to the Brazilian back-waxer under similar circumstances, as if anything could come close to being "similar."

Pursing her lips, Amanda rang the doorbell the way she had rung it since Uncle Edward had announced he had found a man. She'd said she hadn't wanted to invade his privacy, but in fact, she hadn't wanted any surprises. She'd had enough of those—hadn't they all?

She stood for a moment, aware that the driver had dropped the bags in the driveway and driven off. She rang again. Still, no one came.

Applying another light layer of lipstick, she blotted her lips and opened the door.

"Hello? Uncle Edward? Ellie?" She hoped she sounded happy to be there. "Is anyone home? It's me, Amanda-Belle." She used the childlike name Edward used to call her, back when she'd had those dreams about status and jewels. "You dream like an airhead from the south," Edward had said. "A mint-julep-sucking, Tennessee Williams, southern *belle*."

The name had stuck.

She stepped inside, feeling the familiar chill of the foyer, where the local-quarried, cool limestone negated the need for air-conditioning. "Edward? Hello?"

A tall, Spanish-looking woman in a pink dress the color of the peonies came from the kitchen. She seemed vaguely familiar. She wiped her hands on her white apron. "Hello."

"*Hola* to you. Where's my uncle? Where's Edward?"

The tall woman smiled. "Edward is not here."

"Not here?" Surely Amanda did not have the weekend confused. She'd spoken with Ellie only last week.

The woman shook her head. "No. Edward is missing."

Missing? Good Lord, why hadn't he learned to hire people from this country, who understood English? Of course Edward couldn't be missing. It was his birthday and his goddamn party. "Where is my sister? Señorita Ellen?"

The tall woman smirked. "*Señorita* Ellen is out on the boat. With *Señor* Henry. Looking for *Eduardo*."

The housemaid seemed rather sarcastic. "Have any other guests arrived? My sister, Babe? Señorita Movie Star?" Amanda flailed her hands as if that would accelerate the maid's comprehension.

The woman cocked an eyebrow but didn't respond.

Amanda touched her temples. She felt a headache coming on, perhaps from the champagne.

"I'll just go to my room," she said and turned to the staircase that she knew so well. "Our bags are in the driveway. Please have someone bring them upstairs." She did not care if the woman understood what she'd said. Sooner or later someone would trip over the suitcases and they would arrive inside. In the meantime, if Amanda could lie down, she would feel so much better. When she awoke, maybe Chandler and Chase would be there and she could fuss over them and pretend not to notice the rest.

Wes dozed with his head on Babe's shoulder.

She looked out the car window at the steel-strangled boroughs of Brooklyn and Manhattan and realized that sometimes her husband could be a genius. It turned out that Stan-somebody, one of Wes's old stunt doubles, was now a photographer for *Hot Cars* magazine and was based in New York. Wes had made a quick call before they'd left LAX, and lo and behold, Stan had been waiting at JFK with a sleek camera and a huge lens that had attracted attention. Once his shutter had started clicking, others followed suit—cell phones, mostly, but who cared? It was as if other people wanted to get in on the excitement.

In the media world, Stan could sell the photos of Wes McCall and his lovely wife, Babe, traveling back east to attend the seventy-fifth birthday celebration of Edward Dalton, producer of original Broadway hits including *Central Park*, *Seasons*, and *Tunnel of Love*. The accompanying story, however, would no doubt exhume the family dirt, because it had been years and God forbid anyone had forgotten.

Still, it would mean their pictures would be somewhere—that they would be *visible*—at least in the *Post*. Maybe, oh, God, maybe, in the *New York Times*. Visibility was such an important part of not being forgotten. It would be too bad, though, if her family had to suffer for it. Maybe they wouldn't mind. She'd been invited, after all. What would they expect?

"Happy now, darling?" her husband whispered, not that he had to, for the privacy glass was raised high between them and the limo driver.

"Mmm," she replied. She might have rewarded him with sex later that night, but Wes had lost his balls in a motocross accident before they were married, so sex wasn't part of their lives. *Compromise,* Babe once believed, was essential in marriage and in life. Sort of like choosing one's battles.

Luckily the press (or the fans) didn't know about Wes's unfortunate state, any more than Wes knew that sometimes Babe wished . . . *oh, never mind,* she scolded herself. She looked back out the window and forced a smile. "Maybe we'll both have an offer or two by the time we get home." If she only had one more juicy role, life would be so much more livable.

"Or maybe your uncle will find us work in New York."

Babe blinked. The first time she'd met Wes, his trademark royal blue eyes had become Fourth of July sparklers. "You're originally from New York?" he'd asked. "Why aren't you acting on Broadway?"

Naturally, he'd heard of Edward (all those Tonys!) and had had a vague recollection about a scandal, but Wes had been too wrapped up in production (and, Babe suspected, in himself) to pay much attention. Besides, that had been on the East Coast, and Wes had been on the West, and cable TV had barely been invented, let alone YouTube or Facebook or Twitter.

So Babe had laughed and simply said the scandal was a small family matter, and surely he knew that the media sensationalized whatever they wanted.

He hadn't asked further details; he'd seemed more enthralled with her Broadway connection.

"Imagine performing live—applause five nights a week and three matinees! God, I'd give up my left nut for that."

Of course, he'd already given up his left nut and his right one, too, but he hadn't shared that information just yet. Instead, he'd bought her a drink and they went out to the terrace and studied the smogged-in skyline. He seemed nice, and was handsome enough for his age, though Babe had long ago become immune to good looks. After a while, he asked for her number, and she gave him her real one because he was a star, too, and that's how it worked. Unspoken trust. Paparazzi-protected.

Unlike Wes, Babe wanted no part of the theater. Acting to an audience was so . . . *intimate*. It was hardly at all like pretend. With film there were different angles and lighting and a billion takes to get it right. Even after that, they could reshoot if needed, or simply toss the scene out if the director said it didn't work.

No such luck in the theater.

You were who you were. There was no hiding.

Besides, there was more money in films. Or, at least, there once had been.

She bit her lip and lowered her eyes. She supposed some

of Edward's former theater cronies would be at the party. "It will be just like the old days," Ellie had said when she called. "Well, maybe not exactly like those, but it will be fun."

"I thought Edward had given up entertaining."

"This is different. He's seventy-five."

"Is he sick? Is he dying?"

"I don't think so."

"He isn't vying for a comeback, is he?"

"Please, Babe," Ellie had said without answering the question. "I need you here. I've wanted to see you for so long. And I still can't seem to get on a plane to go there."

"Why not?"

Ellie had sighed and explained that she rarely left Kamp Kasteel. She'd tried a few times; she'd had what she thought might be panic attacks. "Let's just say, I'm better off here."

Babe hadn't believed her, but she knew that as long as Ellie believed it, that's how it would be.

And so there was Babe, the youngest sister, the youngest niece, pretending this weekend was about merriment and a birthday and not about resurrecting old ghosts. She was glad Wes was with her, glad she would have him as a diversion, glad that his presence would help remind her of how far she'd come. Yes, Wes was a good enough man, a good enough companion. It shouldn't really matter that she didn't love him.

"I'm going to call the police," Henry announced.

They'd tied up the canoe and left the boathouse, and now were walking up the hill, past the hubbub of decorators who wove tumbles of fairy roses around wire trellises like dollops of confection on a tiered birthday cake.

"No," Ellie snipped. "No police." Though they'd never discussed it, Henry was neither stupid nor blind, nor had he lived on another planet when everything had happened. Surely he knew the last thing they would want now was public attention, law enforcement or otherwise, no matter how much time had passed. "I think Edward has chosen to disappear. If so, he must have decided it's for our own good."

"He's missing. The boat's missing. How can that be for anyone's good?"

"It only means he's gone somewhere. It doesn't mean he's dead. If he drowned, there would be a rowboat and no Uncle Edward." She sounded terse, matter-of-fact. Not at all like the water-logged loofah her stomach had become.

"The police can dredge the lake. Maybe they'll find the boat. Maybe they'll find . . . him." He choked back some tears. If she'd been closer, she might have seen his knobby knees knock.

"No, Henry," she repeated. "Not yet." She tried to soften her tone. None of this, after all, was his fault, no matter how easy it might be to think otherwise.

"Then, when?"

"My sisters will be here soon. We can discuss what to do together. The party doesn't start until noon tomorrow. If he doesn't come home tonight, my guess is he'll turn up in the morning."

"What makes you so sure?"

She could have reminded Henry that he was the first who'd said Edward had run off on purpose. But she sensed he was scared now, no longer trying to be funny. "Once," Ellie said, "when we were children, Uncle Edward said he'd seen a monster in the lake. Years later he admitted he'd had no idea what to do with four small girls. He was terrified we'd all drown, so he figured if he made up a story and frightened us, we wouldn't go near the water. As far as I know, to this day Babe doesn't know how to swim."

"I fail to see a connection."

"He might be trying to distract us from something bigger. Like the fact that his three—maybe four—nieces are getting back together."

They reached the back door. Ellie stepped into the mudroom and removed her straw hat.

"Señorita Ellie," Martina, the caterer, called out in an exaggerated fake accent. "Your *see-ster* has arrived. She *eees* upstairs taking a siesta."

Ellie had no idea why Martina was pretending to speak quasi-Spanish when she'd been born and raised in Westchester County, had graduated from Le Cordon Bleu London, and had returned to New York, where she'd opened her own business that was now quite successful. Ellie would deal with that later. Right now, the important thing was that Amanda was there.

Then the sponge in Ellie's belly twisted again. She pressed her hand up against it and said a silent prayer that the sister who'd arrived indeed *was* Amanda, not Carleen.

Chapter Five

Instead of sleeping, Amanda stared at the ceiling. She'd changed from her linen into a Dior cotton robe that was as white and soft as if it had been washed hundreds of times though it still looked brand-new. She wondered if Jonathan's slut knew enough (had enough money!) to buy quality, and if Jonathan noticed or cared.

Turning onto her side, Amanda gazed at the wall that had been papered with a lavender foil stripe in the eighties and now was painted pea green. Last fall, Ellie had convinced Edward to have the entire house redone, and the decorator had gone wild with shades of vegetable purées. Not that it mattered, Amanda thought. It wasn't as if anyone important went there anymore.

She wondered how many more visits she would have to

endure while pretending her own family was perfect. She wondered if Jonathan would ask for a divorce before Edward died; if so, would Amanda be penniless?

She flipped to her other side.

She wasn't sure if the state of her husband or the state of her finances—or the combination!—was keeping her from a nap. How could she not be worried about both?

For one thing, it might not be long before Jonathan discovered that their checkbook was in ruins.

For another, if she and Jonathan divorced, the kids would be in college, fiscally secure, but what about her? Would she be beholden to Uncle Edward, her existence left up to his whims, her reputation and her pocketbook bankrupt? Would she be destined to move into the pea green room at the lake the way Ellie resided in a room that now resembled a butternut squash?

She could sell her furs, but she already had, feigning a naturalist conscience. She could sell her jewels, but she couldn't remember which ones she'd already pawned and replaced with counterfeit copies. She could try to arrange another equity line on the brownstone, but the bank had said last time was the last time.

Living on Park Avenue had, after all, come with engraved expectations. The charity luncheons and teas and balls included a surreptitious price of wearing proper attire and toting a checkbook. A *big* checkbook.

The truth was, Amanda was nearly insolvent, though hopefully no one had guessed. She'd done such a remarkable job of juggling one credit card against another.

As long as she stayed married, there would be cash flow,

however meager, from Jonathan's job. But if he'd fallen in love . . .

The cream-colored drapes fluttered as if they, too, had caught a chill, the same kind of chill Amanda had felt when she'd seen the business card trapped in the pocket lining of Jonathan's Armani. *Bibiana*, the fancy, swirling type read. *Personal Waxing.* Amanda had frowned and turned the card over. Bibiana had signed *Bibi* on the back, then had written her phone number and added a heart with an arrow through it.

A freaking heart! What the hell was that about?

Two days had passed before Amanda had been able to access her husband's BlackBerry, where, in his words, he stored his life. The contact page had been easy to find. Of course, he had included Bibiana's Web site and home addresses, because even *Ivy-league, schmivy-league* alumni sometimes could be plain stupid.

Back-waxer to Broadway Stars! the Web site had proclaimed in the same swirly, twirly type as on the bimbo's business card. Amanda had never heard Uncle Edward mention that back-waxing was a priority onstage. But she did know that Jonathan barely had chest hair, let alone any on his back. And though they'd been married for so long that they rarely examined one another's follicles, Amanda would have sworn his pubic hairs were exactly as they'd always been: springy and intact.

She'd done a mental scan of his existing underarms and outer arms and his calves that had stayed muscled since his soccer-playing days. Nothing was different, nothing was . . . gone. Which left only one reason for Jonathan to need a back-waxer in his life.

Amanda gripped her stomach now as if she was going to

vomit. She closed her eyes according to the teachings of her yogi and tried to force herself to visualize happy things: St. Barths in April, the Hamptons in August. But even those images could not erase the scene she had witnessed three nights earlier when she'd stalked her own husband to an apartment block in Queens, then watched from an alley—a dark, filthy alley!—for more than two hours until he'd casually exited, straightened his hair, rearranged his Brooks Brothers tie, and checked to be certain he had properly zipped up his fly.

Ellie smelled like a pond and looked even worse. After going upstairs, she'd noticed the door to the green room was closed. Carleen surely wouldn't have usurped Amanda's space, so Ellie's prayer had been answered.

With a grateful sigh, Ellie had grabbed clean clothes and gone straight to the shower, where she now stood, letting the hot spray singe her flesh, wondering what Edward, the sneaky old goat, had done this time and what would happen next. Surely he had disappeared on purpose, as she'd suggested to Henry. Surely he had carefully arranged it to teach his nieces some sort of lesson.

Yes, of course, that was the answer.

She lathered her hair and tried not to wonder, If that were the case, why hadn't he told Henry his plans to trick them? Why had he risked upsetting Henry, too?

"Ellie," Edward had said that morning as they'd sat in the breakfast room, his eyes scanning page one of the *New York Times,* which Kevin, the paperboy, had just delivered. Edward's fingers had been tapping his poached egg at the top, the same way he'd been tapping every day for years. "We're going to have a busy weekend. I trust the caterers and florists are prepared?"

"And the bands and the magicians and the fireworks technicians."

He lifted a small finger. "Pyrotechnic specialists," he corrected.

She smiled, wryly, she supposed, because sometimes Uncle Edward's silliness grated on her nerves. Of course he knew the caterers and florists were prepared: he'd left her in charge, hadn't he?

"And the rooms are all made up?" he asked, that time sipping his tea and flicking his gaze from the newspaper to Ellie with a slight hint of . . . what? Remorse? Regret for having been impulsive?

"Yes," Ellie replied. "Amanda's children will stay in the guest rooms on the third floor. Amanda, Babe, and"—she took a tiny breath—"Carleen will each have their old rooms. As you requested."

He nodded, nibbled on the egg white, then dipped a triangular toast point into the sunny yolk. "And the girls all know to bring a white outfit for the family picture on Sunday?"

"Yes. Of course." Ellie had wanted to ask again if he were sure about having the party, if he were sure it was a good idea to reunite them all under such public conditions. She'd wanted to point out that it was not too late to call it off, that paying cancellation fees might make more sense than going through with it. But except for that one flick of a gaze, Edward was in a jolly mood, and tomorrow was his birthday, after all.

"You still think I'm a fool," he'd said abruptly.

She shook her head. "Whatever you want is fine."

"Including your sister?"

It went without saying that he'd meant Carleen.

Ellie had stood up to clear the table. "Whatever you want," she repeated, then went to her uncle and kissed his cheek. "Have a happy day. I'll see you later. I have a lot to tend to."

And that was the last time Ellie had seen Uncle Edward as he'd dunked another toast point, taken another sip of tea, and turned to page two.

Rinsing her hair now, soaping up her body, Ellie felt slow sadness seeping in. What if Edward wasn't playing a game, what if something had really happened? Was it possible? He could have become ill . . . there could have been an accident . . . though why on earth was she spending time thinking about this now, when obviously the answer was not yet apparent, and she had so much to do? And so many people . . . Amanda, Babe . . . Carleen . . . ?

She closed her eyes and let her tears rain down her cheeks, her throat, and her saggy breasts as she privately called them, though they really were only, what? Thirty-five? Had she been twelve when she'd begun to sprout? Why did she barely recall being twelve? Or fourteen? She only remembered how she'd longed to travel to Egypt, to explore, to discover, to unlock ancient mysteries and reveal hidden truths. It had seemed so romantic to a young girl who'd spent so much time taking care of three younger sisters. Three younger sisters and then Uncle Edward.

Grabbing for a washcloth, Ellie wept. She wept for the childhood that was long past her now, for her unmet dreams of joy and love. Of the four sisters, only Ellie had wound up alone, alone with saggy breasts and thick legs and a spongy bottom and a big bucket of nothing that her life had become.

And now, if Edward was gone . . .

She wept some more, her denial washing away, layer by layer, circling the drain in a great sucking vortex. What was she going to do with her life if, *when*, Edward, her shield from the world—yes, she'd known all along that he'd been a shield—was nothing more than a few cupfuls of ashes sealed in a marble urn?

Twenty minutes later, Ellie pushed herself into a cotton shirt and skirt that were pale aqua and matched her eyes. She brushed her wispy curls, which had once been light brown but were now woven with silver. She applied a light layer of pastel peach lipstick and decided she was as ready as she'd ever be: tears dried, mask of contentment back in place.

After checking with Martina ("No, your uncle *eees no return*"), Ellie took a deep, get-ready-breath and guided her Birkenstocks to Amanda's room.

"I have no idea where Edward is," Ellie announced after Amanda ordered her in. Perching on the window seat that overlooked the driveway, Ellie realized that even as a child, Amanda had always needed an unobscured view, needed to feel in control of something, or at least to be on the lookout in case a shoe dropped. The driveway was quiet now, but it would soon enough be stacked with Mercedes and Jaguars and one or two shiny Bentleys.

"Well, this is absurd." Amanda sat up, plumped a satin pillow, and dangled her legs from the edge of the four-poster bed. She looked worse than she had at Christmas. Two years younger than Ellie, she now appeared older, with pronounced lines at her eyes and mouth and no sign of Botox or even a peel. The lines were, perhaps, a product of marriage or maybe motherhood.

Ellie shrugged. "It's his party. I guess he can disappear if he wants to."

Of course that incensed Amanda, who bolted to her feet and started pacing, an asinine routine the woman had perfected. In the past few years, she'd added a vigorous wringing of her hands. "Don't be ridiculous. He's invited two hundred people—*VIP* people, or at least they once were. Why would he disappear?"

Ellie could have commented, "Why has Uncle Edward ever done anything?" but decided it would be more positive to defend him. Positive for him, annoying as hell for Amanda. "He's probably distressed over the excitement . . . you know, the anticipation. I'm sure he'll be home in time for dinner."

"Is that man with him?"

"Really, Amanda. *That man* has a name. And, no, Henry did not go with him. For what it's worth, Henry is upset. He's afraid something terrible has happened. An accident, maybe."

Amanda stopped pacing. Good Lord, she seemed to brighten. "An accident? Does he think Edward is dead?"

"Don't worry, I'm sure he's fine."

"You're probably right." Amanda dropped back onto the bed. "He'll no doubt be back for dinner. Uncle Edward loves to eat." Then she started to cry.

Ellie hadn't expected Amanda to be distraught. Ambivalent, maybe, but not distraught. "Amanda-Belle," she said, rising from the window seat and walking to comfort her. "He's fine, really he is." But as she put her arm on Amanda's shoulder, her sister waved her away.

"It isn't Edward," she said with a delicate sniff. "It's other things. It's . . . oh, why does life get so complicated?"

Ellie had no idea what her sister was complaining about. Of all of them, surely Amanda had a good life. In some social circles, her life would be deemed the most successful. "If life wasn't complicated, it wouldn't be fun."

Amanda sniffed again. "Well, mine isn't much fun anymore."

It was the first time Ellie had ever heard her sister imply that all was not as grand as it seemed. "Are the kids okay?"

Amanda nodded. "They're fine. It's Jonathan." She inhaled, she exhaled. "Get me a tissue. Please."

Ellie turned to the highboy and snatched several tissues from a fresh box that had been set out when the room had been "made up," as Uncle Edward had called it.

Amanda sniffed again. "Swear to me you won't tell another living soul what I'm about to tell you."

Handing her the tissues, Ellie was about to swear when the sound of a horn beep-beeped outside. She looked down to the driveway, to a white stretch limo. The back door opened and Babe got out.

Chapter Six

"Babe."

"Ellie?"

"Babe."

"Wow. I can't believe I'm really here." Babe burst into tears and flung her arms around her oldest sister's neck. "I can't believe I haven't seen you in so long. You look terrific. You don't look old or ugly or anything. You just look terrific."

"You are such a liar," Ellie said. "It's been almost twenty years." Their cheeks dampened with glee.

After a moment, Ellie extricated herself back and took Babe's face in her hands. "And look at you. You are so beautiful. You are such a star."

Babe dabbed her eyes, though no makeup had dared to run.

"I have missed you—I have missed all of you—so much." She cried again.

Grasping Babe's hands, Ellie gently shook them. "Well, you're here now. That's all that matters, isn't it?"

With a happy nod, Babe said, "Yes," then turned back toward the car. That's when Ellie noticed the gentleman in sunglasses leaning against the trunk, his tanned arms folded, a half smile on his familiar face. "This is Ellie!" Babe proclaimed as she tugged her sister toward the man. "And Ellie, this is Wes McCall."

Ellie let go of Babe long enough to shake hands. When they'd learned about Babe's marriage to Wes, Uncle Edward had rented every one of his movies, and they'd spent four days and three nights hunkered down in the media room eating popcorn and Juju Bears until their stomachs had hurt.

"Yes," Ellie said, "I recognize him." She did not say it would be nice if he removed his sunglasses, that *Hollywood* glasses had no place at Lake Kasteel.

"It's a pleasure to meet you," Wes said dutifully.

"Ellie is the oldest," Babe said, then let out another whelp when she looked past her toward the front door. "Amanda-Belle!" She dumped Ellie like a worn-out boyfriend and darted toward Amanda, who looked more composed than Ellie suspected she felt.

"Babe, darling," Amanda said, warding off a hug with a simple kiss-kiss. "How nice to see you again." She said it as if she'd only seen Babe in the spring. Then she eyed Babe's skirt and was about to speak again when Babe asked, "Where is Uncle Edward?"

Uncle Edward?

Oh, him.

Amanda looked at Ellie, who looked at Babe.

"Well," Ellie said, invoking her most genuine smile, "the truth is, we're not really sure." Then she moved toward the limo to help with the bags.

As they walked into the house, Ellie tried to explain about Edward's unexplained departure. "You remember what a jokester he is," she said, setting a suitcase on the stone floor of the foyer. She laughed. "He's worse now than ever." She hoped Amanda and Babe would be buffaloed by her nonchalance.

Babe grew oddly quiet. "It will be good to see him. When I left he was still a fairly young man."

Ellie laughed again. "And he continues to act like he is. He does T'ai Chi every day, and he walks everywhere. And he plays Ping-Pong with Henry at night."

"Henry?"

"Edward's man-friend," Amanda said, rolling her eyes and marching toward the library.

"Haven't I told you about Henry?" Ellie asked.

"I don't remember," Babe said with a delicate sigh. "I suppose you have. But so much has happened over the years. There's so much I've missed."

No one commented it was her own fault, that, unlike Carleen, she'd been welcome to return any time.

"Well, you're home now," Ellie said, giving her another hug. "That's all that matters."

Babe scrutinized the foyer. "Wow. It looks the same, and yet it doesn't. It looks smaller, you know?"

Ellie laughed. "That's because you remember it when you

were a little girl. Everything seems so much bigger when we're small."

"But it's nice," Babe said. "It's really, really nice." She was wistful, no doubt reminiscing.

Amanda let out a throat-clearing noise that sounded like *Ahem.* "Pardon me for interrupting," she said, "but can we continue this later? Ellie and I have a few things to discuss, and I'm sure the two of you would like to freshen up."

Babe's husband finally removed his sunglasses. "Good idea. I need to recuperate from the flight if I'm going to keep up with you girls."

"By all means," Ellie said. "Go ahead upstairs. Come back down when you're ready."

Then Babe said, "Sounds good. Which room is ours? Oh, wait. I want one of the big, grown-up rooms. It's time, don't you think? We'll take Carleen's! On the north side." The couple began to ascend, with bags in each hand, and Amanda took three steps toward the library.

"No!" Ellie shouted abruptly. "You must sleep in your own room!"

Everyone halted, then all stared at Ellie.

Babe laughed. "That room is too small for us."

Ellie wrung her hands the way she'd seen Amanda do. "But I've had it redone."

"Is it bigger?"

"No."

"Well, then," Babe added and took another step. "It's too small."

"I said *no!*" Ellie screamed, because what choice did she have? She considered saying Carleen's room was under construction or was being fumigated, or had been quarantined—anything she could muster. But sooner or later, they might learn otherwise. So Ellie stiffened her spine, squeezed her eyes shut, and quietly said, "You can't use Carleen's room because it's for Carleen."

Silence.

Then Ellie opened her eyes and saw her two sisters frozen in place, their eyes riveted, their faces pale. Wes, however, kept climbing. He no doubt didn't know any better.

"Uncle Edward invited Carleen," Ellie added. "We don't know if she's coming."

"Why?" Babe asked. "Why did he invite her?"

"He said she has changed. She's married. Has kids. Teaches ninth-grade algebra."

"Ha!" Amanda chided. "She'll come. If she's a teacher, she most likely needs money."

"Look," Ellie said, "Edward invited her, so it's out of our hands. I think he wants us to reunite before, well, before he dies. You know?"

"I thought you said he wasn't dying," Amanda snapped.

"I said . . . oh, Lord, I don't know what I said. But he's seventy-five. He has to die sometime. In the meantime, we don't even know if Carleen will be here. She didn't reply." Ellie was as flustered as she knew she must sound.

"Well," Babe said, hoisting her bag, her cheeks growing pink, her eyes turning to steel. "I hope everyone has a nice time. My husband and I will be leaving." She glared up at Wes, who was on the landing halfway up the stairs. "We're taking the next flight back to L.A."

"Babe . . . ," Ellie said.

"No!" Babe yelped as if she'd been wounded, which, of course, she had been, way back when.

"Don't stop her," Amanda growled. "Let her run away. She does that so well." She folded her arms and looked smug.

"I did *not* run away!" Babe retorted. "I left this crazy family and made something of myself."

"Oh, right. You're an *actress*. How could I forget?"

It wasn't the first time Ellie had heard that Amanda thought Babe's career was shameful. Jealousy, Ellie suspected.

"Good God," Babe said. "You're as much of a snot as you always were."

Amanda snorted and hoofed into the library.

"By the way," Babe called after her, "you look like hell!"

"Babe . . ." Ellie tried to reason, but Babe dropped the suitcase, stomped across the stone floor, and charged out the front door.

"Well," Wes said from above, "I can see the family reunion is off to a great start."

They shouldn't have come. She'd known it, she'd known it, she'd known it since Ellie's phone call and the invitation.

Babe should never have returned to New York, to this house, to this family. What had made her think things would have changed?

Kicking off her shoes, not caring where they landed, she made her way from the driveway to the side of the house. She passed through the tall gate set in the thick hedges and ended up in the rose garden, which was as fragrant and lovely as when she'd been a kid. She tramped on the lawn as if it were a barrel of grapes and she, a vintner.

"Bitch," she muttered. "Amanda-Belle bitch." She flopped on a bench tucked next to a trellis and wondered why Edward had been so unkind as to invite the one person Babe never wanted to see again. Ever.

Carleen.

Argh.

Not Amanda, the bitch, but Carleen.

Plucking a red rose, Babe lightly touched its soft petals. Arguing with Amanda was nothing new. Still, Babe supposed it wasn't right to take out her frustration on her when Carleen was the culprit. Carleen, who had once been Babe's idol, the sister closest to her in age, the one she'd emulated.

Carleen, after all, had been the most vibrant. Her eyes had been big and green and framed with dark lashes; her posture had been straight, her aura, confident. Her hair had been a blend of auburn and copper, the colors of oak leaves in autumn. "Carleen's our natural beauty," their mother had often proclaimed. When Carleen was thirteen and Babe was ten, that type of comment had not bolstered Babe's self-esteem.

It might have been easier if Carleen had not used her "natural beauty" to her advantage.

When Carleen was a freshman, she had a boyfriend named Louis. He was a junior, the star of the basketball team.

"Take your sister with you," Father had ordered Carleen when she was dressing for the winter carnival game.

"No," Carleen retorted, pulling on fuzzy leg warmers for which Babe would have given a whole year's allowance. "Louis and I have a date."

"He's playing basketball, you're sitting in the bleachers. That's not a date. Besides, your mother and I are going out. If you don't take your sister, you will stay home and babysit her."

"Where's Amanda?"

Father hadn't answered because he had given his orders, and he never liked it when Carleen sassed him back.

Babe had hardly been able to contain her excitement. She'd scurried around the room that she shared with Carleen, looking for something that might make her look grown up and pretty. She hadn't been to the high school before—seventh graders didn't usually have the chance.

Carleen shook a stern middle finger at her sister. "You'd better not ruin this for me."

Babe shook her head. "I won't. I promise." She opened another drawer and took out her *Ride, Sally Ride* T-shirt to put on over a black turtleneck.

"No," Carleen said with a big, huffy sigh. "You are not wearing that to the game."

It was Babe's favorite shirt, the one Mother had bought her the summer before when the famous astronaut, Sally Ride, was the first American woman to go into space. "You girls can do anything," Mother had said, "not like in my generation." Babe loved the T-shirt and all that it stood for. She wore it on special occasions.

She began to protest when Carleen tossed a pullover at her. It was pale blue and the neckline was torn in a Jennifer Beals, *Flashdance* sort of way. "Unreal," Babe said, because she couldn't believe Carleen would let her have something she prized.

"Just wear it," Carleen said, "and don't embarrass me."

By the end of that school year Babe was into Carleen's nail polish and eye makeup, though not when Mother was looking or when Father was home. Babe's friends envied her for having the coolest sister on the face of the earth.

Plucking a rose petal now, Babe let it float to the ground. *Yes*, she thought, *Carleen had turned into the villain, not Amanda.* She supposed she should apologize to Amanda.

She stood up and walked toward the back of the house. That's when she noticed the tent and the tables and several set-up people moving about on the lawn.

Right, she thought. *Two hundred guests are expected.*

Bypassing dozens of folding chairs that had been draped in fabric, Babe headed toward stacks of wooden cases labeled Dom Perignon. Maybe a bottle was already on ice and would make a suitable peace offering. Or maybe Babe should just drink it herself.

Chapter Seven

"I can't believe you didn't warn me," Amanda bristled at Ellie after the two finally settled into the Hepplewhite wing chairs in the library and Wes said he'd go outside for a smoke and try to settle Babe down.

"Edward asked me not to tell either of you," Ellie said. "He was afraid you wouldn't come."

"He was right about me. I mean, what does Carleen plan to do? Show up after all this time, after all she did, and expect to collect a quarter of Edward's fortune?"

Which confirmed the real reason Amanda was there.

Ellie smoothed a worn spot on the dark leather armrest. "Edward invited her, Amanda. Not the other way around." She hated that it seemed she was defending Carleen.

"How did he find her? Where does she live?"

"I have no idea. He didn't tell me."

Amanda stood up because she'd been seated all of maybe five minutes, a record of sorts when she was in such a state. She strode to the bookcase that held the nineteenth-century American collection, removed a thin volume of Hawthorne's little-known *Doctor Grimshawe's Secret*, and pushed the well-worn button on the back of the bookcase. The wall rotated forward, exposing a small room laden with racks of chilling wine. Years ago, Edward had selected the Hawthorne to conceal access to his own special secret. The girls—Carleen, actually—had discovered it when she was twelve and thought spying on their uncle was a rite of summer.

"Well," Amanda continued as she stepped into the narrow wine room, made a selection, then emerged with a bottle in hand, "I can't believe you've allowed it, after all Carleen cost you."

For once, Amanda was not speaking of money, at least not overtly. Ellie knew she was referring to Paul, the quiet, kind man Ellie had married at a small evening ceremony at the Temple of Dendur inside the Met. Paul had been only an inch taller than Ellie's five-foot-five, and his hips had been more narrow than hers, but his eyes had been soft brown and his smile had been kind and he'd loved her in a companionable way.

Paul had been a librarian. He'd worked at the mammoth public landmark in midtown; she'd worked forty blocks north at a similar behemoth structure. They'd claimed that twenty-eight limestone stairs had brought them together—the identical number of steps that scaled from the sidewalks up to the front doors at both the library on Fifth Avenue and Forty-second Street and at the Met, uptown. Actually, they'd been introduced at a money management seminar one Saturday morning at the YMCA.

"I'm not very good at handling money," Paul had admitted during the breakout session.

"Me either," Ellie said, not wanting to reveal that Uncle Edward provided a financial cushion. "I do know I'll never get rich as an historian."

"Or me as a librarian."

"But if that's what we love doing, it's what counts, isn't it?"

They decided it was. They also decided to skip the rest of the seminar and feast on coffee and Everything Bagels, throwing financial caution out the window to the pigeons in Central Park.

Three months later they married. Their time together was pleasant and steady, sedated with books. He was a sweet lover, and Ellie enjoyed the closeness of him, his light scent of musty old books, the way he took off his glasses just before making love, then put them back on right after he climaxed, as if, for those moments, he did not need to see clearly, as if he allowed himself to become lost in the pleasure of her.

For a wedding gift, Edward had given them cash for a honeymoon. "Go to Egypt," he said to Ellie. "Just because you're now a missus, doesn't mean you should give up on your dreams."

Ellie and Paul put the money and a few travel brochures in a small brass box, promising each other they would honeymoon on the Nile when they could arrange month-long vacations.

In the meantime, they were content to work, read, make frequent love, and listen to nascent poets at coffeehouses in the Village. Some people, including Ellie, might have said her life was not very exciting, but she did not need excitement. Growing up as the eldest of four sisters, she'd had excitement enough.

But then came the blood and thunder Carleen had wrought.

For a while, Paul withstood the cameras and the questions, and the media presence outside their apartment building. Ellie hoped that living among the masses in Manhattan would render them mere flecks in the multitude. But Edward Dalton was Edward Dalton, after all, and the lights of Broadway that followed him everywhere then followed his family. And Ellie was his niece, Carleen's sister.

One day, Paul packed up and left. He didn't stop long enough to say he was sorry.

Ellie now watched Amanda pour a large glass of Pinot Noir and reminded herself that Paul had made the right choice for himself. He'd been a smart man, after all.

"Any other surprises?" Amanda asked. "Any other spurious creatures who've been invited?"

It was not a good time to mention anyone else who might raise Amanda's waxed eyebrows. "Please, Amanda. It's Uncle Edward's birthday. His party. Try to remember that."

Amanda took a long—too long—drink and set down her glass just as Babe swept into the library, her husband in tow, his sunglasses returned to the bridge of his nose. He smelled like a Cuban cigar.

"I'm sorry, Amanda, but I loved her so much," Babe announced as if she were in a movie and this was a new scene. "Carleen. I loved her so much when we were kids, I wanted to be just like her."

Ellie silently groaned.

Amanda said, "God, can't we change the subject?"

"I agree," Ellie said. "Let's not make this weekend about her. For starters, we need to decide what to do about Uncle Edward. Should we cancel the party? Should we move it to Sunday?" She didn't ask if they should call the police. They would all know that wouldn't be wise.

"Okay," Babe said, "let's talk about Edward and the party."

"And not Carleen," Amanda added.

"Right," Ellie said. "Her name is off limits. Okay?"

The others started to nod, just as the front doorbell rang.

It seemed like an hour before one of the staff answered the door, another hour before they heard muffled voices, another before Amanda gushed out a sigh and said, "For God's sake, it's only Chandler and Chase."

The boys paraded into the library with perfect posture, shoulders back, chins up. They were attired in khakis and golf shirts, little clones of their father, and wore their hair in the latest short style that was favored by Choate Rosemary Hall. Introductions were made (Babe had never met her nephews!), and the air in the room finally gained momentum when Chase realized Wes McCall really was his uncle, though Amanda could tell by her younger son's puckered brow that the man's obvious age was a little surprising. He looked so much younger on-screen.

Chase said it was awesomely cool to meet him, that he'd known they were related somehow but never dreamed they would meet, not really. Chase was such a sensitive boy that sometimes he made up for Chandler, who affected aloofness when he wasn't impressed. At seventeen, aloofness might be popular, but Amanda knew the real reason was that Chandler was too much like her. Conversely, at thirteen, Chase was like Jonathan, more comfortable with life and with people. She wondered if his future would include adultery.

"Where is your father?" she interrupted.

"Tied up," Chandler answered. As the older, more somber boy, he was often the designated mouthpiece. "He'll be here in the morning."

Amanda turned back to her wine without comment.

"Where's Uncle Edward?" Chase asked because he adored him: last Christmas, Edward had taught him a few magic tricks. "Has he met Wes?"

"We're not sure where he is," Ellie said. She followed with a condensed version about Edward making off with the rowboat. She didn't mention the possibility of postponing the party or canceling it altogether.

"Let's go find him," Chase said. "Maybe Wes can come with us! Did Uncle Edward leave the canoe?"

Ellie nodded.

"Don't look at me," Chandler said. "Three is too many in a canoe."

"Not where I come from," Wes said, peeling off his glasses as if he were Superman and the library was a phone booth. No one commented that without his sunglasses his face looked as if it was time for more plastic.

"Where are you from?" Chase asked.

"British Columbia. I logged in more hours kayaking around Vancouver Island than I did sitting in school."

Even Chandler seemed roused by that.

"Cool!" Chase cried. "Mom, can we go?"

Amanda said, "By all means. It will give us time to get reacquainted with our long-lost sister."

Of course she meant Babe, but how could they all not think of Carleen?

Chapter Eight

The last time Carleen had been on a bus was when she'd left New York City on a Greyhound. She'd had a one-way ticket, the promise of a job in a costume factory, and paid-up tuition at UMass Boston.

"Make something of yourself," Uncle Edward had said. He'd refrained from kissing her good-bye at the station: he'd wrinkled his brow as if to say something more, then shaken his head and had left. That was the last time they had seen each other.

Still, the bus had been more relaxing back then.

Staring out the tinted window at the bus stop in Amherst, Massachusetts (not even a depot, merely a stop in the center of town, with tickets purchased inside a bookstore), Carleen knew it would have been easier if she'd have let Brian go with her. Instead, she watched as he crossed the town common, paused when he reached their eight-year-old Ford Explorer, turned back to the bus (a Peter Pan, not a Greyhound), and gave a big wave. Her husband was never embarrassed to show affection in public: he was always himself, delighted with life more often than not, delighted with her and with their two daughters. They lived on the other side of the hill from Emily Dickinson's Amherst, in a place called Belchertown, famous not for its colleges but for its reservoir, the Quabbin, a pristine lake that had been formed in the 1930s when four towns had been flooded so the people in Boston could have clean drinking water. The act had been a political scandal. Carleen laughed when she heard the story: any scandal was worth laughing about, as long as it did not involve her. Besides, the name *Belchertown* was itself humorous, though she no longer laughed about it in public. She was not that Carleen anymore. She had tried very hard to rid the world of that caustic, inappropriate person.

Medication had helped. Brian had, too. So had finishing college, becoming a mother, getting her master's, and teaching ninth graders.

She waved back now, checked the closure of the paisley quilted bag that she had made by hand (wouldn't her sisters be shocked to learn she'd picked up a few sewing skills at the costume factory?), and waited for the bus to finish loading and head to New York City, with stops in Springfield, Hartford, and New Haven. In New York she'd change for Tarrytown, then take a cab to Mount Kasteel and the lake. She'd arrive around ten o'clock, in time for dessert and not dinner, thus avoiding having to stretch awkward small talk over several courses.

She had no idea what to expect. The only thing for certain was that they were older.

She'd seen Babe in the tabloids over the years and had been so surprised, proud, envious, that her little sister had really made a name for herself. It seemed only yesterday that Carleen had taught her how to walk in high heels, how to blow-dry her hair, how to apply mascara without sticking the wand in her eye. Who would have known that Babe, not Carleen, would turn out to be the real beauty in the family? When Babe's first film was released, Carleen spent every afternoon for two weeks at the cinema watching the larger-than-life image of her sister. In the darkness, Carleen's tears flowed nonstop. Hopefully, no one had noticed, because the film was a romantic comedy, not suited to crying.

She was sad that Babe never had children.

As for the others, Ellie and Amanda, Carleen didn't know if they were married or had kids or had gone to the moon.

She had, after all, done as she'd been told. She had left; she had never returned. Not once had any of her sisters tried to contact her. Not once had any of them tried to find her, to see if she was okay, to say they were sorry for all that had happened, to say they understood and that they forgave her.

Not one of her sisters.

Not once.

She gripped her quilted bag again and wondered why she was going this weekend.

Then the big engine rumbled to life and the door squished closed on its hydraulics. Carleen jerked forward, ready to lunge from her seat, race to the front and beg to get off.

Then she remembered her decision to finally tell her sisters the truth.

"Your husband must be a busy man," Babe said to Amanda once Chandler and Chase had left the library with Wes.

"And yours is still handsome," Amanda mocked. "For his age and all."

"Do you think he's dead?"

"Your husband?"

"No. Uncle Edward."

"Who knows. When we saw him at Christmas he looked rather peaked."

"Perhaps people look peaked to you unless they've wintered in the Caribbean or the Aegean."

"Better than the fake bronze tans of L.A."

"Enough," Ellie said sharply before any more barbs could be traded. "We need to decide whether or not to cancel the party."

Amanda sipped her wine. "I think we all have a better chance of survival if we leave things as they are. Two hundred guests will be a distraction."

"From the fact Edward's missing?"

"No. From each other."

Babe toyed with her hair. "What if he doesn't come back? What will we tell everyone?"

"Babe has a point," Amanda conceded. "The only thing worse than the gossip that would start if we cancel the party is if we act like it's a big deal that he's not here. Someone is bound to call the police. Someone will be convinced he is dead."

Dead. There was that word again.

Ellie shifted uncomfortably on the Hepplewhite. "Edward is fine, he has to be. I suggest we have the party and see what happens. In the meantime, let's talk about something else."

Amanda stood up again and traced her steps back to the wine. "So now we can't talk about Edward and we can't talk about Carleen. Have you compiled a list of acceptable topics?"

Ellie looked at her sweet sister, Babe. She smiled. "Yes. Why don't we talk about Babe. We haven't seen her in a while, remember?"

"It's no fun to talk about someone when they're in the room," Amanda retorted. It might have been funny if it weren't the truth. "Oh, all right," Amanda continued, "do tell us, Babe. What have you been doing for the past twenty years?"

"Actually, it's only been nineteen," Babe said. "And I'm sure you've read or heard most of it. Three husbands, no kids, two Emmys, no Oscars."

"Four nominations," Ellie interrupted.

"Two gone to Meryl Streep, one to Nicole Kidman, and the latest to that newcomer, Kate Winslet."

"She's hardly a newcomer."

"Time flies."

"So what's the real dirt?" Amanda asked. "What's life really like in Hollywood?"

Ellie could tell Amanda was being sarcastic, because she knew Amanda had no patience with the disingenuous film world. It was the one trait she'd inherited from Uncle Edward.

"You could have visited anytime," Babe replied.

"Ouch," Amanda said and poured herself more wine. "Well, sorry. I've been busy tending to my charities and raising my three children."

If the remark was meant to be cutting, Amanda succeeded.

"Amanda," Ellie said, "sometimes you are a pompous ass."

Babe laughed and stood up. "Well, this has been lovely, but while my husband is off on a search party and Amanda is getting drunk before dinner, I think I'll go upstairs and rest. I'm sure you understand. It's been a long day."

Ellie stood up, kissed her sister's cheek. "I'll call for you in time for dinner."

"I'll be in my old room. The one in the back."

Ellie felt a sting but reserved comment.

"Pleasant dreams," Amanda called after Babe. "Oh, by the way, I hope you've brought something more appropriate to wear. You're in New York now, you know. Civilization."

"Yes," Babe replied. "As I recall, it's where the world revolves around you. I'll try to keep that in mind." She swept from the room in a graceful departure befitting a dramatic actress of an earlier time, Bette Davis, perhaps, or Elizabeth Taylor.

Ellie had to stop herself from laughing out loud.

"Well, apparently she's still a princess," Amanda said.

"Funny," Ellie said, "that's not quite how I saw it." Still, she was considering asking Amanda to pour wine for her, too, when the doorbell rang again. Instead of asking for wine, Ellie held her breath.

"I guess we're going to have to get used to this for the next couple of days," Amanda commented, and Ellie agreed.

Chapter Nine

Once again, it wasn't Carleen. And it wasn't Edward.

This time it was Heather, Amanda's daughter, the eldest of her brood, her contribution to Wellesley. The last time Ellie had seen the girl had been at Christmas, at which time her thick coppery-red hair had not been twisted into a loose top-knot. She had not worn black eyeliner as she did now, or eye shadow of what appeared to be glitter. Ellie also did not recall that the girl had a large tattoo of a monarch butterfly on her upper left arm, or one that resembled a camilla in full bloom on her right.

Judging by the widening of Amanda's eyes and the veins that popped symmetrically on either side of her throat, she did not recall those things, either.

"Hi, Mom. Hi, Aunt Ellie. This is Shotgun."

It appeared Heather was indicating that the name of the young man next to her was Shotgun, not that he was toting one by his side, though it might have complemented his slicked-back black hair.

"Hello," Ellie said, because Amanda was mute. "Come in. Sit down." She half-wondered if the mass of tattoos that painted most of Shotgun's flesh not covered by a black tank top or black leather chaps would rub off on the upholstery of Uncle Edward's Hepplewhite chairs.

"We missed lunch," Heather said. "Can we raid the kitchen?"

"Sure," Ellie said. "Dinner's not until eight. But you can probably find something for sandwiches."

"Cool," Heather said. "Any beer? Shotgun promised not to drink and drive, and now he's absolutely dying of thirst!"

It was hard to focus on what Heather was saying instead of being transfixed by her sparkling eyelids. Still, Ellie wondered if she should ask if Shotgun was of legal age. Then she realized she didn't even know what legal age in New York was anymore. Being a recluse could be so informationally limiting. "Ask Martina," she said. "She's the caterer for the party. She should be in the kitchen."

"Cool. Oh, is anyone around to take our duffels? I promised Shotgun we'd get the room on the third floor that overlooks the lake. He absolutely loves the water, you know? He's a Pisces."

The two tattooed young bodies then departed from the doorway and moved toward the kitchen.

Amanda remained mute.

Ellie was not sure what to say, so she just said, "Well."

Then Amanda came to, jumped to her feet, and said, "What

did she say? I mean, she doesn't really expect to share a room? With that . . . that boy? In this house?"

Ellie didn't know if she'd be more concerned about that or the tattoos or the transformation of Heather's once pretty face. "Well," she said again.

Amanda's two visible throat veins grew larger and more purple. "Well, nothing. Won't Naomi just love that."

It took a second for Ellie to remember that Naomi really was Babe, that Amanda had often called her by her given name whenever she'd been filled with what came off as hatred but really was envy.

"Amanda, please. We can work this out."

"She's my daughter! I'm the one who has to work this out, not you! I'm the one! Not even her father! Because where is he, anyway! I'll tell you where he is! He's screwing a Brazilian back-waxer named Bibiana!" She flung her wineglass onto the Hepplewhite, where it bounced once, then landed on the floor and shattered—*to smithereens* their mother would have said. Then she marched from the room toward the kitchen shouting, "Heather! Heather! Come back here!" over and over the whole way.

The room was different from what Babe remembered. A thick coat of eggplant-colored paint had replaced the princess-themed wallpaper; a large, queen-size bed stood where the canopy twin had once been. Instead of a pink organza bed-spread, a beige comforter was topped with piles of throw pillows in shades of eggplant and olive; instead of ruffled, rib-boned pink curtains, wooden blinds with wide slats hung at the double windows.

Tucked in the corner, however, where the slant of the ceiling accommodated the angle of the eaves, a child's oak table and two chairs still sat, as if waiting for little-girl-Babe to glue sequins onto her summer T-shirts, string glass beads into bracelets for her sisters, serve tea to her Cabbage Patch doll.

If Babe closed her eyes, she might smell the bubble gum scent of the cologne she'd once loved.

It was in this room that Babe had decided to be an actor. There had not been a specific date or a time, but it had been in this room, a sensation, a feeling, a *knowing* that had been present.

She moved to the small chair now and sat down, her knees poking up toward her chin. The sequins, the bracelets, even the pretend tea had been part of a ritual she'd developed and perfected, a ritual of a make-believe world where there had been no older sisters to measure up to or compete with.

"What did you think of the play, Mrs. Minerva?" Babe would ask her Cabbage Patch doll, who'd come with a name she couldn't remember but who had been dubbed Mrs. Minerva by Uncle Edward. "Yes, yes, I thought so, too. A little weak in the third act. Not quite enough motivation for the resolution."

They were words she had learned by listening to Uncle Edward and his friends—just as she'd observed the nuances of great Broadway stars: the tilts of the heads, the gestures with cigarettes, the red lips that overworked syllables with each breathy word. Day after day, year after year Babe practiced the tilts and the gestures and the lip work in the maple-framed mirror that still stood on the bureau next to the table.

The summer before Amanda started college, she had walked

in on Babe rehearsing her ritual. "Oh, grow up," Amanda had scoffed. With big hair and access to Edward's sports car and her own credit card, Amanda thought she was someone special.

Ellie had come up behind her and told her to mind her own business and leave Babe alone.

Right after that Babe paid more attention to Carleen, who was only three years older than she was, three years more grown up.

Babe remembered those early days and the innocence that had defined them. Choosing Carleen as her mentor had been her first big mistake. Falling in love at fourteen, her second.

His name was Ray Williams, and he lived on the lake year-round. He was the same age as Carleen and had his driver's license and use of his mother's car, an old, beat-up Rambler whose front seats folded down. They spent a lot of time hugging and groping on those seats. But it wasn't until the following summer, when Babe was fifteen, that Ray covered the upholstery with his mother's crocheted afghan and they, at last, *did it.*

Over the winter, she had planned the event. Staying in touch hadn't been easy: her mother and father said she was too young for a boyfriend; Ray's parents were fiercely protective of their only child and did not want him with one of Edward Dalton's nieces. Edward, of course, was one of those wild *theater* people, one of those *summer* people who interrupted their lives for three months each year.

But Babe was in love. Having followed Carleen's growing-up lead for some time, Babe knew that to keep Ray, sex had to come next. She enlisted Carleen, who'd been happy to dish out advice: she said it must happen soon after they arrived at Kamp Kasteel for the season—that would guarantee Ray's allegiance for the whole summer, no matter how hard his parents might try to keep them apart.

Carleen, of course, knew everything.

The Dalton nieces were shipped off to Edward's on June twenty-first. On June twenty-third, Babe was lying on her back in Mrs. Williams's Rambler, cushioned by the afghan.

It was clumsy but lovely. Best of all, Babe didn't have to pretend. She loved Ray, she knew it, with each touch, with each kiss. He was real; he was hers.

When they were finished Ray held her and rocked her and told her he'd never met a girl as beautiful as she was or as sweet or as wonderful. He said he'd missed her so much over the winter that sometimes he'd felt sick deep inside.

They made love all summer until the end, when Ray left for Virginia Tech, and Babe was left maimed, and Carleen took off for Poughkeepsie. Then everything changed. Abruptly. Painfully. With no turning back.

Except for attending public high school, Babe spent most of the next three years in her room at Uncle Edward's with the sequins and the glass beads and the Cabbage Patch doll that she had outgrown. She'd outgrown the house, too. Maybe they all had, because it had become silent. The parties had ended, the laughter had ceased. She never heard from Ray. She learned through the mailman that he was staying at college year-round. She was certain his parents had done that on purpose. She thought about going to Virginia but knew that was a daydream, another lapse into *pretend*.

Three years later, Babe finally let go and moved to Los Angeles.

With a small sigh, she stood up now, went to the window, and looked down to the grounds and the perky white and gold tent. It was good, she supposed, that she had come back. It was good there was going to be a celebration, a catharsis needed for so long. Perhaps it might not be so bad. As long as Carleen didn't come.

Chapter Ten

"*I don't care what you did on Nantucket. You* will not sleep together in Uncle Edward's house. You will have some respect for this family. You will have some respect for him."

"Mother, no offense to him, but Edward's an old queer. Do you honestly think he cares who sleeps with whom?"

In another world, at another time, Amanda would have raised her hand and slapped her daughter's face, right or left cheek, it wouldn't have mattered, anything to have let Heather know she was being a brat and that Amanda would not, absolutely not, tolerate her insubordination. Amanda suspected, however, that her daughter was trying to show off for the tattooed prince who now stood next to her in the kitchen, a fistful of Spanish almonds in one hand, a lager in the other.

"I have said what I've said and that's final," Amanda replied. "If you don't like it, you and your friend are welcome to leave." She would not call the boy *Shotgun*, not if Heather begged her. Surely that was not the name on his birth certificate. Not if his family summered on Nantucket.

"I'm cool with it, Mrs. Delaney," whatever-his-name-was said. "I brought my sleeping bag. I can camp out."

She hadn't expected the boy would take her side. "Well," she said quickly, "you can put your sleeping bag in the boathouse. It's probably not fixed up, but it would be better than sleeping outside. In case it rains."

"Mother, Shotgun is not sleeping in the boathouse. It's moldy and damp and it stinks in there."

Amanda did not want to ask her daughter how she knew what the boathouse was like. Heather looked too much like— *was* too much like—Carleen, after all. And Carleen had a history of seeking out hideaways for boyfriends and sex and drinking and smoking pot.

God! Amanda thought. How she hated thinking about Carleen! It was bad enough she was reminded of her each time she looked at her daughter and her daughter's godforsaken hair, which Amanda had tried more than once to get Heather to dye. Black. Purple. *Anything.*

She turned from the children—they were children, weren't they?—and said, "I don't care where he sleeps, as long as it isn't with you." She went into the hall and headed back to the library when she bumped into Babe, who was coming down the stairs.

"I thought you were napping," Amanda said.

Babe shook her head. "Too much going on in my head."

Amanda sneered. "Tell me about it."

Babe went outside in search of fresh air again, in search of good feelings that surely would stir from watching the party come together—tables being set, chairs being arranged, flowers and champagne and crisp linens being staged. She was going to have a good time if it killed her.

Making her way across the manicured grass, she decided to welcome Wes and the boys back from their adventure. Hopefully, Edward would be with them. She said hello to several of the staff and set-up crew and headed toward the boathouse. That's when she spotted a young man in black walking with a young woman with a shock of red hair—Carleen-like hair, or at least the way Carleen's hair had looked when they'd been young.

Babe stopped, caught her breath. The girl had a slim back and long legs and a cute little strut. *Good grief, she could be Carleen twenty years ago.*

She must have been imagining things.

Still, Babe watched the couple link arms and bump comfortably against each other as they walked, their light laughter drifting over the lawn, their carefree youth reminding Babe of her own, of when she'd loved Ray and he'd loved her back.

Ray.

She smiled. She sighed.

She wondered what had happened to him. There had been a well-worn path to his house . . . off to the right . . . a few yards from the boathouse. Her eyes slowly pivoted toward that direction. Surely the path was gone by now, crowded by weeds and time and memories that were best left alone. Still, she took one careful step, then another, her gaze searching, her heart softly beating.

Suddenly, there it was.

The entrance was narrower than she remembered, more secretive, more alluring. It was framed with clusters of tiny white wildflowers that seemed to invite her in, seemed eager to beckon her to Ray's house, to his smile, his arms, and his love.

She looked around.

The young man and the Carleen clone rushed into the boathouse; Babe could not see the canoe on the lake. She glanced back to the path. Did she dare? Why not? It wasn't as if Ray still lived on the other side. Yes, why not? She put one foot forward, followed by another, and then, good grief, another, and soon Babe was swallowed up by the trees and cattails that ran along the shore and hid her from onlookers who might see her sneak off to the place where she'd met him that summer day.

Babe had been exploring, looking for her own world of pretend far from her sisters and the noise and the people of Uncle Edward's world. She'd found the path, her private escape. She'd matted down cattails, made a soft seat by the water. Obscured on either side by the high walls of grasses, she'd sat down, dangled her young legs into the lake, and watched the featherweight water bugs skim the silent surface. In the quiet, Babe had daydreamed that her true love would appear beside her, his reflection in the water, the way she had read in a fairy tale. Of course, it hadn't been possible; of course, it had only been make-believe.

And suddenly, there was the image. It was a boy, older than

she was, a handsome boy, with dark hair and blue eyes framed by dark lashes, and freckles that dotted his creamy skin. She blinked. The reflection didn't dissolve. Babe squealed. She jumped up, slipped on the cattails, and fell into the lake.

When she came up for air she dog-paddled like crazy but didn't dare get to the shore. She had on a white cotton shirt and pants, after all, and it would be soaked and all her girl parts would be showing clear through.

"Sorry," he said. "I didn't mean to scare you. I'm Ray Williams. From over there." He pointed somewhere, but Babe didn't pay much attention. She was too busy trying to make her feet locate the bottom of the lake.

"Do you need any help?"

She shook her head. If only she knew how to swim! If only Uncle Edward hadn't told them about the lake monster, she might have taken lessons.

Suddenly her arms tired. Babe slipped below the surface.

Finally, she touched the bottom.

But she was running out of air.

She felt pressure on her chest and an odd, floaty sensation inside her head.

Then an arm grasped her waist and pulled her up with one swift, unfaltering motion until the surface broke through and she could breathe again.

Ahhh.

Her hero propelled her to the shoreline and up into the cattails and took off his shirt and wrapped it tightly around her because she was shivering. And then he held her close against him and stroked her hair and she coughed and he rubbed her back and said she'd be all right.

And that was how Naomi Dalton had met her true love.

Babe laughed again at the sweet sadness of it all, of the relationship that followed, of the sorrow of the end.

She stopped then, knowing it wasn't wise to continue. She took a deep, nostalgic breath, turned around, and headed out of her daydreams, back to Uncle Edward's, and the world as it had become.

Chapter Eleven

It was only six o'clock and Ellie had already had enough of her sister Amanda. What was that business about Jonathan and a Brazilian? *Oh,* Ellie thought, washing her hands at the copper kitchen sink, she would be much happier once this weekend and its players had come and gone.

"I can stay and help you with supper," Martina said. "Everything is ready, but I can help you serve."

Ellie shook her head. She wanted something to do, a purpose that would help her keep upright and focused and stop her from screaming. "You need to go home. Tomorrow will be a busy day."

Martina nodded. She took off her apron and folded it neatly. "Your sister didn't recognize me."

"Amanda?"

"*Sí.*"

Ellie sighed. "Don't tell me. Amanda doesn't think you speak English."

"She never did. It was bad enough when we were kids. Now it's plain rude."

"Yes, Amanda can be rude. I am sorry."

"Don't apologize for her. I was the daughter of Edward's housekeeper. In Amanda's mind, I am Latino, ergo, I shall always be inferior."

Ellie remembered the long-ago altercation when Amanda had suggested that Martina go "back to the island where she belonged." Ellie had told Edward, who had erupted. She had never seen him so angry. He stomped through the house until he found Amanda. He shouted that he did not allow such small-minded behavior under his roof, and that if Amanda did not apologize immediately, she would not be allowed to return to Kamp Kasteel. *Ever.* Amanda had been about twelve, still young enough for him to take her by the hand and march her back to the kitchen, where Martina waited for her mother to finish work for the day. After Amanda emitted a weak "I am sorry, Martina," she lifted her chin and pranced, self-righteously, from the room.

Ellie had been so embarrassed, so ashamed of her sister. Edward had assured her that someday Amanda would regret her actions. Until recently, Ellie hadn't known what had become of Martina—or the huge success Martina now enjoyed. Uncle Edward had greeted her warmly, and Ellie had realized he had hired her not only because her catering business was now one of the most sought-after in Manhattan but also to teach Amanda a long-deserved lesson. He'd winked at

Ellie and said Martina would be "their little secret" until he was willing to divulge it. He liked having secrets, God help them all.

"If you're here by eight," Ellie said, "you'll have plenty of time." Martina was only going to tend to the family; her staff would wait on everyone else.

"I'll be here at seven forty-five," Martina replied as she went to the door.

Ellie waved, then turned to the refrigerator and removed the platters of chilled chicken salad, sliced cheeses and apples, and two smoked brook trouts, Edward's "catch of the day" a few days ago that Martina had expertly preserved. Ellie set it all on the poured concrete countertop (the poured concrete had been Henry's idea, along with the small, gleaming river rocks that had been embedded), next to a green salad and thin slices of marinated beef tenderloin with roasted red pepper strips and garlic cloves.

It all looked *so divine*, as Amanda would say. It was too bad that sometimes a family gathering had a way of reducing one's appetite.

Ellie counted the bundles of utensils to suit those who would be in attendance: Amanda (not Jonathan), Chandler, Chase, Heather, the boyfriend (whose name Ellie had already forgotten); Babe and Wes; Ellie; Henry (apparently, not Uncle Edward). Nine. That was all. Why was there so much commotion if that was all?

Then she realized she hadn't yet heard Chandler and Chase return with Babe's husband. Good Lord, Ellie hoped they hadn't disappeared, too. Perhaps there really was a Lake Kasteel monster after all.

Then again, three less would mean only six for supper. Surely six would be more manageable. Especially when at least one of them was not hungry.

Babe waved to Wes and the boys as she emerged from the path and they emerged from the boathouse at the same time.

"Any luck?" she shouted.

"Tippy Canoe and Tyler, too!" Wes called back and Babe forced a laugh, but the boys didn't seem to be in good humor. In fact they—and Wes—looked wet. He swaggered toward her with the stride of a man who had paraded in front of too many cameras over too many years, as if he'd forgotten how Wesley Jamison McCall had walked when he'd been, say, seventeen, as Ray Williams had been when Babe had met him. Wes had swaggered into her life at a vulnerable time, after husbands one then two were long gone, each only having wanted to be attached to her fame and her money. Wes liked the fact that, in many ways, she was his equal. He also liked that she was respectable arm candy, not so young that he could be called lecherous, old enough to understand that sex didn't always matter. In short, she'd been around the block a couple of times and was no longer naïve.

"That's an old presidential campaign slogan," Wes said now as he reached her. "For us, it simply means we capsized the damn canoe. Lost our paddles. Had to go ashore on an island and grab some pine boughs to paddle back. Christ, talk about embarrassing."

He gave her a hug, leaving behind a trace of gin. He must have packed a bottle when she hadn't been looking. "As for your uncle Edward, I think he has rowed down to the Hudson and right about now he's passing Forty-second Street and tipping his cap. Where were you? Hiding in the weeds?"

It took Babe a second to realize he must have seen the direction from which she'd come. "I was looking for wildflowers," she replied quickly. "The prettiest wildflowers always grew along the path." She turned toward its entrance as if she expected the flowers would bow in confirmation.

"Hmm," Wes replied. "Seems to me there are enough goddamn flowers up at the house to open an arboretum."

Now and then Wes startled her by using a big word. More often than not, it was the wrong word. But, *choosing her battles* as Mother had instructed, Babe didn't correct him.

"How are the boys?" she asked, cupping her arm through Wes's slightly damp forearm. "Are they snobs like Amanda?"

"I think the younger one might have escaped her genetics. God. Where does that come from, anyway? Was your mother so . . . hoity-toity?"

It wasn't a big word, but it suited Amanda. Babe tried to recall if their mother had been like that. She'd been polished and proper, but she'd been the wife of a plumbing supply salesman who hadn't done anything significant except have a mistress he'd entertained at the Algonquin.

"And what's the deal with Carleen? The boys told me she killed your parents. That she burned the house down when they were in it. Why didn't you tell me?"

In that single, unexpected moment, grief covered her heart the way a dark cloud can suddenly block the sun on a grand summer day.

Babe averted his eyes. "Tabloid trash," she said, then tugged his arm. "See why I didn't want to come home?"

"But . . ."

She pressed a finger to her lips. "Sssh. No more talk." She led him toward the house, deciding she needed to treat the weekend as if it were a film and she was an actor playing a part. The *denouement*, of course, was as yet unpredictable, but guaranteed to be over by seven thirty-three Sunday night when the plane would lift up from the runway and ferry her back toward the West, toward the place that now was her home.

Supper was genial, considering the absence of the host and Amanda's husband and the unspoken, looming concerns about Carleen's intentions and Edward's whereabouts. Henry had complained of a headache and hadn't come to the table.

Throughout the chicken salad and cold trout, the conversation was more like a question and answer period in which Chase interrogated Wes about his cinematic successes ("How did you make that building blow up?" "When those cars flew off the bridge, was anyone in them?"). No one seemed to mind. Chandler seemed committed to not speak to anyone, which might have annoyed his sister, who was seated next to him, except she was too busy fondling her boyfriend, who was seated on the other side of her. Which left the three sisters—Ellie, Amanda, and Babe—lined up like wooden dolls in a carnival booth at one of Edward's famous parties, waiting for someone to take a chance for charity on three balls for a dollar and see who could be knocked off the bench for a Kewpie doll, or whatever the prizes were today, perhaps one of those handheld video games that irritated Amanda because they gave children the ability to detach from others, the way Amanda supposed all of them at the table, except

Chase and Wes, were trying to detach from one another right now.

Amanda checked her watch. It was after nine thirty. Whew. Almost time to bid everyone a pleasant goodnight.

"Lemon meringue pie?" Ellie finally offered.

The males all said yes, the ladies said no, a weight-related injustice in life, Amanda mused. She got up and helped clear the dishes, a pottery collection that looked French or Italian, another change her elder sister had wrought in the household. A sudden thought jumped into Amanda's mind: What if Edward left Ellie the mansion and he put all his money into a fund to keep the place going as long as Ellie lived? What if he died but Amanda still wound up broke?

She grew faint and light-headed; she blamed the trout. Why had she eaten cold fish that had been hooked by Uncle Edward? Was it part of his plan? Was he going to poison them all, or only her, because of her fiscal irresponsibility?

Suddenly queasy, she clutched the edge of the table. The pottery platter with remnants of the suspect-tainted trout slid from her hand and crashed to the floor. Without stopping to clean up the evidence-mess, Amanda raced from the dining room toward the powder room that was now under the wide staircase and had once been a hiding place for the four young girls. . . .

She slammed the door behind her, lifted the lid of the toilet, then *tossed her cookies*, as her mother would have delicately called it.

Oh, Amanda thought as she crumpled to the floor, she should not have eaten, she should not have pretended that everything was fine.

It was cold on the floor. Her stomach felt better; she reached up and flushed, then examined the tiles that surrounded the bowl. Some type of polished stone, she deduced. Not ordinary marble or locally bred limestone but something exotic, more than likely European.

Resting her head against the base of the pedestal sink, she wondered why she was pondering tile when her entire future was at stake.

She thought of her husband. She did not like him right then. How could she? Could she ever have sex with him again, or see him naked, for that matter, knowing the back-waxer had seen him naked, too, had probably touched him *there*, had probably . . . *oh*, her stomach rolled again.

To get her mind off Jonathan, she thought of her children, and of the fact that Chase was the only one she presently liked. Amanda had never minded admitting that sort of thing to herself—whom did it hurt? Even though Chase was not her style or her likeness, he was an enjoyable boy with a curious, unaffected personality that would take him far. He was not as book smart as his brother, but he wouldn't need to be. Chase had genuine charm, and if the bastards of the world didn't get him, he would be fine.

Chandler was an ass, just like she was. Amanda knew that. She also knew she didn't much like herself right now, either, so it would figure she would not care for him.

Heather made her shudder. She looked—had always looked—so much like Carleen that it was quite disconcerting. Yet if Heather ended up pregnant, she would probably not have an abortion but would expect her family to embrace her and help her raise (i.e., *pay for*) the baby the way Bill and Mazie Dalton would not have done for Babe had they known Babe had been pregnant, had Carleen not convinced Babe to have the abortion and not tell their parents because *they would all get in trouble*. Amanda knew that Carleen had told Babe's secret to Ellie and Amanda so *she* wouldn't have been the only one to be in trouble. Surely their parents wouldn't blame *all* the sisters for a conspiracy to rob Babe of her innocence.

Yes, Heather not only looked like Carleen but often acted like her as well, which was even more disconcerting.

Amanda stared at the imported, polished stone floor and wondered if one day Heather would kill her parents the way Carleen had.

"Amanda-Belle?" Ellie called from the other side of the door. "Are you all right in there?"

Amanda hauled herself to her feet and looked at her pale, tired face in the mirror. "I'm fine. I'll be out in a minute."

"Everyone's finished with supper and they're going to their rooms. I'll be in the kitchen if you need anything."

As if I could possibly need anything, Amanda thought with a nauseous laugh.

Chapter Twelve

"Did my daughter go down to the boathouse with that tattooed creep?" Amanda asked once she had vacated the powder room and joined Ellie in the kitchen.

Ellie drew in a deep breath and counted to three. Sometimes dealing with her sister required a short pause. "He seems like a nice, boy, Amanda. His father is a professor at Harvard."

Amanda's eyebrows went up. "Really? I didn't know that."

Of course not, Ellie thought. *You haven't bothered to make any conversation.* She loaded the last platter into the dishwasher and wiped down the counter. "Tomorrow will come quickly. It looks as if the weather will hold."

Amanda pouted. "Please. Let's not talk about my daughter or the weather. I think there is a more important issue at hand. Like where is Uncle Edward and what are we going to do about it?"

How could Ellie admit she did not know what to do? How could she tell Amanda that she was so stressed she couldn't think straight? These years at the lake had been so quiet and nice. Even when Henry had arrived, it had caused little disturbance: they'd simply glided from one day to the next without uproar or expectations. Decisions, too, had caused minimal disruption, except for the redecorating Ellie had orchestrated last fall. Picking out paint colors, though it had seemed taxing, couldn't compare with the goings-on of today. This weekend. The whole mess.

She put her face in her hands and felt her shoulders start to tremble. She hoped beyond hope that she wouldn't cry. *Oh, God, please, don't let me cry, not in front of Amanda.*

God must have been out for a late supper or an after-dinner liqueur, because before Ellie knew it, tears plopped from her eyes like rain from the eaves that were blocked up by leaves.

"Ellie!" Amanda screeched and lunged for her, as if Ellie had been having a heart attack or a stroke. "Don't!"

Well, of course Amanda would shout "Don't!" She detested displays of raw feelings.

Ellie waved her sister away. "It's all right, Amanda-Belle. I'm fine." *As fine as you were in the powder room*, she wanted to add but did not. Ellie wiped her eyes, and Amanda stepped two steps away.

"Let's sit down," Amanda said, as if sitting would solve everything.

They moved to the breakfast nook overlooking the backyard, which was bathed in security lights now that it had grown dark.

"Where is Edward?" Ellie asked with a leftover sniff. "Why has he done this to me?" She'd meant to say *Why has he done this to us?* but, she supposed, she'd really meant *me,* so it didn't much matter.

"He's always been a bastard," Amanda replied.

"Amanda! Don't be a prig."

"Well, it's true. Rich, famous Edward Dalton. Where did that ever get any of us? He's hoarded his millions except for an occasional crumb here and there to keep us plugged in so he can abuse us with this kind of behavior. Face it, Ellie, the man is self-centered."

"Amanda, that's not true. Edward is generous and kind—"

"Generous? To whom?"

"To me. To you. To Babe, I think. When she was young."

"He's only generous when it serves him, Ellie."

"Stop. It's not true."

"Well," Amanda said, staring out at the tent and the chairs and the foreboding of tomorrow, "I don't like anyone very much right now."

That's when Ellie remembered Jonathan and the Brazilian. "Amanda, about Jonathan . . ."

But just then Babe appeared in the doorway. Her makeup had been cleansed and her curls were loosely pinned to the top of her head. She wore a thin chiffon robe and, apparently, very little beneath it. If Ellie were Amanda, she'd be glad her husband was not present to imagine what accompanied Babe's visible curves.

"Oh, am I interrupting?" Babe asked. "Wes fell asleep and I could use a cup of tea."

At least Amanda didn't comment that either Wes was a minuteman, or they hadn't had sex.

"Help yourself," Ellie said. "It's in the upper cabinet to the right of the sink." She was done waiting on people for the day.

Amanda and Ellie fell silent while Babe rummaged through the boxes of herb teas. Ellie supposed she shouldn't stand up and say goodnight now that she'd broached the subject of Jonathan's mistress. Not that she needed to know.

Turning her gaze back to the yard, she hoped that no matter where he was or what he was doing, Uncle Edward was safe. It would be appalling if anything happened the night before his big celebration. The thought of it made her stomach grumble. She realized she hadn't eaten much supper; she'd been too distraught about, well, about everything and everyone at the table. Maybe she should ask Babe to pour tea for her, too.

That's when a shadow moved through the security light in the yard. Ellie stood up. "Uncle Edward?" she said and Amanda stood up and Babe stopped what she was doing and floated to the window.

"Is it him?" Babe asked.

"I don't know," Ellie said. "I only saw a shadow."

Amanda dropped back to her chair. "It's probably my daughter, coming back to the house after a good screw."

For a woman who pretended to be so refined, sometimes Amanda was surprisingly crass.

A light knock knocked on the back door.

"Yes, it must be Heather," Ellie whispered. After all, Heather, not Edward, would not have a key and therefore need to knock. "Amanda, are you going to open the door?"

Amanda let out a rough sigh. "I suppose I should be grateful she didn't spend the night down there with him."

"I suppose," Ellie said.

"Oh, for God's sake," Babe said, "I'll let her in." She swished her chiffon toward the back door, unlocked the lock, and opened the door. But it was not Heather, and it was not Edward. Good Lord, it was Carleen.

Chapter Thirteen

Babe slammed the door and uttered something profane that had eight or ten syllables.

Amanda fanned herself as if she were going to faint.

Ellie felt something stab her in the vicinity of her heart: anguish, pain, loss, something like that. Still, she was the oldest. She needed to take charge.

Reluctantly, Ellie stood up. "Babe," she said. "Stop it. Carleen is our sister. You must let her in."

Babe stared at her in horror, no longer the movie star she'd become but the little girl afraid of the monster in the lake.

Amanda stood up, too. "Well, *I'm* not going to let her in. She simply has no business being here."

They stood there, eyes bouncing from one to the other, three sisters in a standoff, a fourth on the back steps.

"Well," Ellie said, "wouldn't Mother and Daddy be proud. Here we are, grown adults, acting like children."

"Leave them out of this," Amanda said. "They're not the ones who invited her."

"Not to mention that they're dead," Babe chimed in. "Because of *her*."

It was interesting, of course, that Amanda and Babe were now on the same side, two adversaries suddenly best friends for a common cause. "The state of New York said it was an accident," Ellie said.

Amanda blinked with condescension. "The state of New York did not know Carleen."

As if that ended the discussion, Amanda and Babe began to leave the kitchen.

"Wait," Ellie said. "What about Uncle Edward?"

"What about him?" asked Babe as both of them stopped.

"He invited Carleen. He wants her here for his birthday. Maybe he's sick after all. Maybe he wants his whole family here for reasons we don't know yet." She purposely teased Amanda with the possibility of Edward's death, hoping it would trigger her penchant for greed.

"I don't care about his motive," Babe said. "She left this family years ago, and it's best that she doesn't come back." An odd pitch to her voice made it sound as if Babe had been referring to herself and not Carleen.

Amanda hesitated, her greed busily grappling with the heat of the moment. "Wait, Babe," she finally said. "Maybe Ellie's right. Maybe we should be congenial, for Uncle Edward's sake." Greed, of course, triumphed, because when it came to Amanda, it usually did.

Babe re-anchored a curl that had sprung loose. "Do what you want," she said. "But this is about more than the death of our parents for me. This is about the death of *my baby*."

Ellie braced herself. Since Babe had arrived, Ellie had noticed the change. She realized that her youngest sister no longer followed the leader, no longer automatically did whatever the older ones wanted. She had become an adult with a mind of her own.

"You have your kids, Amanda," Babe continued. Her cheeks became pink, her breath short and wispy. "Ellie, I have no idea why you never had any. But I wanted kids. I wanted a family. But Carleen made me have that stupid abortion. None of you knew that my cervix was damaged in the process. I was only fifteen; it wasn't fully developed.

"After I got married the first time, I had four miscarriages. My doctor finally told me to stop getting pregnant, that I couldn't have children the 'natural' way. No kids for Babe! Not then! Not ever!" Her voice dramatically cracked on the *ever*. But she remained stalwart and did not cry. "So don't expect me to unlock that door and welcome my long-lost sister with open arms. Not for a minute. Not on your life.

"As for this place, why do you think I haven't been back here in all these years? It's because I couldn't stand the memories. Of Carleen. Of everything and everyone. Even of Uncle Edward, who, by the way, had a big fat nerve inviting Carleen and not telling us.

"Enjoy the party, ladies. I'm gone on the next plane." She stomped from the kitchen, her chiffon billowing behind her.

Amanda and Ellie looked at each other a moment, then Amanda called out, "Babe! Babe, wait for me!" and went off after her, leaving Ellie to sigh a sad, heavy sigh as another knock rapped on the door.

"I've seen all her movies," Carleen said to Ellie after Ellie finally broke down and let her in and the two were seated in the nook where Ellie and Amanda had been. "She looks terrific."

Carleen, however, did not look terrific, she looked mediocre. Her big eighties hair had deflated and was gathered into a small auburn ponytail; her once-black-lined eyes had light mascara on their lashes but otherwise were unadorned. Her fingernails were short, painted with clear polish. If she'd had lipstick on earlier in the day, it had worn off. She seemed a little weary, but not nervous or upset. She didn't ask where her sisters had gone after Babe had opened, then slammed, the door.

"Babe has been very successful," Ellie said. "She always was talented." She did not say that neither Ellie nor Amanda had seen Babe in years, that Carleen's behavior had impacted each of them differently. Let her think the three sisters had remained close, that they had closed ranks and been a support system for one another.

"What about you, Ellie? You are talented, too. Are you still at the Met?"

It took Ellie a second to remember that she had been working, had started her career, had met Paul and been what she'd thought of as in love when everything had happened, when everything had changed. "No," she replied.

Carleen folded her hands on her purse, an odd quilted thing that looked as if she had bought it at a garage sale. Amanda would have a heyday with that.

"This is awkward," Carleen said. "Me. Being here."

"Yes." Ellie was not going to lie. She was too tired already, and it was going to be too long a weekend for lying and trying to remember what she'd said to whom.

"Has Uncle Edward gone to bed?"

Ellie wished Babe had finished making the tea. If she had, she would have inserted a hefty shot of scotch. "I expect so," she said and stood up. "Well, it's getting late."

Carleen nodded. "I only brought a small bag. It's on the steps. I came around back because I saw the lights. I wasn't sure if the party had started early."

"Tomorrow. The party starts at noon."

As Carleen unfastened a pink ribbon from her ponytail, Ellie remembered that she'd traded her big hair for the trial, that she'd sacrificed style in order to appear demure. Harmless. Innocent.

"Well, then," Carleen said, standing up, too, "I guess I should retire."

Retire was a frumpy word to come from Carleen. *Frumpy?* Ellie wondered. *Who was she kidding?* Then she checked her annoyance. She needed to leave being rude to Amanda. For Ellie, unkindness was just too exhausting. "I'll get your bag," Ellie said. "Did you come far?" It wouldn't hurt to be civil. For Uncle Edward's sake. For the sake of the headache she felt starting to blossom.

"Five hours on a bus," Carleen said.

"Ouch."

"Yes."

Ellie retrieved the bag from the back steps—it was a small, overnight thing, ideal for someone traveling light. She hoped

Carleen had packed something white for the family picture session—if she wasn't run out of town before then.

"It was twenty years ago, Babe," her husband said. "You're different people today. For starters, you're adults."

"Which is exactly why I get to think for myself. Which is exactly why we are going home." She had tried to reason with Wes when she'd gone upstairs. She had tried to get him to buy into her *theatrics* (his word, not hers).

He had talked her into waiting until morning.

But now it was the morning and Babe hadn't changed her mind. She packed her clothes, her shoes, her trunkload of cosmetics. She took a last glance at the table where she'd once held high tea for her dolls. She felt no remorse.

"We can't go," Wes said as he pulled his legs from under the big white comforter and swung them to the floor. "It would look ridiculous. Besides, we should be sure your uncle is all right."

"Because you think he can help your career?" There. She'd said it. She'd gotten the issue out in the open.

"Excuse me?"

She flipped the suitcase lid closed. She zipped. She sniffed. She parked her hands on her slender hips as if she were Amanda. "Did you think I wouldn't get it? Did you think I'd actually believe you came here—*that you coerced me to come here*—for my benefit? Or that the stunt at the airport had anything to do with me?"

"Babe . . ." Sometimes Wes said "Babe" as if it were a sarcastic endearment, not practically her given name.

"Don't 'Babe' me, Wes McCall. All you want is a ticket to

Broadway. You want to use my Uncle Edward to resuscitate your career."

"I think in that department, we both could use some help."

"You could use help, not me. I have a plan."

"Right. Fragrances."

"Or jewelry. Maybe handbags. The point is, I don't expect a handout."

He stood up. "Fine. You have your plan. I have mine." He grabbed his shaving kit and clothes and headed toward the door. Unlike Ellie and Amanda's rooms, Babe's was without an attached bath, an *en suite* luxury reserved for the older, more important girls. He stopped and turned back to her. "Look, we can argue about this all day and still not solve anything. For now, I'm going to shower. I promised the boys that if Edward isn't back, I'd take them out looking again."

Babe couldn't believe he wasn't taking her seriously. But then, had he ever? "You're taking Amanda's boys on another fruitless expedition?"

"Maybe we'll find your uncle this time. Anyway, I promised Chase. Chandler will probably pull his head out of his butt and come, too. There won't be much going on around here until the party."

"So you're determined to stay. Do I have to remind you this is my family, not yours?"

He shrugged. Laughed. "I'm just trying to make the best of this, Babe. You might consider doing the same."

She threw her suitcase onto the floor. "Do what you want. I'll be here in my room. I'm not going to be anywhere near that sister of mine. You can't make me." *You can't make me?* Had she really said that, as if she were seven years old?

Wes laughed again. "Christ, I can't believe you let 'tabloid trash' rule your life. Wasn't that what you called it? Well, honey, you're acting as if it was much more than that."

Babe flung herself onto the bed—another wretchedly overacted antic for which she immediately hated herself.

Chapter Fourteen

Carleen was huddled under the covers, frozen in the same position she'd been in all night, the blankets tight under her chin, her gaze fixed on the ceiling. She hadn't slept. Seeing her sisters, feeling their wrath, being in this room again—it was as if time had never passed.

She shivered. Bright sunlight wedged itself between the blinds, an indication that the day was beginning with summer perfection, that it would be warm and wonderful for the party, just as Uncle Edward probably thought he deserved.

Still, she shivered.

"Are you sure you want to go alone?" her husband had asked when she'd told him about the invitation and her intent. "I can go with you. We can bring the girls!" He said their cocker spaniel could visit his mother, that she loved spoiling the dog. He said the girls might have fun meeting their cousins—didn't one of her sisters have children?

Carleen had told Brian long ago about all that had happened, but he'd married her anyway, a testament to his kindness and compassion. But along with his virtues, he could sometimes be dense: he didn't believe her sisters would hate her forever.

When their daughters (now fourteen and twelve) had been born, Carleen had been disappointed. It would have been easier if she'd had boys: no future comparisons of looks or attitude, no need to reminisce with each landmark of their childhoods. Thank God, both Savannah and Elizabeth took after Brian's side, though Savannah often displayed Ellie's empathetic nature, which Carleen knew was fortunate, given all the other traits that could have surfaced.

Sometimes, when Carleen least expected it, one or both of them looked and sounded like Babe, the way she had been once, sweet and innocent.

Still, Carleen was grateful that so far her girls were into horses and gymnastics instead of beer and boys. Carleen, after all, had had her first drink when she was eleven, the morning after one of Uncle Edward's parties. She'd crept down to the gazebo, where she'd been sneaking cigarettes since she'd been nine. That morning, she stepped inside the structure and almost tripped over Toni Parker—a buxom Broadway star— who was passed out cold, half naked, covered by what looked to be a man's jacket. Carleen knew it wasn't Toni's husband's jacket because he was on the West Coast shooting a made-for-TV movie, or so she'd overheard the night before.

Toni roused and peered at Carleen with one eye. Carleen lit up and blew out a long stream of smoke.

"Have a good time last night?" Carleen asked.

Pulling the jacket over her boobs, Toni laughed. "You tell me." She brushed a few wavy curls off her forehead. "God, my head is splitting. I don't suppose you have an extra one of those?"

Carleen lit another cigarette and handed it over. It was her last one, but it would be worth it to watch the diva in distress.

The woman took a drag, coughed, then spotted a champagne bottle on its side on the floor. "That thing open?"

Carleen picked it up. "Nope."

"Well, then. Looks like this is our lucky day." She grabbed the bottle from Carleen, rocked it back and forth, then gently forced the cork. *Pop.* A thin, wispy cloud snaked out. Toni raised the bottle to her lips and took a giant swig. "Ah," she said. "Hair of the dog."

Carleen studied her. "Don't mind if I do, too," she said, and Toni laughed and passed the bottle back. Carleen took a swig the way Toni had done, and they both laughed and took another drag off their cigarettes.

It had been fun to feel like such a big shot.

Carleen closed her eyes now and wondered what had ever happened to Toni Parker. Today the woman would have been arrested. The last time Carleen had seen Toni's name in the rags, the story said she'd gone to Europe and disappeared into the streets of Paris, an act that had seemed romantic. Today it seemed insane. Still, Carleen couldn't blame Toni Parker for her own behavior. Carleen had seem destined for it, somehow, for lying, cheating, stealing, smoking, drinking, drugging—the blue ribbon winner of the black sheep competition.

What if the fire had never happened? she wondered for the millionth time in twenty years. Would she, too, have disappeared into the Parisian streets?

"Make something of yourself," Uncle Edward had said, and so she had. She had made herself respectable. She had made herself into a teacher, a wife, a mother. She had thanked her husband for offering to come with her, but this was her past, her responsibility to finally make right.

But now, back here, shivering in the bed, she did not feel like any of those things. She felt like Carleen Dalton, black sheep, bad seed, whatever.

Closing her eyes, she tried to think about the relief she would feel once she told the truth about what really had happened, why she'd lit the fire, why their parents had died, and why they'd still have been one big, happy family if it hadn't been for Uncle Edward—the man they all seemed to adore.

Ellie was in the kitchen, where she'd been since dawn. She'd given the grounds a final once-over. She'd rearranged the order of the buffet table. She'd reviewed the guest list, then snapped it onto a clipboard and parked it at the front door so she quickly could check off who showed up and notice who (how dare they!) did not.

Now, she was at the sink again, pouring coffee into a thermos for Babe's husband. She'd already packed a bag of cheese and fruit and sports drinks for Chandler and Chase, who'd bounded down the stairs earlier and told Ellie that Wes was taking them out again to search for Uncle Edward. She'd wanted to add some of her famous rum cake, but was surprised that most of it was gone. She hadn't thought Edward was capable of consuming that much between when she'd made it Thursday night and when he'd disappeared.

She screwed the top onto the thermos and didn't mention the cake to Wes, who leaned against the counter, arms folded, studying Ellie as if he were Secret Service and she was going to serve the president. He'd been acting like a doting uncle, though Ellie sensed it was only because he was savoring Chase's hero worship. She didn't suppose he had many young fans left.

Still, it was the most animation Ellie had seen out of Amanda's boys since they'd been in preschool. Amanda had such a way of burdening them with daily expectations.

"Coffee will wake me up," Wes said. He didn't say he'd argued with his wife on and off during the night. Though the walls of this old house were pretty solid, Ellie's bedroom was right next to Babe's. Last night, the words "Carleen" and "No" had been quite audible.

Ellie wondered if the marriage was in trouble.

"Edward's been gone a whole day now," Wes continued, as if Ellie didn't know. "Maybe it's time for the police."

"I think he's fine," she said—again—trying to act as if she was convinced. But the truth was, in addition to Babe's rants, Ellie's mounting worries about Edward had kept her awake most of the night. She was worried, and yet . . .

"We don't need the police here," she added matter-of-factly. The reasons, of course, were wide and varied, starting with two hundred guests and ending with Carleen.

"But they have techniques," Wes continued. "And dogs."

"No," she insisted. She handed the thermos to Wes and

looked him square in the eye so he'd know she was serious.

"Okay," he said. "Then the boys and I will scout around the lake again. Any advice?"

"The reeds get pretty tall and thick in some spots along the shoreline. If he's not on the island, he might have found a protected inlet, left the boat, then made his way to the road and hitchhiked into town."

Wes's eyebrows went up. "Hitchhiked?"

"It used to be one of Uncle Edward's pastimes. He said it was a good way to meet interesting people outside your own circle of friends." She waited for Wes to make a derogatory remark, but all he said was, "Okay. We'll check the shoreline for abandoned rowboats."

"And you won't phone the police."

"No, ma'am."

Ellie nodded. "Thank you." She wondered if not phoning the police would be considered negligent. Elder abuse. Something like that. Still, didn't an adult need to be missing for a couple of days before law enforcement would get involved? *Oh, God,* she thought for the millionth time, *what's the right thing to do?*

Wes hoisted the thermos. "I don't know what time my wife will come downstairs," he said. "She didn't sleep very well."

Ellie suspected none of them had.

"Thanks for the coffee," he added. "I'll see you later."

"Before noon, please," Ellie called after him as, sunglasses intact, he trotted from the kitchen and dashed out the back door as if this were a movie. Through the window she saw him dart past the bustling caterers, then head down the hill, just as Amanda's daughter emerged from the boathouse, her clothes a mess, her hair askance, as if she hadn't slept very much, either.

* * *

Martina arrived and said she would take over in the kitchen, that she'd prepare breakfast for anyone who wanted it, that Ellie should go outside and supervise the carnival people who had arrived. So Ellie went out onto the steps, surveyed the backyard stage, and tried to determine if all was as Edward had dictated: tent, tables, chairs, food stations, dance floor, band shell. Off to the left, several carnival booths—trademarks of Edward's parties—were being assembled: a popular favorite had once been called Dunk the Director, though Ellie had no idea what was in store for today.

If Edward had anything in store.

Beyond his disappearance.

And the arrival of Carleen.

As if those weren't enough.

"He didn't come home last night." Henry had crept up beside her.

"No," Ellie said. "I didn't think so."

"And now it's too late to postpone the party."

"I'm not giving up on him yet. Amanda's boys went scouting again with Babe's husband. They're going to search the shoreline." She realized her voice sounded thin and weak. She hoped Henry hadn't noticed.

He didn't answer, so the two of them stood in silence, watching the entertainment come to life.

"Do you have any ideas?" Ellie finally asked. "Did Edward say anything that might have foreshadowed this?"

Henry turned his gaze toward three young men who were affixing broad, hanging ribbons from two poles that looked thirty feet high. "No," he said. "I've asked myself that over and over."

"Me, too," she said. "Me, too."

A birdlike girl appeared next to the young men. She climbed up one ribbon, then wrapped it around and around her lithe, young body in a singular, fluid motion—a trapeze act updated in the style of Cirque du Soleil.

"Sometimes he forgets things," Henry said. "The other day we went into town and for a minute he forgot why we were there. I told him he was meeting his banker, and he laughed and said he was teasing me." The girl swung back and forth. "I didn't believe him, though. I should have told you, Ellie." Then Henry started to cry. "Do you think he has dementia? Do you think he wandered off by mistake? That he doesn't know his party is today?"

Ellie put her arm on Henry's shoulder. "No," she said firmly. "Uncle Edward is fine. And this certainly isn't your fault. He's seventy-five. It's natural for him to forget things now and then. Good Lord, I forget things. Don't you?"

Henry quieted down, and Ellie was grateful. A weeping man in madras shorts didn't do much for a party mood.

"Look at these games!" Ellie continued, sweeping her arm across the air. "How Edward loves games! He's playing another one with us right now."

"Maybe," Henry sniffed. "Maybe he is. But do you think his iPod is involved?"

Ellie didn't understand. "His iPod? The one you gave him for Christmas?"

"It's missing. Didn't I tell you? He keeps it on the nightstand in case he can't sleep. He likes to listen without disturbing me."

"Henry!" Ellie cried, grasping his shoulder again. "His iPod is missing?"

"Yes." Then a smile crept over his lips as if a revelation had just occurred. "His iPod is gone. Just like the rowboat. Just like him."

Ellie would have hugged him, but she didn't want to waste the time. "Come on," she said, "let's see what else is missing—starting in the library. Edward wouldn't plan to go anywhere without a good book." She turned and fled back toward the house, Henry's moccasins pat-pattering behind her.

Chapter Fifteen

"What in God's name are you doing?" Amanda asked.

"Looking for Dickens," Ellie explained and went back to her task. She was at one end of the library, Henry was at the other. They were alternately reciting titles of volumes, trying to determine if any were missing like Edward and the rowboat and the iPod.

"And Trollope," Henry chimed in. "Lately he loved Anthony Trollope. *He Knew He Was Right. Orley Farm.*"

"I don't know enough Trollope," Ellie replied, "to know which ones might be missing."

"I'll get a list," Henry, newly enthused, exclaimed. He darted from the library toward the office, where the computer was docked.

Ellie riffled past *Great Expectations, Dombey and Son, Martin Chuzzlewit.*

"What *are* you doing?" Amanda demanded again. "It's nearly ten o'clock. Two hundred guests will be here soon."

"We have time, Amanda. Right now, we're looking for clues about Edward's disappearance."

"On the bookshelves?"

The Old Curiosity Shop. Nicholas Nickleby.

Bleak House.

Hard Times.

Little Dorrit.

If only she could remember all of Dickens's works!

"Stop this right now!" Amanda shouted.

Ellie closed her eyes. "Have you had coffee?" she asked. "Martina made breakfast."

"What I want is a reasonable answer. Why are you digging through these tedious volumes?" Amanda had always thought reading was tedious. Ellie suspected that was because reading required sitting still.

"If you must know, we're trying to reassure ourselves that Edward planned his disappearance, the way he did when we were kids. To get away from the commotion."

Amanda huffed and puffed.

Ellie scanned and scanned again. *A Tale of Two Cities*! *Our Mutual Friend*! And then it hit her. *Oliver Twist* was gone. It was one of Edward's favorite editions, nestled comfortably inside a leather spine and boasting quirky illustrations of Oliver, Mr. Bumble, and poor Nancy, the caring whore.

"I've decided he must be sick," Amanda announced.

"Oh?" Ellie half-listened to her sister while continuing the hunt for Oliver.

"Yes. I think he's ill and knows it. He planned this party as a 'going away' party, a kind of Irish wake. At the last minute, he decided not to attend. For all we know, he's too sick to be here."

"Are you sure you don't want him to die so you will come into money?" Ellie was surprised she'd said that out loud.

Before Amanda could respond, Henry thankfully reappeared.

"The binoculars are gone," he said in a rush. "That old fart really did take off. But where is he? We already checked around the island. And the boys went ashore and got the pine boughs when they lost their paddles. Wouldn't they have seen him?"

"If he hasn't hidden the boat on the shore, I suppose he could have rowed his way off the lake. No, wait. That wouldn't be possible. There's only one way out by water, and that's down by the castle, over the falls." At first, she started to laugh, then realized what she had said. "Oh, dear," she said. "The falls."

And then the doorbell rang and footsteps pounded down the stairs and Amanda's daughter, Heather, shrieked, "Daddy's here," and Amanda said, "Oh. Great."

"Let's get another boat," Jonathan said.

Ellie was glad to have another body on board, so to speak, which was why, when Jonathan entered the library, she immediately pounced, sidestepping Amanda's agita and rattling off the story of Uncle Edward and his mysterious vanishing act, explaining that it might have included a nosedive over the waterfall on the south end by the castle.

"We don't have another boat," Ellie said now. "Edward has the rowboat, and Wes took the canoe."

"What about the neighbors? Surely you have neighbors."

"It's the end of June. Most don't arrive until July." She didn't understand why she was bickering with Amanda's husband. Perhaps it had to do with the back-waxer, whoever she was.

"So our only options are to go to Sears and buy another boat or call the Coast Guard, which I, for one, have never seen patrolling Lake Kasteel."

"Stop trying to be comical," Amanda snipped. "This is important."

"I agree. Which is why I am going to get back in my rented SUV and check out the neighborhood. Someone else must be around." He jangled the keys and headed for the door.

"Wait!" Amanda shouted.

Jonathan stopped, his back to his wife. Ellie wondered if he had any hair under his Callaway golf shirt, or if the lady in question had removed it—the *Trollope* in question, Ellie mused, not to be confused with Anthony of London letters. She laughed.

"This isn't funny!" Amanda ranted as she stomped one foot.

Ellie tightened her lips and regained her composure. She wondered if Amanda ever knew how ridiculous she sometimes looked.

"I'm going with you," Amanda said to her not-yet-erstwhile husband, who apparently didn't know that his cover, so to speak, had been blown.

"Why?" he asked.

Amanda frowned a second, then pressed the lines from her forehead as if she feared they would stick. "Because I said so.

Because I've been coming here a lot longer than you have, and I might know some of the neighbors. If you're going to ask to use their boat, it might be nice if you had someone credible with you."

Yikes, Ellie thought, though it was hard to determine by Jonathan's unchanged expression if he'd caught the barb about credibility and if he wondered why his wife had slung it at him.

"Actually," Jonathan said, "I'll help myself to a boat. There might not be time to ask." He moved toward the door without waiting for her response.

Amanda pushed out a wallop of angry air and shook her finger at her daughter. "As for you, young lady, we are not finished." Then Amanda clicked her heels and traipsed after her husband as if she really intended to help.

"I hate her," Heather said to Ellie and Ellie shook her head, and Heather went out the back way, no doubt to her tattooed love interest, as if hatred validated her behavior.

Babe was determined to spend all weekend in her bedroom. Surely she could find something to occupy her time for these mere hours—thirty-two—before she and Wes left for JFK. She didn't care if the others thought she was sulking. She hadn't needed them all these years; she didn't need them now. After the party she'd sneak downstairs and fix a plate of leftovers. Maybe there would be a bottle of champagne. It would be better than socializing with *them.*

In the meantime, she could review the business plan she'd written for the fragrance line. It was a dull task, compared to thinking about Ray, but she could always pretend it was a script. She did so much better with scripts.

She did, however, have to pee. Hopefully she could hold it until she was certain everyone had abandoned the second floor.

Carleen sat at the old vanity table and stared into the mirror. It had taken all her strength to haul herself from beneath the covers, all the self-talk she had mastered over the years to convince herself that she belonged here as much as the others. It had been her summer home, too, the place where excitement had happened, not like dreary Poughkeepsie, where she barely remembered one year to the next.

But Lake Kasteel! This was where the fun was. This was where the magic happened, where Carleen had sat in front of this very mirror and watched her transformation from a gangly preteen to a *hot potato sexpot*, as her favorite boyfriend, Earl, had often called her.

She'd thought he was pretty hot, too. It had helped that he drove a motorcycle and smoked cigarettes and had manliness, as *Cosmopolitan* called it.

Carleen sighed. She touched the lines under her eyes, tried to smoothe them with her fingertips. She didn't have to wonder where the time had gone. Every year had been a blessing, another year distanced from the past. This past. This place and the people in it.

She supposed she couldn't stay in the bedroom all weekend. Sooner or later, she'd at least have to use the bathroom, which would mean leaving the room and going down the hall. Maybe she could hold it for just a little while.

She pulled her hair into a ponytail and wondered how long she could wait.

Chapter Sixteen

"She's here," Amanda said to Jonathan. "My sister, Carleen."

He let out a low whistle.

"It was all her fault. The fire. My parents dying. Babe's abortion. All of it. And now she's come back." She'd thrown in Babe's abortion because she didn't think she'd ever told him about that. It had been so embarrassing, so distasteful. Now, however, it might help deflect any fantasies Jonathan might conjure about his glamorous, movie star sister-in-law. Amanda, after all, could no longer trust him.

"What's she like now?" he asked.

"Babe?"

"No, Carleen."

"She looks like our daughter."

They drove from the driveway to the narrow, unpaved road that circled Lake Kasteel and provided residential access, rutty though it was.

"The boys are with Wes McCall," Amanda said, not that Jonathan had asked. "Babe's husband."

"Oh, right," Jonathan said. "The actor."

She checked her lipstick in the mirror on the visor.

"Well," Jonathan continued, "Chandler must be excited to meet McCall. He's always been one of his heroes, hasn't he?"

"Chandler outgrew him years ago. Now it's Chase who likes those kinds of movies." Her words were purposely sour, both for her husband, who didn't know his own sons better, and for Babe's husband, for whom she did not hold a grudge; she simply was annoyed that he was there interfering.

She was about to muster the nerve to ask what kind of business had kept Jonathan in Manhattan last night when he took a sharp right and they landed in a driveway.

"Donnelly," Jonathan said, reading the mailbox perched on a post. "Sound familiar?"

She shook her head: Amanda had never befriended the neighbors the way a couple of her sisters had, especially Babe, who'd had that boyfriend, Ray, for a while, the father of the aforementioned aborted baby. Ellie once told her that he still lived there, that he was the head of the lake association or something upstanding like that.

Jonathan pulled up to an old brown Jeep that was parked, unregistered, next to a rickety garage. The garage was attached to a large stone house whose lawn needed mowing and whose gardens needed tending.

"Summer people," Amanda said. "Not here yet."

Her husband stopped the car and jumped out. He started to walk around the garage when Amanda opened her door and shouted, "Hey, what are you doing? You really can't take someone's boat if they're not home."

He looked at her oddly. "Your uncle is missing. He might have drowned."

"That's no excuse to turn into a thief."

He laughed. "Then call the police and have them arrest me. Oh, wait, I bet no one has called the police on account of no one wants to stir up any trouble. Or alert the media that the Dalton girls have returned to their uncle Edward's."

She got out onto the pockmarked driveway. "That's not very nice."

He laughed and waved her away. "Stay there or come with me. It's up to you."

For a moment she stood her ground, her life-with-Jonathan flashing before her, her future a blurred vision of thrift shops and food stamps. Her only choice, as she saw it, was to take control and confront him, to be the aggressor rather than the victim.

"Wait up," Amanda shouted at last. "We might as well be arrested together."

They must have opened their bedroom doors at the exact same time, because Babe had been listening for sounds of life. She hadn't heard any. Not one little peep.

Which was why she shouted, "Jesus," when she nearly collided with Carleen.

"Babe," Carleen said. "I'm sorry."

Babe figured she meant she was sorry that she'd almost

bumped into her, not sorry about all the other stuff. She clutched her towel and looked away. "I'm going to use the bathroom. You need to use the one in Ellie's room."

Carleen juggled shampoo and powder and reached out and touched Babe on the arm. *Touched her on the arm.* "Babe," she said. "Can't we at least be polite? For Edward's sake?"

Now that Babe saw Carleen up close, it was nice to know the years showed on her, that she wasn't nearly as pretty as she'd once been, that she had bags under her eyes and crow's-feet at the corners, and her skin looked pretty dry. "I don't have anything to say to you," Babe replied.

"That's too bad," Carleen said, "because I have a lot to say to you." She started down the hall toward Ellie's room; at least it didn't seem she would argue about that.

"You have a lot to say? Like what?"

Carleen stopped. Carleen turned around.

"Like how are you?"

"Well, you're looking at me. You can see I'm fine." *Better than you,* she wanted to add.

"You didn't used to have a chip on your shoulder."

"Didn't I? Maybe I got it from you."

They stood there in the hall, each clinging to a towel. It might have been better if they'd both been holding pistols.

"Why are you here?" Babe asked.

"Because I was invited."

"Edward's mistake."

"Maybe," Carleen said. "But I have as much of a right to be here as you do, Babe."

"That's a matter of opinion."

"Yes. I guess it is."

"Why are you alone? Don't you have a family?"

"A husband, yes."

"And children?"

She hesitated. "Yes. Two."

"How nice for you."

"It is. They are."

"Boys or girls, or one of each?"

"Girls. Two girls."

"Are they like you?"

"No," Carleen said. "They're nice, like Ellie is. The way you used to be." With that she turned again and walked toward Ellie's room, leaving Babe standing in the hall in a small cloud of talcum powder dust.

Few people might understand that, despite her fame and fortune, Babe would have traded everything if she could only have had a child. Ray Williams's child. If she only could have turned back time and instead of saying yes to Carleen, Babe had said, *"No. I will not kill my baby, I don't care what Mother and Father think or say or do."*

She'd asked the doctor—the *abortionist*, a female physician whose name she could not remember but whose stern face she would never forget—if the fetus had been a boy or a girl. The doctor would not say; she'd said it had been too early to tell.

Not that it mattered by then. And Babe was sick. She'd lost a lot of blood when her cervix had been damaged because she was so young, too young.

"Not uncommon," the doctor had sighed.

Only Babe's therapist knew that seventeen motion pictures (five of which were TV originals), three husbands, those damned awards and countless accolades later, Naomi "Babe" Dalton had still not moved on, not in her heart, where it counted.

She turned the shower to steam, as hot as possible. She thought about her parents, burning in the fire, "smoke inhalation," the fire chief had called it, adding that the heat had been unusually intense because it had been a dry summer and firewood was stacked against the side of the house where the fireplace had been and one thing ignited the other and *whoosh,* everything went up in flames. The house. Mother and Daddy. Not Carleen, because she escaped.

"I didn't mean to do it," Carleen had whispered soberly at the trial. She'd worn a tailored Liz Claiborne suit and had pulled her wild red hair into a ponytail and tied it with a pink ribbon. She had on very little makeup and sedate Capezios. She did not look like Carleen but like a Miss Porter's imitation. Amanda said her attorney must have told her to dress like that to garner pity from the jury.

But who would take pity on the rest of them?

"I didn't know the flue was closed," Carleen continued from the stand. "The house filled up with smoke; I got scared and I ran."

"You didn't think to alert your parents?" the district attorney probed.

"I didn't know they were home. They go away in summers. We stay with Uncle Edward . . ."

"So you should have been at your uncle Edward's house?"

"Yes."

"That is Edward Dalton?" The D.A. swung and faced the audience, pointing at Uncle Edward.

"Yes."

"So you were supposed to be at Edward's, but you snuck home to Poughkeepsie . . ."

"I . . . I went to find my birth certificate."

"Your birth certificate? For what purpose?"

"To prove I'm eighteen. So my boyfriend and I could go to North Carolina to get married."

The courtroom got quiet. Until then, no one—not Ellie, Amanda, Babe, or, apparently, Edward—had known that Carleen and Earl intended to run off and get married.

"That's all," she whispered. "I just wanted my birth certificate."

"Did you find it?"

"No."

"But you went looking in the attic?"

"Yes."

"What did you find there?"

"Old things. School papers, mostly." She toyed with the ribbon wrapped around her ponytail.

"What did you do next?"

"I tried to burn them."

The D.A. moved a few paces to the left, then a few back to the right. "So you went home for your birth certificate. You went upstairs to the attic to look for it. But though you couldn't find it, you found some old school papers and decided to burn them?"

"Yes."

"And that made sense to you?"

Her hands moved from the pink ribbon. "I . . . I was angry," she said. "I was angry I couldn't find what I wanted."

"So you burned your school papers."

She shrugged. "Yes." She admitted it had been foolish. "But I was angry with my mother. I wanted to marry Earl, and I knew she wouldn't want me to. But I didn't want to live with them anymore. I was just being stupid. I didn't mean to hurt them."

Then she cried, which was something to see. None of them had ever seen Carleen cry; she was always the tough one who held both laughter and tears deep inside.

Luckily for her, the jury believed her. Luckily for her, they knew who Uncle Edward was—indeed, they spent most court sessions with their eyes shooting from Carleen to him to the many supporters he'd brought along, most of whom having had their larger-than-life portraits plastered on billboards in Times Square at one time or another.

"Not guilty of manslaughter," the foreman read once they'd made up their minds.

Later that day, Uncle Edward escorted Carleen to a bus. That was the last they saw of her—*Good riddance*, Babe and Ellie and Amanda said simultaneously under their breath as they watched the silver Greyhound start its stop-and-go trip out of town.

Babe leaned against the tile wall of the shower now, sweating from the steam, withered from the heat, exhausted from remembering. She wondered if she should retreat to her room again or join Ellie and Amanda, who must now be hurting, too.

Chapter Seventeen

Oliver Twist and the binoculars and Edward's iPod were missing.

Ellie and Henry stood in the small room that once was the butler's pantry. Edward had converted it into an office when he stopped giving parties and fired the live-in staff. He could have chosen any of the bedrooms upstairs, but this was close to the kitchen, where he could fetch tea and spirits whenever he wanted.

"He's on the island," Ellie said as she ransacked a dilapidated wooden filing cabinet in search of more clues—not that she needed any, not that she wasn't sure.

"He can't be. We already ruled that out."

"He is. Think about it. A book. His iPod. Binoculars, for God's sake. He might be hiding out, but Edward is too nosey not to want to know what else is going on. Even if it's just to watch other boaters. Did I say watch? *Snoop* is more like Edward." She sounded frenetic, almost as if she were as loony as Edward. The truth was, she was relieved.

"But where's the boat?"

"Maybe he hauled it out of the water and hid it. Covered it with branches. Or buried it. He could have pulled it far enough onto the shore so we couldn't see it. Maybe Wes and the boys will find it."

"I don't agree."

"Why not?"

"Because he's seventy-five, Ellie."

"And he's in great shape for seventy-five."

Henry sighed and sank on the creaky rolling chair that Edward insisted on keeping at his desk. It was a far cry from a Hepplewhite, but it had come from Edward's office in Times Square, and he'd insisted it was where he had always done his best thinking. "He isn't in great shape," Henry said.

Ellie stopped fiddling and turned to him. "What on earth do you mean?"

After a long, too long, drawn-out sigh, Henry said, "Edward has cancer, Ellie. The big *C*."

She blinked. She would have sat down, but Henry was parked in the only chair in the room. In addition to saying he had always done his best thinking in the old wooden chair, Uncle Edward had said he'd done his best thinking alone.

"What are you talking about?" she finally managed to ask.

Henry closed his eyes. "I'm sorry. I promised Edward I wouldn't tell you."

Turning back to the file, she tried slamming the drawer,

but some papers were stuck and got jammed in the process. She ripped the drawer open, yanking too hard. The contents tipped out and dumped onto the floor.

"*Goddamnit,*" she said, and Henry didn't comment. With her gaze fixed on the mess, Ellie asked, "Are you sure?"

"Yes," Henry said quietly. "It's in his colon."

Ellie suddenly smiled, as if this were good news. "But that can't be right. Edward isn't sick."

Henry shrugged. "It works that way sometimes. We went to New York-Presbyterian, Ellie. They found it in his colonoscopy. They know what they're doing."

"But when did you go?" If she challenged him on the details, he might admit he was lying. "You and Edward rarely leave the estate."

"Late April," he said. "We were gone a whole day. You were with the gardeners preparing the summer beds."

She remembered. It had been a Tuesday, not that it mattered.

"Would you like to sit down?" Henry stood.

Ellie sat. "I can't believe this."

"I know."

"When was he planning to tell me?"

"I don't think he wanted you to know. At all."

She stared at the rubble on the floor.

"That's when he decided to plan this party," Henry continued. "That's when he realized he wanted his friends and family together one last time."

It was believable. And yet, it was not.

"There's more," Henry added. "Edward doesn't want treatment. He says chemotherapy will ruin his good looks." Then

Henry's narrow shoulders started to quiver and he lowered his head and cried.

"No," Ellie said, but Henry nodded, *Yes.*

She knew she should go to him, comfort him, reassure him that somehow they'd get through this, that maybe Edward would live a long life and everything would be fine. Instead all she said was, "So he is on the island."

"I don't know. I don't know where he is, or what he's done."

"Yes," Ellie said. "That's where he is. And he wants us to leave him alone."

"Unless he decided to end things his own way . . . on his own terms . . . that would be so like him. . . ."

Ellie stood up, looped her arm through Henry's, and sighed. "I will not believe that, and neither should you. For now, we will do what Uncle Edward wants. We will host the party. And celebrate his birthday. He left on his own terms; he should come back the same way."

Ellie had no idea how she was staying composed. She only knew someone had to, and, as usual, it would be her. Which was why she decided right then not to tell her sisters. She owed Edward that much, after all.

Besides, it was really annoying that Amanda was right.

Before getting into the boat, Amanda tossed off her ballet flats. They were only Cole Haan, but it had taken forever to find the exact match for the pink capris and the knit top she wore. Unfortunately, the strappy sandals she'd chosen to complement the pale cherry halter dress for the party would do little to conceal the two nicks on her pedicure.

God, she thought, trying to smooth the damaged edge of her right foot's big toenail, how she hated all things relating to the outdoors. Bugs and birds. Raccoons and skunks. Rickety boats like the one her husband now steered toward the south end of Lake Kasteel.

It was hard to believe she had once liked it here at the lake. She had actually liked swimming and canoeing—in spite of Edward's warnings about the mythical lake monster. But around thirteen or fourteen she'd stopped wanting to get her hair wet, and it had been downhill from there. Oh, sure, she'd loved watching the theater people and the glamorous ladies. But, deep down, Amanda had been disturbed that they weren't refined, that they weren't more sophisticated.

There was the scarlet-lipped woman who always toted her small dog whose curly white hair was a dead ringer for the coif of his mistress.

Or Mrs. McGuire, who arrived at each party on the arm of a different young man and whose husband no one seemed to know much about—like who he was, what he did for a living, or if he existed at all.

Or who could forget *Lovely Lydia,* as Uncle Edward called the twenty-something-year-old who always accompanied Jacob Hines, who was eighty-something if he were a day, or so Uncle Edward chuckled aloud whenever the couple arrived?

They were imposing characters, slices of Edward's dramatic life. Amanda wondered if any of them were like Bibiana, the woman who might have made off with her husband's heart.

She should ask him now while they were alone on this godforsaken lake with no one within shouting distance.

"I had hoped the nonsense with your sister was over and

done with," Jonathan said, interrupting her thoughts, circum-
venting her intent.

"Carleen? I will never forgive her."

"Jesus, Amanda. People change."

"I haven't changed."

He laughed. "You? You of all people have changed. You
used to be more relaxed. Happier."

She couldn't very well tell him she used to have dreams
about a husband who was someone and a life that was special.
When she'd finally understood the dreams were not going to
come true, yes, she'd lost happiness then. Why wouldn't she?
"When we are young we are naïve," she said.

"You should give your sister a chance. It probably wasn't
easy for her to come here."

Amanda stared at the water, trying to grasp what he had
said. Of all people, Jonathan knew what the family had gone
through—he'd been in Amanda's life then, they'd been planning their wedding, they'd been choosing their crystal, he'd
been parlaying her around Princeton as if he'd won the regatta.
Didn't he remember the pain Carleen had caused? Didn't he
remember the damn *funeral*?

"How quickly you forget," she said.

"Be realistic, Amanda. Haven't you ever done anything you
regretted?"

She didn't know if he was talking about Carleen or the slut
from Brazil. She pursed her lips, stared into the lake water,
and said, "I didn't kill my parents. Carleen did."

"God, Amanda. You are so intolerant and unforgiving."

She whipped her head around. "Intolerant and unforgiving? Is that how you see me? You would rather I ignore it

when people in my life—people I *trust*—betray me?" She was moving precariously close to announcing that she knew about his slut, close to grabbing one of the oars and whacking Jonathan over the head. Instead, she said, "Take me back to the house."

"No. We're going to find Edward."

"Find him or don't, for all I care. But first, take me to the house. I don't want to continue this conversation."

"Stop making so much of it."

But Amanda shook her head to indicate those were her last words on the subject. If he didn't comply, she would jump overboard and start swimming, which would not bode well for what was left of her pedi, though her sisters would no doubt be amused.

"They still hate me." Carleen stood in Ellie's bedroom, looking out the long window at the party preparations scurrying below. She had used Ellie's bathroom and planned to wait there until Babe went back to her room. Thankfully, Carleen had tucked her cell phone into her robe pocket and had been able to get through to her husband.

"Maybe they need a little time," Brian said.

"It's been twenty years. I'm trying to be nice, but it isn't working. I shouldn't have come." She meandered to Ellie's bureau. Her eyes surveyed the top: an antique glass-globed lamp, a faux suede jewelry box, a white crocheted runner like the kind Mother had displayed on every side table in every room of their Poughkeepsie house.

"I should have come with you."

"That wouldn't have solved anything," she said. She lightly

touched the crocheted piece, then moved to the jewelry box. "They'd only hate me more. It doesn't help that it looks as if I'm the only one with a normal life."

"And a handsome husband?"

"Oh, yes. Definitely." Lifting the lid, Carleen peered inside at a jumble of small, yet classic, earrings, two or three gold bracelets, several simple, yet sparkling, pins.

"More handsome than Wes McCall?"

"I'm sure, though I haven't seen him yet. I haven't seen my uncle yet, either." She poked at the earrings, wondering if they were real or fake. So many of Carleen's adornments were from QVC; she doubted that Ellie even watched television.

"Your uncle didn't greet you last night?"

"No. I guess he'd gone to bed." She scooped up a few items and studied the way the sunlight danced off the facets.

"You have a strange family."

"Finally, you get it."

That's when the door opened and Ellie came into the room, and there stood Carleen, sifting the gold and silver and sparkling jewels through her fingers.

Chapter Eighteen

"Carleen?" Ellie didn't ask what her sister was doing. It was pretty obvious.

The lid to the jewelry box slammed shut. Carleen moved to block it. "I'll call you later," she said into the phone, then clicked it off. "Ellie."

"Yes," Ellie replied, her gaze fixed on the dresser. "This is my room."

"I know that."

"Why are you here?"

"I came to use your bathroom."

"There's one in the hall," Ellie said, as if Carleen might have forgotten.

"Babe was there."

"And so you came into my room to . . . ?"

"To use your bathroom."

Ellie pursed her lips. She wondered if she should ask to search Carleen's pockets for her jewelry.

Carleen stepped forward. "Ellie," she said, "I know what you must be thinking. But I was talking to my husband. I was waiting for Babe to finish so we wouldn't bump into each other again. She still hates me, you know?"

After a long, slow blink, Ellie managed to shift her eyes from the dresser to Carleen.

"I was looking out the window. I walked over to your dresser. I was talking. I wasn't paying attention. I only looked inside your jewelry box because I, oh, I don't know, I needed to do something while I was on the phone, I guess. To fidget. You know. This weekend is so surreal to me."

It could be true, Ellie supposed. But *Carleen* and *innocent* never had been two words that had gone well together, no matter what the jury had said. "In case you think otherwise," Ellie said stiffly, "I have nothing of value. And certainly no jewelry of Mother's. Everything that was hers is gone now. If you forgot."

Carleen moved toward the door. "I'm sorry," she said. "I'll leave you alone. I know you must want to get ready for the party."

Ellie glared at her sister. "Edward is missing," she said, stopping her sister. "I don't need your shit, because Edward is missing and that's more important to me than you or what you were doing."

"What do you mean, 'Edward is missing'?"

"He's been gone since yesterday. We've sent out search

parties, because, after all, we can't call the police. You, of all people, know why. Now get out of my room and get out of my way."

Carleen hesitated. "I'm sorry that Edward is missing, Ellie. But it isn't my fault."

Ellie glared a moment longer, then hissed, "*Just get out of my sight!*" Carleen did, and Ellie was too worn out to wonder if she'd ever attacked any of her sisters with so much venom in her heart. She closed her eyes and hung her head. Later, she supposed, she should check inside her jewelry box to see what was there and determine what wasn't. Later, not now. She did not have the strength to do that right now.

There was only one thing for Carleen to do. Two, if you counted suicide, but she had never felt that desperate, not even back then.

She returned to her room and safely shut the door. She sat down on the old vanity table, where she'd once tucked Earl's photo into the frame of the mirror. But this time, she was thinking about Edward, not Earl.

Edward is missing.

Carleen supposed that somehow her sisters would blame her for that, too.

She wanted to call Brian and ask him to come get her. But she could not ask him to step into this muck.

No, the only thing left for Carleen to do was call a cab— if she could find one in this place. She would make her way back to the city and wait for a bus back to Amherst. Yes, she decided, she needed to leave, the way she'd once done. It was not as if this time she'd end up alone, in a strange town, with only a suitcase, a few hundred dollars, a paid-up tuition, and instructions not to return.

She remembered those first days and weeks. The early morning gagging smell of donuts being baked next door to the brick boardinghouse in Back Bay. The rattle of the "T" as it shuttled her back and forth to classes amid somber faces of students and working people. The drone of sewing machines in the costume factory, second shift. The Cheetos and root beer she had for dinner because the vending machines offered few choices.

Boston had been her penance, the prison for *not guilty of manslaughter.*

She'd done her time. It would be different now. She had a home to go to now, a loving family, a long-haired spaniel named Puppy.

Yes, Carleen should leave.

Or there was a third choice. She could stay and do what she had planned, whether Uncle Edward surfaced or not.

Ellie stayed standing in the same position in her room for several minutes, trying to make her mind go blank, wishing she had come upstairs later, earlier, any time that would have erased the scene she'd just witnessed.

They were right, Amanda and Babe. They were right not to trust Carleen, to be angry that Edward had invited her. Ellie was such a fool! Such a pushover when it came to her family. They'd been together so few years; had it been wrong to hope for more?

Someone knocked on the door. Softly.

Was it Carleen? Come to return things? The gold bracelet Edward gave Ellie to comfort her the day her divorce became final? The brooch he said had been his mother's—her grandmother's? He'd said that because Ellie was the eldest, she should have it. It was so sad, after all, that none of the girls had anything of their mother's, that everything had been destroyed in the fire. *A total loss*, she'd heard one of the firefighters say.

The knock came again, followed by a small whisper.

"Ellie?"

It was Babe's whisper.

Ellie turned and slowly opened the door.

"Henry said you came upstairs to change. I'm all ready. Can I help? I don't want to bother the caterers, but I need something to do."

Ellie managed a small smile. She knew she couldn't, wouldn't, tell Babe or Amanda about what had happened with Carleen. She must hold it together, for Uncle Edward's sake. "You look so pretty," Ellie said. Babe had on a light blue dress that hugged her curves and accentuated her eyes, their mother's eyes. She'd done her hair up loosely and wore teardrop aquamarine earrings. "All you have to do is mingle with the guests and be the star that you are. I'm sure many of them are hoping you'll be here."

"Oh," Babe said. "I hate that part. It's easier to be in the spotlight when it's among total strangers. I guess it's too much to ask that Edward's guests will be strangers?"

Ellie shook her head. "Most will remember us from when we were girls."

"Which is why the party starts at noon and not eight o'clock."

"They all have white hair. Some have none."

Babe laughed, then closed her pretty blue eyes. "This is hard, isn't it? All of us being together? Wondering what's happened to Uncle Edward?"

"Yes, honey, it's hard."

Babe's eyes flew open and her mouth widened into a grin. "Well, I've decided to stay. I figure you and Amanda must be hurting and worried, too. I'm sorry I haven't come home before now. I only hope I get to see him. I hope he isn't . . . you know."

"He's fine," Ellie repeated, for the hundredth time.

Babe nodded and brushed a hand across her cheek. "Well, enough of that, anyway. There are other things to talk about. Like what are you going to wear today?"

Ellie supposed she should invite Babe in. If she did, she risked breaking down and telling her about Carleen and the jewelry box. And then she might tell her about Edward's cancer. Babe had always been easy to talk to. "A simple beige sundress," she quickly said. "With a little jacket."

Babe wrinkled her nose. "Sounds boring."

Ellie giggled. "It is! Just like me!" She didn't say she'd ordered it from a catalog because the thought of shopping in stores usually triggered an onrush of panic.

Suddenly, Babe pushed past her and was in the room. "Well, as long as I'm here," she said, "I won't allow you to look boring! You're my sister and I love you and I don't think I've ever told you that."

She hadn't. Ellie smiled.

Then Babe marched to the wardrobe (the big house had so few real closets) and pulled open the doors. A fast shuffle through the hangers only revealed how pathetic, and, yes, boring, Ellie's clothes really were.

Babe groaned. "Uck. Okay, so it's a little late for a trip to Rodeo Drive. Let me see the sundress."

Ellie went into the bathroom, where she'd hung the dress on the back of the door after she'd ironed it Thursday. Thankfully, Carleen hadn't stolen it. Perhaps she hadn't found jewelry to match.

After checking the dress, Babe said, "Wait here." She, of course, wouldn't know that Ellie wouldn't risk stepping into the hall, where Carleen surely lurked.

God, Ellie thought. *I'm becoming as freaked out about her as my sisters!*

She turned her thoughts to the dress and quietly agreed that it was, indeed, boring, with its modestly scooped neckline and square-cut bolero that had been embroidered in threads the same shade of beige. *Understated* would have been a compliment.

Babe was gone only a minute when she returned, holding up a delicate scarf in soft shades of seafoam, aqua, and sand, laced with twinkling silver and gold. "Throw away the jacket and wear this. It will brighten your face." She looped the scarf around Ellie's neck and stepped back to admire.

"Perfect," she said, turning Ellie to face the mirror. "You look like Mother."

Ellie smiled. "I always thought you were the one who looked like her the most."

Babe shook her head. "You look just like her now. Standing here. Wasn't she about your age when she died?"

Yes, Ellie thought, with a gentle memory. "It was a lifetime ago."

They were quiet a moment, then Babe asked, "Hey, Ellie, do you know whatever happened to Ray Williams and his family? Like where they went after they left Lake Kasteel?"

Ellie supposed she should have anticipated the question sooner or later. But with everything else going on . . ." Oh, Babe," she said. "We never socialize." Avoiding the truth was so much easier right now. "Besides, sometimes it's best to forget the past."

Babe nodded, rearranged the scarf, and smiled again. "I know. It doesn't matter. I was just wondering."

Ellie forced a return smile and wondered if she could—should—bring herself to tell Babe the rest, that she knew Ray still lived there because his son, Kevin, was their newspaper delivery boy, or that Ray was the environmental manager of the lake association and sent Edward newsletters from time to time, not via e-mail but the old-fashioned, Mount Kasteel way, printed on a sheet of plain paper and tucked in the mailbox. Not to mention that—with all the to-do about Carleen coming and Uncle Edward going—Ellie forgot that Uncle Edward had been oddly insistent on including Ray's name on the guest list. But Ray hadn't replied, so Ellie assumed they were "safe." Now, however, she remembered that Carleen hadn't replied, either.

Chapter Nineteen

Amanda scrambled from the flimsy boat without giving Jonathan the satisfaction of a good-bye. She marched onto Uncle Edward's dock, stopped at the boathouse, and loudly knocked. "Open the door, Heather. Get out here this instant." Perhaps there were some aspects of her life she still could control, to salvage a few pieces from the ruins.

There was no answer.

Inhaling a stiff, shoulder-raising breath, Amanda knocked again. "I'm coming in," she barked and pushed open the door. Her vision quickly adjusted to the darkness and to the fact that the boathouse was empty. Amanda let out a low growl and stormed away.

She stalked up the hill, Cole Haan flats in hand, more concerned with damaging the shoes than her pedicure. She could always, after all, repair her toenails herself, unpleasant as that would be. But if she was left without fiscal resources, she was damned if she'd let her wardrobe or her shoes suffer. It would be humiliating enough once word got out that Jonathan had chosen a foreigner over her.

Darting through a swarm of people in white serving jackets, Amanda kept her head down, focused on her mission. Then she heard "Mother!" in her daughter's voice.

Amanda slowed her pace.

"Did you find Uncle Edward?" Heather asked as she caught up to her.

Amanda did a double take at the young woman, who had, sometime in the last hour, transformed herself back to the Wellesley girl. She was dressed in a clean, pretty skirt and top, and her hair was brushed neatly. The boyfriend, however, was nowhere to be seen. Oh, wait. Was that him standing next to Heather? The handsome boy in khakis and a long-sleeved cotton shirt that covered hideous tattoos?

She looked back to her daughter and blinked. "Heather?" she asked, as if needing an introduction.

"Yes, Mother. Who did you expect?"

Amanda's spine stiffened. "You look nice. Both of you." She'd show Jonathan who was intolerant and who was not. "What are you doing?"

"Jarred helped the carnie people reconfigure the dunking booth. They were having trouble with the water."

Jarred? Who the hell was Jarred? Apparently the boyfriend's name had changed along with his suit of clothes.

"Well," Amanda said, avoiding the melodramatic or the re-active, "that's nice. Have you seen my sisters?"

"No. I've been inside with Martina. Helping her stuff mushroom caps. But what about Uncle Edward?"

Amanda shrugged. "Who knows where the hell he is," she said, then resumed her hustle toward the house. After all, she only had a short time to change into her cherry halter and preserve what was left of her dignity.

Inside the house, she was about to mount the stairs, when she spotted a clipboard next to the front door. A few sheets of paper were held under a wide silver spring. Two columns of type were printed on page one.

"The guest list!" Amanda said in a hush, then grabbed it. If she was privy to who would be coming, she'd be better able to position herself in the crowd, to spend time with those folks who might be relevant to her future.

Her eyes searched up and down, as if she were a man checking out a woman.

Antoine, Mark and Sybil.

Athas, Bob and Laura.

Custer, Rodney and wife.

The names weren't familiar, but then, it had been years.

Goldsmith, Farrington, Lyons.

She flipped the page.

Slater, Toomey, Williams.

She stopped. *Williams?*

Ray Williams.

She sucked in her breath. "Holy shit," she said, just as Carleen rounded the corner.

"Interesting reading?" the prodigal sister inquired.

Amanda dropped the clipboard. She laughed. "It is as if you're shocked that Ray Williams was invited."

A wave of distress flitted across Carleen's face. Amanda did little to hide her amusement.

"Ray Williams?" Carleen finally asked. "Oh, no. Does Babe know?"

Amanda tossed her a satisfied look. "I have no idea. But something tells me I doubt it."

"Oh, no," Amanda heard Carleen say again, but by then Amanda was ascending the staircase, hopefully leaving Carleen to feel as upset as she deserved.

Ellie decided to call off the search. Whatever Edward was up to, he apparently was up to it with forethought and reason. Wherever he was, he wanted to be there. Later she'd decide what to do about the hurt that she felt because he hadn't told her about the cancer.

Cancer.

Uncle Edward?

Uncle Edward.

She shook her head, as if the act of shaking would dispel her distress. Adjusting Babe's scarf around her neck, Ellie decided that yes, the scarf added a healthy glow to her cheeks. Perhaps it would help others think she was happy, relaxed. She checked her watch: it was after eleven. Less than an hour until the party.

It would be strange not to have the guest of honor, but those who'd been invited knew Edward and should not be surprised. They might expect that later he would leap from a cake, which Ellie highly doubted under the circumstances with the cancer.

Oh! she thought. *Stop thinking about that!*

Making her way downstairs and through the kitchen, she stepped out to the backyard, where everything had magically come to life. Two jugglers paraded past her, their colorful props dancing lightly in the air; a gold-painted Statue of Liberty took a practice stance atop an orange crate; a strolling musician tuned up his banjo and harmonica simultaneously. Over by the games the young woman floated and spun and swung from the ribbons; a young man lined up bowling pins; a clown of questionable gender tested the dunking booth with the help of someone who looked like Heather's boyfriend without biker-wear or tattoos.

Edward would have loved the action.

With a small sigh, Ellie turned her attention to the caterers. She'd helped select the menu. Edward had requested simple fare: a barbecue with chicken, ribs, corn on the cob and slaw. And baked beans, his favorite, though he preferred them from a can. For a man of sophisticated tastes in art and literature, sometimes he gravitated toward being common.

Then she smiled as she remembered that he had insisted on Dom Perignon, because even Edward Dalton had a limit to his folksiness.

Ellie meandered among the tables, checking the linens and place settings and the "six chairs per table" per Uncle Edward, who'd always felt that too many people at a table discouraged conversation except between the loudmouth (there was always one of those) and the busybody (ditto). There would be no table for gifts: Edward had insisted on *no gifts*. "If you feel you *must*," he'd asked Ellie to write on each invitation, "then please make a donation to the Actors' Equity Association. God knows everyone is underpaid, compared to the players for the Yankees and the Mets." He often enjoyed weighing the contributions to society made by Broadway versus baseball.

Henry was near the cake table, looking forlorn, despite having changed into a crisp linen suit. Ellie joined him. "He still might show up," she said.

But he looked bewildered and wandered from her, the way Edward had wandered from the estate.

Ellie sighed again. More than anything, she wanted this day to be done—even more when she saw Carleen approach.

"Have you given up looking for him?" Carleen asked.

Ellie's mouth went dry, but she answered anyway. "Yes. We are going to let Edward be. I'll tell Babe's husband and Jonathan and Amanda as soon as they come back."

"Amanda is back. That's why I thought the search was called off."

"I didn't see her." Ellie suspected her tone sounded like a challenge.

"Oh, she's here, all right. She's in the house. The way she stares at me makes my whole body shiver."

Ellie ignored the comment. "So they didn't find Edward?"

"I didn't see him. Besides, Amanda was more interested in conveying the auspicious news that Uncle Edward invited Ray Williams."

Oh, Ellie thought. *Oh, dear.*

"I thought she was testing me," Carleen continued. "But she was holding the guest list and wearing a smirk. Does Babe know?"

Ellie's mouth was parched now. "No. I hope he won't come."

"Well," Carleen said, "I've never seen a party where people who are wanted aren't here, and others who were invited aren't really wanted." She turned away.

"Carleen," Ellie said. "Wait. Where are you going?"

"First, I am going to set something straight. Then I am going to find Edward."

"I meant what I said. I don't want anyone else looking for him. You don't have all the facts."

Carleen stopped; she spun around. "Then share them with me."

"I can't. Not right now."

Carleen leveled her gaze with an icy look. "Then you do what you want, and I'll do what I want. It's a free country, remember?"

So, Ellie realized, it seemed that the old Carleen still simmered beneath her timid ponytail and her hand-quilted purse.

Chapter Twenty

At three minutes before noon, a dark green, vintage Jaguar delivered the first guests: David and Myrna Goldsmith, who, like Edward, once had been young but now were not.

Ellie stationed herself at the front door with her game face and her clipboard that held a list of names of everyone who'd been invited. She did not expect to recognize them all, so Edward had prepared her a line: "Hello, thank you so much for coming! Uncle Edward will be so pleased that you've come all this way." The remark would suit everyone, because most of the guests were from Manhattan and most were over sixty, seventy, and more, and traveling twenty-eight miles for a party had been a commitment.

It was nice, however, that Ellie could easily identify the first arrivals. She checked their names off on the list, set down the clipboard, then went outside to the top step. "David! Myrna!" she exclaimed. "Thank you so much for coming!"

Heather's boyfriend had volunteered to valet park the vehicles, for which Ellie had been both surprised and appreciative. He scooted around her now and jumped into the driver's seat that David Goldsmith had vacated. Thankfully, the boy did not look as if he might make off with the car, and he didn't tattoo the driveway with rubber as he wheeled away.

Ellie directed the Goldsmiths past the arborvitae and the burgundy roses, then toward the peonies and through the gate that led to the backyard. "Uncle Edward will be so pleased that you've come all this way."

"I know he said no gifts." David patted the pocket of his seersucker jacket, which looked like a Ralph Lauren. "But I've brought Havanas. I was hoping Edward would join me in a smoke before the party gets under way."

Oh, great, Ellie thought. The first guests, and already she would have to lie. "Actually," she said, shielding her eyes against the sun that seemed to grow brighter in the summer sky, "Edward isn't in the garden yet."

"Oh?" David and Myrna Goldsmith asked in unison.

Realistically, Ellie knew the Goldsmiths would not have any cause to think something was wrong or that Edward was gone. Still, Ellie knew David had once been a celebrated playwright for several of Edward's productions and was therefore a smart man who knew her uncle quite well. When Edward had packed up and left Broadway, David had tried negotiating numerous futile tricks to change his mind.

"Actually," Ellie said carefully, "we think Edward is planning to stage a grand entrance later, so please enjoy your-selves until then." She smiled, as if she were part of a glorious scheme. To seal the deal, she winked.

God, had she really winked?

The Goldsmiths studied her briefly, then chuckled simulta-neously. David put his hand at his wife's elbow and guided her toward the champagne.

So far, so sort-of-good, Ellie thought as she returned to the driveway at the front of the house. *Only one hundred and ninety-eight people left to greet.*

And then a Rolls pulled in, followed by a stretch Mercedes. Ellie took a deep breath and made ready to lie again.

Carleen needed to find a way to make this right. She needed to find a way to prove to Ellie she was not the old Carleen, that she had grown, she had changed, and, above all, she could be trusted. She was a mother of two! She was a wife! A freaking algebra teacher! What made Ellie think she would stoop so low as to prowl through her box of junk jewelry?

Because she caught you, Carleen reminded herself.

It didn't matter that Carleen hadn't intended on lifting a brooch or a bracelet or two. Seeing was believing, and Ellie certainly knew what she'd seen.

And what was this business about Edward being missing? Did they blame her for that? Why was he gone? Because of her? Had he kept tabs on her all these years so that one day he could lure her back, then thrust her into the claws of her unforgiving sisters?

Obviously, it was time for Carleen to come clean with them.

Trudging along the lake road from the house toward her

first destination, she reminded herself that the outcome of this weekend shouldn't matter. She and Brian were fine. They didn't need her family and they didn't need Edward's money. They didn't need her to do this to make their life right.

But she did.

As she slipped out of her sandals that were not made for walking, Carleen tried not to think about the party sounds wafting behind her: the music, the laughter, the people having fun. She tried not to feel the loneliness those sounds once evoked.

Long ago, *fun* had seemed like the answer to her loneliness, to the fact that she'd never felt she'd fit in. Not before the fire, when competing for attention was mandatory; not after the fire, when she was alone in a world where most people honored their fathers and mothers, not caused their deaths.

One night in Boston, the fun stopped. It was during her first semester in college, her first weeks since being banished from the family and all things familiar. During the night, Carleen woke up sick. Her belly and her head ached with distress; her heart compressed in pain. She blamed the cheap wine she'd consumed at a frat party. She reached across the mattress for the boy she'd brought home. John. Jahn. Not that his name mattered, because he had left.

She climbed from her bed and crawled to the window, clutching her midsection. Outside, snowflakes danced in the streetlamp; the ground was blanketed by two or three inches, maybe more.

Another pain stabbed her. Carleen knew she needed a doctor. She couldn't call her landlady because the woman was probably drunk. It was after midnight, after all, and this was Back Bay, where the only thing more predictable than the narrow streets and brick brownstones and too few parking spaces were the Irish pubs on every corner.

She could call an ambulance. But to get to a phone she would need to make her way down the carved mahogany staircase that had been majestic in the 1890s but now seemed steep and foreboding.

That's when Carleen realized how alone she really was. She knew all she could do was wait to see if the pain would pass. Wait to see if she would live or die. There was no other choice.

She sank onto the window seat, staring into the night. "Make something of yourself," Uncle Edward had said. In that moment, on that window seat, Carleen understood that her future was up to her.

She kicked a small stone away from her footstep now. As difficult as that lesson had been, it had been her turning point. She'd made it through that horrid night and had been able to get to a clinic in the morning.

"You have the flu," the doctor had said. An ordinary flu.

To her, it was not ordinary.

The following week she moved into a boardinghouse for women—a place she would have laughed at before. But it had security and a housemother and someone to be there if needed. No smoking, no drinking, no drugging allowed. It hadn't been easy, but she'd succeeded.

And now, as Carleen took another step, she knew it was time for amends. She hoped Ray was home. It would be better to see him before he showed up at the party and shocked the hell out of Babe.

* * *

By twelve twenty, dozens of people combed the backyard of Kamp Kasteel, telling tales, reliving good times, sipping Dom as if it were midnight and they still were players on a big, SRO stage. *Kamp Kasteel.* Babe smiled at the name the girls had once given their home away from home, their exclusive playground.

Happily for her, Wes was garnering more attention than she was. Then again, he was putting himself in that position, shaking hands, introducing himself as Edward's nephew-by-marriage, showing his sparkling teeth, poised (posed!) with his champagne glass, schmoozing Hollywood schmooze at which he was so adept.

"Nothing's the same," she could hear him say, and his listeners agreed, perhaps because they were of a similar generation. "We shoot in Canada today. Or New Zealand. Imagine that. It costs less to ship essentials than to hire stateside." He adjusted his sunglasses frequently for emphasis. "Those of us who made our money in the eighties and nineties are grateful we don't have to jump through those exhausting hoops." He spoke with authority, as if it had been his choice to shrink his career.

Babe took a step back, closer to the roses, though she would have altered her direction if she'd seen Amanda standing there.

"I suppose your husband will sign autographs next."

"Amanda," Babe said, "I don't know why you don't like me, but we're adults now. Can't you let it go?"

Amanda kept her eyes on Babe's husband and snorted. "Don't take it personally, kiddo. I don't like most people these days."

Babe didn't know how to respond. "Well," she said, after a few seconds. "It isn't very becoming." If Babe hadn't let Carleen scare her off, surely she would not let Amanda. "Not to mention you're not setting a very good example for your children. How would you feel if one day they behaved like this toward one another?"

Amanda folded her arms in a haughty stance. That's when Babe noticed how thin the woman was, perhaps more from worry than dieting. Amanda had always been such a worrier.

"Have you had anything to eat?" Babe suddenly asked.

With a flick of her head, Amanda sized up her sister. "Who can eat with this turmoil?"

Babe laughed. "It's a party, Amanda-Belle. It is supposed to be fun, not tumultuous."

One eyebrow cocked. "Aren't you worried about dear Uncle Edward? Apparently your husband's recent expedition with my sons has yielded nothing."

"I agree with Ellie. Edward will find his way home when he's ready."

Amanda scanned the crowd. "In the meantime, Carleen seems to have gone into hiding. Let's hope she stays where she is and saves us from mortification."

"Apparently Edward doesn't think she is mortifying."

"He must be losing his marbles. It would be just like Ellie not to tell us. That way, she could control his estate."

A whoop of delight rose from the arena where Wes was entertaining. "Okay," he said (too loudly) to a woman. "One more glass of champagne, and you can try to dunk me."

The woman whooped again as if he'd agreed to seduce her, which, of course, she did not know was not possible, at least not in the traditional way.

"Amanda," Babe said, turning back to her sister. "Why on

earth would you care whether or not Ellie controls the estate? I've always had the impression Jonathan does very well."

Amanda rotated her chin in an upward direction. "It's not the money, Babe. It's the principle."

"Ellie has more principles than the rest of us put together."

"Don't count on it. It's usually the ones you least expect to betray you who will."

Babe got the impression Amanda was referring to someone other than Ellie. "Well," she said, "I don't need Edward's money. Did you know I'm planning to start my own fragrance line?"

Amanda laughed.

For a moment, Babe thought Amanda must have been laughing at something she'd overheard one of the guests say. The announcement of a fragrance line wasn't grounds for laughter, was it? Then Babe remembered that Amanda had rarely been supportive of anything any of her sisters had done or had wanted to do.

"My agent is trying to convince me to add a clothing line," Babe added, not caring that it was a lie. "And handbags. They are so popular today."

"In that case, you might want to help out Carleen. Have you seen that quilted thing she's toting around?"

"Maybe she can't afford to buy her clothes. We really don't know much about her life, do we?" Babe couldn't believe that her irritation with Amanda had resulted in her defending Carleen.

Amanda elevated an eyebrow. "We know she's returned to the scene of many of her crimes, Poughkeepsie notwithstanding. By the way, do you know your old boyfriend is on the guest list? Ray Williams? Wasn't that his name?"

Babe slow-motioned her gaze from Amanda back toward Wes. But he had moved his performance to the girl with the ribbons, who now seemed as enrapt as the rest.

"Excuse me," Babe said, then walked away, Amanda's smugness casting a dark shadow behind her.

Chapter Twenty-one

Okay, so it was mean. But Amanda was sick to death of this weekend and of trying to put on the show of all shows. Besides, seeing Ray's name on the clipboard had been too juicy not to share, first with Carleen, then with Babe.

That would teach them both to think Amanda wasn't on top of the real things that mattered.

She stayed by the roses now, trying to determine where, and with whom, her time would be best spent.

From here she could see her boys, both working to get the golden Statue of Liberty to flinch. She could intervene but did not have the interest.

Heather and *the boyfriend* were not in sight. Hopefully they were not fornicating in clear view of the crowd assembled

under the tent. Just because the two lovebirds had showered
and changed did not mean they were fit for society, even Edward's.

Amanda's gaze trailed down the hill toward the dock and
the boathouse. Jonathan still had not made his way back in the
stolen rowboat. Maybe he and Edward had both gone over the
falls and Amanda would stand to inherit.

A third (a quarter?) of Edward's estate.

The two-million-dollar life insurance policy the firm had
on Jonathan.

A trace of a smile flitted over her lips. Did she dare wish for
such a glorious outcome to this asinine weekend? Resolution
to her debt, a new fiscal future free from a cad of a husband?

If Jonathan died, would she be obligated to notify the back-
waxer?

"Amanda, darling, whatever are you doing over there in the
bushes?" The woman who called out looked vaguely familiar.
She wore a great deal of what looked like peacock feathers,
including a few in her shock of white hair. Her thin lips were
painted too red and her rouge (yes, rouge, not blush) seemed
to have been extracted from the same pot. She sat in a cluster
of wide-eyed ladies. "Come tell us if it's true that Carleen was
invited." She patted the eggshell-colored, padded fabric that
covered the plastic folding chair and was supposed to look like
upholstery. "She worked for my sister in Boston, you know.
Mostly stitching ready-to-wear."

That's when Amanda realized the woman was Nola, the
costume designer who'd been known for her gossip as well as
her getups. Amanda hadn't known (or cared) that Nola had a

sister in Boston where Carleen had apparently worked. No doubt Edward secured her the job.

And now the ladies-in-waiting wanted to dish about the decadent sister.

Why the hell not? Amanda trotted to the champagne table and snatched a bottle. Chitchat would be more fun than pondering her mess of a life.

Besides, she thought, as an added attraction she could ice the gossip cake with a tidbit about Babe's old boyfriend who might make an appearance—wouldn't that be a hoot?

Babe had no idea what to do, where to hide, and if, in fact, hiding was what she wanted to do.

Ray.

She stole her way to the path that led to his house because it was safe, or at least it always had been. She supposed, on a subconscious level, that she hoped he'd once again step into her reflection and into her heart.

You are not a teenager, she reminded herself as she slipped through the overgrowth, further from the party. *And you are married. Your life is not here.*

That, of course, was from her sensible-self sitting on her right shoulder, whispering in her right ear. On her left side, however, was her emotional-self, who now said, *But wouldn't it be wonderful to feel love again?*

And then she found her special place. She sat on the ground, not caring if it ruined her dress.

When she'd first gone to Hollywood, thoughts of Ray had been the catalyst for each performance: maybe he would hear she had a part in a movie, maybe he would see it, maybe he would realize he was still in love with her and had to be with her. Maybe he would go to California and rescue Babe from herself.

One film, then another, and another. Her star rose high; surely he'd learned what she was doing. But he didn't come. After several films, several years, she tucked his memory away. She married, divorced, married again. She was nominated for an Oscar. Still, he didn't come.

Looking into the water, Babe started to cry. Slowly, at first, the way she'd cried for so long after the baby, after Ray. She sat there, a grown woman, an international film star, her dress getting soiled, her cheeks streaking mascara, not knowing what to do next, yet knowing the fairy tale had ended long ago and Ray's reflection would not appear again.

Carleen sat on the steps that led to the back porch at Ray Williams's house. She pulled up her knees and gathered her long skirt around her ankles. There had been no answer when she'd knocked on the screen door, but the inside door was open, so someone must have been around. Waiting was better than going back to Edward's house, back to the party, where she wasn't wanted.

She didn't have to wait long.

A young boy about twelve lumbered up the hill from a pontoon boat that was tied up at a pier next to a boathouse. He carried a blanket, a bottle of Gatorade, and what looked like a walkie-talkie. Beside him, a chocolate Lab pranced.

"May I help you?" the boy called.

It was nice to see he had manners. Carleen stood up and laughed at herself for thinking as Amanda would have.

A few hours back in Amanda's aura was clearly not good for her brain!

"Are you Ray Williams's boy?"

As he grew closer, Carleen realized she hadn't needed to ask. He looked so much like the boy she remembered, with thick, black hair and Irish blue eyes and freckles scattered across his nose.

"Kevin Williams," he said, though he did not set down his things and offer to shake hands. "Ray's my dad."

Carleen nodded. "You look like him. Is he home?"

"He's working."

"On a Saturday afternoon?"

"His office is here."

"I knocked."

"He probably didn't hear you. He turns on his music sometimes." The whole time they stood there, Kevin was sizing her up like a cop working a suspect. "Maybe I can help you. My dad's busy this time of year."

If she told him who she was, the kid would go inside and tell Ray, who would probably instruct him to lock all the windows and doors. Carleen smiled and said, "Thanks, but I really need to talk directly to him."

A small scowl appeared. "Can I at least tell him your name?" Just then his walkie-talkie started to crackle. A gravelly, distant voice came through the speaker and asked, "Kevin?" The boy flicked his eyes from Carleen to the phone, back to Carleen, back to the phone. He fumbled a second, then flipped a switch. The static was cut off. "Look," he said, "I'm kind of in a hurry."

She decided he left her no choice. "I'm sorry to bother you. But please tell your father that Carleen is here."

The boy eyed her another quick moment, then went onto the porch, the screen door slapping behind him, the dog left sitting, watching her.

She listened but couldn't hear anything.

Looking back toward the lake, Carleen wondered why Edward had invited Ray. Had he wanted Babe and Ray to reunite? As far as Carleen knew, Edward had not known that Babe had been pregnant. The sisters had all known, not the adults. She'd been so careful when she'd brought Babe back to Edward's after the procedure. She'd told him Babe had cramps—a word guaranteed to make Edward vanish, to not expect Babe for dinner, to not inquire about details of her condition. So Babe had stayed in her room. The sisters took turns bringing her tea and chicken noodle soup, though she wouldn't eat, and she wouldn't drink. For the first time in Carleen's life, she'd been afraid. She did not fear her parents, or that they'd learn about the abortion. No. Carleen had been afraid that Babe would die and it would be her fault.

Which was the real reason why, three days later, she left for Poughkeepsie in search of her birth certificate so she could elope with Earl and run away from the rest.

But Edward had no way of knowing that Babe was not merely suffering from cramps. Did he?

Was Ray's invitation to today's party merely a coincidence?

"Carleen."

She laughed and turned back to the porch. "I never need

to use my last name. I just say 'Carleen,' and everyone seems to know who I am. Especially around here." He looked pretty good for a guy who, as she remembered, was the same age as she was, three years older than Babe. His hair was still dark, though his freckles seemed muted. He wore jeans and a brown T-shirt that had a picture of a tree with a caption that read Every Day is Earth Day. He didn't look dressed for a party.

"You look well," Ray said.

"We thought we might see you next door."

He smiled. "I could lie and say I'm too busy."

"But?"

"But the truth is, I've only seen Edward a handful of times over the years. I didn't think that warranted being part of his celebration." He scratched the dog's left ear, then the right.

"Babe is here." She blurted it out so quickly that she startled herself.

"I wondered if she would be."

"It's her first time back."

"And?"

"And I thought it might be nice if you saw each other again. I always felt there was unfinished business between the two of you. That maybe you needed closure or something."

He folded his arms, concealing the line about Earth Day. "You're kidding, right? I mean, Jesus, Carleen, we were kids back then."

"Not really," she said. "You weren't kids, not really."

He frowned. "Did she send you over?"

Carleen shook her head. "As far as I know, she doesn't know you still live here."

Looking past her, then down toward the lake, to the shore,

then across the water, Ray said, "Come on, Carleen. She's a big-time movie star. I'm sure I'm the last person she wants to see."

"It was my fault," Carleen suddenly said, as she lowered her voice, her eyes, her chin. "The abortion. It was my fault. I convinced her not to tell our parents. After I came over here and told your father that Babe was pregnant, well, I made all the arrangements."

Ray narrowed his eyes. His hands grasped her arms. "What abortion, Carleen? What the hell do you mean, you told my father?"

Chapter Twenty-two

"Well?" David Goldsmith quizzed Ellie, who stood by Martina, overseeing the removal of the entrée chafing dishes. The guests seemed to have had their fill of barbecue; it was time for desserts—birthday cake, ice cream, brownies, more all-American food for this odd-American group. "Where is he?"

Ellie smiled, as if she had no idea to whom David was referring. But he carried a half-smoked stogie in one hand, and his seersucker had started to wilt. It was only two o'clock, but it was apparent this party would not last into the night the way Edward's parties had once done.

The guests were older, after all. Wiser. More sensible.

Ellie felt older, too, from keeping up appearances.

She spotted Amanda chatting with the costume designer and her cronies. At least Amanda seemed content.

Carleen was nowhere to be seen; neither was Babe. Hopefully they were not somewhere together, scratching at each other's eyes.

"You don't know where he is, do you?" the former playwright asked.

Ellie shook her head. "I haven't got a clue. He left yesterday morning." Relief washed over her. Saying the words out loud—to someone other than the family—seemed somehow cathartic.

"Good for him," David responded. "When I turn seventy-five, I hope I have the balls to disappear, too."

With his wrinkled face and his saggy jacket, he looked older than Edward. She had a fleeting thought about how quickly Edward would age once the cancer really took hold. "It would be nice to tell someone you're going, though," she said quietly. "It isn't right to deliberately cause your family worry."

He puffed on his cigar. "He didn't leave a note?"

"Nothing. Henry and I figured out he took his iPod and his binoculars and *Oliver Twist*."

"Henry. Ah, yes, that little man."

"Excuse me?"

David puffed again and chuckled. "Before you blame Edward, you might be wise to do a background check on Henry. You might learn this isn't the first time one of his lovers has disappeared."

Two pastry chefs arrived, carrying a three-layer sheet cake decorated like Times Square—not the one with Toys "R" Us and the Virgin Megastore but the old Broadway district, with marquees for the Shubert and the Biltmore and the Booth; for *Cabaret, The Odd Couple,* and Edward's *Central Park.* Mini LED lights blinked and flashed and cast a happy glow; guests from every table rose from their chairs and wove around one another for a closer look. If Edward had been present, he would have blown out the single candle that stood atop One Times Square, home of the New Year's Eve ball. In view of Edward's absence, Ellie quickly extinguished the flame.

A tenor in the crowd began to sing "For He's a Jolly Good Fellow." Perhaps he didn't realize the birthday boy wasn't there. Still, almost everyone joined in halfway through the stanza, including David Goldsmith, as if he hadn't just presented a frightening thought.

Henry?

Had Henry done something to Edward?

The singing abated, and Ellie said everyone should please return to their tables, that the waitstaff would cut the cake and deliver generous pieces. As David turned to leave, she grabbed his shoulder.

"What did you mean?" she asked. "Henry is harmless and quiet. You must have him confused with someone else."

David bent to the ground, where he tamped out his Havana. "All these years," he said. "Did you think we no longer came here because Edward didn't want us? Or because of that unfortunate incident with your sister Carleen?"

Ellie didn't know what to say. Of course she'd thought the parties had ended because of Carleen. Because Uncle Edward had left the theater because of the fire and the trial and the scandal.

"No, child. Edward stopped entertaining because of Henry.

None of us wanted to be around the little twit. He had such a disagreeable side. He enjoyed butting into other people's business. Like the way he intervened when your mother wanted to leave your father. Oh, I see I've said too much."

Ellie felt herself pale. She stared at David, her eyes unblinking. As far as she knew, Henry had not known her parents. What on earth did David mean? But just as she started to ask for details, a *whip-whip* of helicopter blades sliced through the air.

Voices gasped.

Necks swiveled toward the sky.

Hands elevated to visor the sun.

"It must be Edward!" someone cried. "He's here at last!"

Thank God, Ellie thought, dabbing her brow with Babe's scarf. *Thank God.*

The enormous metal insect dipped and bent toward them without attempting to alight. Then, from one of the aircraft's open doors, a man in fatigues thrust a long-lensed camera and pointed it directly at the crowd.

Ellie followed the invisible line of sight that led straight to the photographer's subject: Wes McCall.

So Edward had not returned, after all.

Amanda assumed her creditors had flown in to capture her, that the camera was an automatic weapon, and the man behind the trigger had her in his crosshairs. Who knew what collection agencies would resort to these days?

She supposed it would serve her right for wearing the cherry-colored sundress when she should have planned something less conspicuous.

But, alas, the shooter seemed more interested in Babe's husband than in a run-of-the-mill deadbeat like her.

With a hasty excuse to the costume lady and her friends (whose interest had been diverted by the helicopter before Amanda had had the chance to snitch about Babe's carnal teen years), Amanda clambered over to Ellie. "I suppose this is a standard Hollywood party occurrence," she griped.

"I thought it was him, Amanda-Belle. I thought it was Uncle Edward."

"I do believe the old coot has abandoned us. It looks, however, as if we'll be featured in a celebrity rag." As soon as she'd said it, she wondered if her creditors stooped to reading the rags. If so, they might see her picture and project that, as Edward Dalton's niece, she had access to the means to pay them off.

Oh, no! They would expose her to the world! She never could show face on Park Avenue again!

She slapped her hands over her face as if she were Britney Spears or the late Michael Jackson. Peeking through her fingers, she saw the man in fatigues change equipment, then arm himself with a video camera, a big one, like television stations used. *The Insider. Celeb. Hot Gossip.*

Argh! She'd be on cable as well as in print! YouTube wouldn't be far behind!

The cameraman took aim in one direction after another while the deafening metal beast dove in for a close-up.

That's when all hell broke loose.

The cyclone from the blades whirled the paper tablecloths and the padded chair covers.

Ladies whooped and grabbed their hats and hemlines.

Men held on to their toupees.

Ellie waved and waved, as if she could shoo the thing away. "Wes must be behind this!" she shouted to Amanda. "He needs to stop them!" She stumbled through the wind and the flying paper debris until she reached the celebrity in question, who stood, calmly gazing around, his sunglasses perched in place, a tiny smile revealing hints of his trademark dimples.

Amanda charged after her sister, and her two sons charged after her, their cheeks flush with helicopter-excitement. "Stop them!" Ellie screeched at Wes. "They're ruining the party!" The miniature Palace Theatre blew off the cake and landed at Ellie's feet. She looked like Dorothy without ruby slippers.

"No control," Wes hollered back, resting a condescending hand on Amanda's half-naked back. "These boys do what they want."

"Bullshit!" Amanda needed to end the intrusion before her picture showed up on the worldwide freaking web. "Get rid of them now! We're worried sick about Edward! How dare you orchestrate a publicity stunt!"

"Mom, don't . . . ," Chandler said, but his mother quickly hushed him.

Wes removed his glasses and glared at Amanda-Belle.

"If you care anything about your wife and her family," she ranted, "you'd know that the last thing we want is publicity. This is New York, not California. We are respectable people, not movie business trash. Edward would tell you as much if he was here . . . if he's okay . . ." If she deferred to the feel-sorry-for-us-we're-worried-about-Edward card, maybe the damn cameras would leave.

"Mom!" Chandler shouted, more loudly this time. "Stop. Uncle Edward is fine. We saw him."

Even the blades of the helicopter seemed to hush with that remark. All eyes turned toward the boy.

"Shut up!" Chase, the younger one, screamed at his brother.

"What's going on?" Amanda demanded.

"Shut up," Chase repeated, this time through his teeth.

"He made us promise not to tell," Chandler declared.

Chase put his hands over his ears and fled. Chandler started to follow, but Amanda stopped him in his Air Jordans. "*What's going on?*" she repeated. "*Where is Edward?*"

Chandler turned back to his mother with a self-righteous look—gee, where had he learned that? "He's on the island," he yelled above the chopper blades. "But he said if we told anyone, he'd cut you out of his will. I've seen your bills, Mom. I know how desperate you are for money. But, please, this is so juvenile."

Amanda turned what must have been a lovely shade of mortification, which must have blended nicely with her sundress. The guests emitted a collective gasp: imagine! Amanda Dalton Delaney desperate for money!

Wes laughed and turned back to the crowd. "He's kidding," he said. "The boy has a vivid imagination. A chip off his old uncle's block!"

No one corrected the fact that Edward wasn't Chandler's uncle but his mother's.

"You were kidding, right?" Wes asked, his eyes drilling into the boy's. "We were on the island. We got pine boughs to use for paddles. But we did not see Edward, did we, son?"

"Right," Chandler muttered. "We didn't see him. I was kidding." Then he sauntered off toward the lake, hopefully to drown himself in waterlogged shame.

Wes signaled up to the cameraman, who hollered something to the pilot, after which the chopper lifted up, up, and away, over the treetops and the lake, rippling the water in its wake. "Now!" Wes continued, turning back to the guests. "Let's eat cake!"

"Thank you," Ellie mouthed to Babe's husband, but he had started to lead a small parade toward the dessert table. Ellie looked at Amanda and said, "Well, I suppose we should be grateful. In spite of the jugglers and the ribbon-wrapping girl, without Wes McCall, the party would have been dull."

Amanda did not know how to answer.

Chapter Twenty-three

*Ellie grabbed two Happy Birthday, cowboy-*themed paper dessert plates (Uncle Edward's selection) and meandered toward Amanda, who had taken refuge at the gazebo. As she walked, she overheard the guests twitter (not on the Internet, but the old-fashioned *psst-psst,* face-to-face kind). Well, why not, Ellie supposed. After all, in addition to the paparazzi, they'd been treated to a juicy tidbit about Amanda, compliments of Amanda's own son.

She needed money?

Edward would cut her out of his will?

Gasp.

Gasp.

Twitter some more.

The guests would be slow to leave now. They'd stick around

for the last drop of Dom, for the last morsel of cake, because who knew what spectacle would unfold next?

"What do you think?" Ellie asked Amanda as she settled onto the wooden bench and set the cake slices between them. "Did they find Uncle Edward?"

"Probably. Wes doesn't know my son. The last thing Chandler has is an imagination, vivid or otherwise."

Ellie didn't comment that Chandler took after his mother. "Is Jonathan back yet?"

"I have no idea." Amanda picked up one of the plates and poked at the frosting with a plastic fork.

"Amanda," Ellie sighed. "Is it true? Are you in financial trouble?"

"Yes."

"Can I help? Can I offer you money?"

Amanda laughed. "Unless you have a secret stash, I doubt you have enough."

"I have a few thousand put away." She didn't add it was the money Edward had given her for the honeymoon that never had been.

"Thanks. But a few thousand won't do it."

Ellie sighed again. First Jonathan's infidelity, now this. She did not know what to say to her sister on either topic— Amanda had always been so stubborn, so staunchly independent about her private business. Ellie changed the subject. "Amanda-Belle, I need to ask you something. Did you ever hear anything negative about Edward's Henry? David Goldsmith implied Henry was some sort of criminal. He also said Henry was the reason Mother and Father never divorced."

Amanda frowned. "What are you talking about?"

"Mother and Father. Did you ever sense they wanted a divorce?"

"Our mother and father?"

"Well, yes." Apparently it wasn't the time to hold such a curious conversation with her sister, at least, not with *this* sister.

"I don't know what you mean. They had a perfect marriage, didn't they?"

Ellie blinked. She didn't know if she'd ever wondered one way or the other.

"I, for one, have always tried to emulate what they had," Amanda continued. "With Jonathan, you know? I always wanted a marriage like theirs. And I wanted the financial security."

"We weren't financially secure, Amanda. Thank goodness we had Uncle Edward." By the bewildered look that crossed Amanda's face, Ellie realized she might as well have said they'd been paupers. "Without Uncle Edward, our lives would have been very different. We wouldn't have had college educations. Not to mention the house in Poughkeepsie."

Amanda blanched. "What?" she asked. "What?"

"Edward bought our house. Didn't you know that?"

"The house Carleen burned down?"

She needn't have added that. Ellie sighed again. "I overheard Mother and Father talking about it once. She said Father should let Edward buy it, that he really wanted to."

"I never knew that."

Ellie shrugged. "I don't think it was a big deal. Uncle Edward had money; we didn't."

Amanda seemed to ponder that a moment.

"Enough about that," Ellie said. "What about Henry? Did you know he knew Mother and Father?"

Amanda sniffed and dabbled with her cake. "I've paid little attention to the man. Wasn't he a chorus boy or something? Maybe he befriended Mother because he wanted Edward. Maybe she told him she wanted to leave Father and he convinced her not to. Who cares. We all have secrets, don't we?"

Well, the last part certainly was turning out to be true. And it seemed that if Henry was such an ogre, there would have been signs before now. He'd lived there for years, for God's sake. The only time she'd heard him utter anything noteworthy was when Connecticut legalized gay marriage.

They'd been having breakfast in the morning room.

"Now we have no excuse," Henry had said to Edward after he read the headline from the newspaper. Edward only chuckled; the issue wasn't mentioned in Ellie's presence again.

Nor had there been any talk about whether Henry's former lovers had disappeared or not.

As for Mother, she'd been a housewife from Poughkeepsie. Had she even known any gay men other than the few Edward brought to Lake Kasteel for the holidays? That must have been when Mother met Henry. Still, it was surprising that if Henry had known Mazie, he'd never mentioned her.

But Amanda was right, everyone had secrets, even Ellie, who had once harbored an obsessive passion for the mysteries of King Tutankhamen and a neurotic envy of Cleopatra's beauty and grace, excluding, of course, the curious unions the Queen of the Nile had enjoyed with her brothers.

"I suppose it's a moot point about Mother and Father," Ellie said. "For now, I want to concentrate on believing Chandler was right in saying they found Edward. At least it would mean he's all right and Henry is not an ax murderer."

"Hallelujah," Amanda said with a sniff. Then she stood up. "In the meantime, I've had all I can take of the festivities. Will anyone notice if I slip away?"

"You, too?"

"Only to the bedroom. I have another migraine coming on."

"Go ahead. I'm going to try and corner Wes. But Amanda-Belle?" Ellie's sister looked back at her. She looked so much older than when she'd arrived yesterday. "I meant what I said about the money. Whatever I have is yours. If you need more, maybe I can help you get it from Edward."

Amanda laughed. "I already asked him. Twice. His answer was no." With that she left the gazebo and the slice of birthday cake behind.

From her refuge on the path, Babe heard the helicopter. She assumed Edward was making the grand entrance they had anticipated. She assumed he'd be distressed that she wasn't there. Still, she could not pull herself up off the ground. She couldn't pretend to be merry now that Ray's name had been mentioned. Now that she knew he was close by. Despite Hollywood kudos, she simply was not that good an actor.

So she couldn't get up, and she couldn't pretend. All she could do was think about . . . then. About them.

She'd gotten pregnant sometime at the end of June, maybe the first time they'd done it. By the third week of August, she'd realized the inevitable. The night before Ray was to leave Lake Kasteel for college, she knew she had to tell him. She knew they were too young to get married, but maybe she could keep their baby. It was 1988: the world was filled with single mothers.

She'd worn her white, lacey big shirt with her black leggings that Carleen had said made her look older than fifteen. Of course, Carleen hadn't yet known that Babe would need the stretchy pants sooner than later: Babe hadn't yet told her about her predicament. Like Ray, Carleen had been packing for college, and Babe hadn't wanted to disturb her.

Ray had held Babe's hand as they sat on the small manmade beach, listening to the crickets, hearing the soft plop as a frog or a fish or a duck jumped out of or into the water. They had not crammed themselves into the back of the Rambler. Summer was almost over; the sun was setting early; they could make love in the fresh air and no one would see them.

"Sweet Naomi," he whispered. "My Babe. I don't want to go away without you."

She wanted to say she could go with him, that they could get married and live in an apartment while he went to architectural school.

"The good thing," he said quickly, "is I'll have so much work to do, it will keep me distracted. I'll need a good job if we want any kind of a future."

"A future?" she'd whispered.

"I love you, Babe," he said. "I've been thinking about us. By the time I'm done with college you'll be out of high school. You'll be nineteen. I'll be twenty-two. I know we'll be young, but maybe we can get married. Then later, after my career is established, we can buy a house. Have a couple of kids. Buy a station wagon and a dog." He laughed. "I know it's a long time from now, but if we're patient, we can make it work. What do you think?"

In spite of the dusk, she saw his eyes twinkle. Maybe it was love. Maybe it was excitement about making plans. How could she spoil their last night together? So she replied, "Sure, that sounds swell."

He let go of her hand and slipped his arm around her. "Not that you'll want to wait for a guy like me."

She looked up to the slate sky and said to the evening star, "I'll wait, Ray. I'll wait."

The next day he was gone, and she told Carleen, and Carleen told their sisters and made the arrangements, and then Friday came and Babe hardly remembered anything except for the doctor saying she would have no more babies. And then it was Labor Day. And the house burned down. And the last thing she'd heard about Ray Williams was that his parents had moved to Virginia to be close to his school and they'd rented their house to a literary agent who'd had a breakdown and needed to get out of Manhattan.

The sun moved behind a thick cloud now. Babe felt a chill. She rubbed her arms; she closed her eyes; then she heard his voice.

"Babe? Is it really you?"

She nearly laughed out loud at how foolish she'd become, that she thought she could hear Ray's voice, hear how it would sound today in his grown-up body.

"Babe?"

Opening her eyes, she looked into the water. The figure reflected was tall and straight and . . . *oh*, she thought. *Oh, no . . .*

The figure bent down and tapped her shoulder. She closed her eyes again.

"Babe? It's me. Ray Williams."

Her tears spilled freely. "Don't," she whispered. "Please don't tease me."

"Are you okay?"

She blinked. She turned. She scanned his face, his mouth, his eyes. "My God," she said. "It's you."

He stood up and jammed both hands into the pockets of his jeans. "Yeah," he said. "And it's you, too. Hey—I've seen some of your movies. You're really good, you know?"

She summoned the strength to pull herself to her feet. She faced him, a foot, maybe two feet away. "Ray. You still live here."

He looked at her without words.

"I can't believe it," she said.

They stayed in their positions without moving, without speaking.

Finally, he worked one hand through his hair. "I was taking the path over to Edward's. Carleen came to see me."

"My sister?"

"She told me, Babe. She told me about the abortion. I didn't know. Why didn't you tell me?" He took a step back.

"Carleen told you? Just now?"

He nodded and moved his hand across the crown of his head again.

"I tried to find you. Your parents moved."

"They told me they wanted a change. Carleen said she told my father about the baby."

The world shifted then, tipped on its axis, and went a bit out of focus.

"Carleen told your father?" she heard her voice whimper.

"She said before she made the . . . . arrangements . . . for the abortion, she went to my father. He called her trash. He slammed the door. Then my parents went to Virginia. God, Babe, I'm so sorry." He reached out and lightly touched her shoulder, his fingers warm against her skin.

"She never told me she'd told your father. She never told me he knew."

"She was trying to see if there was a way for you . . . for us . . . but he was so stubborn. He told me you left town after the fire, that you'd sent him a letter saying you had a new boy-friend and didn't want to see me again. Oh, God, I believed him. I am so sorry." His blue eyes glistened with tears.

Babe knew that later she'd have to think about what Ray had just said, that Carleen had gone to his father, that she'd never told Babe he'd called her trash and slammed the door. Babe had not known Carleen had tried to help Babe and Ray. She'd only known that her sister arranged for the abortion and said it was better that way.

One tear, then another, spilled down Ray's cheeks. Babe gently wiped them away. "We can't change the past, Ray. No one's to blame. We were careless and foolish, but we were kids. We're not kids anymore."

"I feel like a kid," he said, "when I look at you."

Chapter Twenty-four

"Wes?" Ellie sandwiched Babe's husband by the table where extra slices of cake had been displayed. "We need to have a conversation."

Wes smiled the way he'd smiled for the camera that had hung from the helicopter. "I am sorry for the fuss," he said. "That damn paparazzi seems to find me everywhere."

It was not the time to say she doubted that. "It's about Edward," she said. "Did you find him or did you not?"

"It's like I said. The boy has a vivid imagination. I didn't want to bring it up in front of everyone, but we capsized the canoe. We lost our paddles. But we managed to get to the island. All we found there were a few pine boughs to help us paddle back. We didn't find your uncle."

"Really?"

His smile broadened. "I have no need to lie."

"So Chandler invented a coincidental story about his mother's bills?"

"As I said, I have no need to lie. Other than to omit the part about capsizing the canoe, which wouldn't do much for my image of mister macho rugged man." He laughed.

She smiled and turned away. She did not believe him for a minute.

Then she spotted Henry: she might have better luck with him.

Henry was by the tent, disposing of used paper plates and napkins as if he'd worked for Martina. Ellie meandered over to him, wondering if David Goldsmith would consider garbage duty suspicious.

"I want the people to leave now," he said as she approached. "Don't they understand it's time to go? They've eaten every morsel, drunk every bottle. They devoured the cake like deprived sugar addicts." Henry had changed back into his madras shorts and had added a straw bowler that looked ridiculous. Ellie wondered if he hoped his new attire would alert the guests that the party was over.

"They're drinking coffee."

"They need to stop. They need to go."

"They will, sooner or later. In the meantime, I want to ask you something." She paused. "About my mother."

He yanked the huge trash bag from the barrel he'd been stuffing and tied the flaps into a knot. "I'd think there were more urgent things to talk about right now. Like where on earth Edward is and when—*if*—he is coming home."

"David Goldsmith said my parents never divorced because

of you. I didn't know divorce had ever been an issue. I didn't even know that you knew them."

He set down the bag with a heavy, old person's sigh. "I knew your mother. She came to the theater to watch rehearsals."

He could have said the sky was green and the lawn, purple. "My mother? My mother went to your rehearsals?" She'd known Mazie enjoyed an occasional night out at the theater. But rehearsals? "When?"

"You expect me to remember? I don't know. Maybe when she was in the city shopping. Or waiting to meet your father. He had business in the city, didn't he?"

Ellie didn't think she should mention the time Babe had seen Father at the Algonquin. "But why would my mother want to leave my father?" *And what did you have to do with it?* She began picking post-helicopter debris from the lawn and dropping it into another receptacle. Cleaning up helped her feel nonchalant, as if the questions she was asking weren't really important.

"Maybe she became enamored with the theater life. People used to think it was glamorous." He pulled another trash bag from a container and stared into the discarded rubble. "Broadway hardly gets that kind of respect anymore. On opening nights, women came in furs and jewels; men in suits, sometimes tails." He snorted. "Now they show up in jeans and T-shirts, eating pizza while they stand in queue. It's disgusting."

Ellie wanted to ask about his previous lovers and if any had disappeared like Uncle Edward. But this wasn't the time or the place and Henry was edgy already. "What about my mother? Did she go to opening nights? Did she wear furs and jewels?" She'd rarely seen Mazie Dalton in anything but a spray-starched housedress, the quintessential housewife—Amanda had been right about that.

"I don't remember what your mother wore or what her theater-going habits were." *Snap, snap,* went the flaps of the plastic bag.

"But David specifically said you were the reason she didn't get a divorce. I wonder what he meant?"

"Mr. Goldsmith is wrong. If I were you, I'd leave it alone. Talking about the past will upset your uncle."

At least he had referred to Edward in the future, *he's-still-alive* tense.

Hoisting the two bags, his knobby knees buckling, Henry waddled off, leaving Ellie with the rest of the rubbish and too many unanswered questions.

Carleen was heading back to Edward's when she heard hurried footsteps approaching from behind.

"Heather? Honey?" a man's voice called out.

She turned and saw a forty-something-year-old man running toward her. She stopped. "I don't know who you are, but I'm not Heather."

He slowed his pace, then halted when he reached her. "Oh, Christ, you're Carleen."

She laughed. "I'm not quite as scary as you make that sound."

He shook his head. "No. No, it's that my daughter looks so much like you. The hair. The height. Everything."

"You're Amanda's husband. It's been a long time." She vaguely remembered the lanky Ivy Leaguer who'd tagged after her sister, who had been busily picking out china and crystal. He did not resemble the same nerd.

He shook her hand. "Jonathan Delaney. Guilty as charged."

His choice of the word *guilty* did not seem malicious.

"It's odd, isn't it?" Carleen asked. "You have a daughter who looks like me. I have two daughters, one of whom often reminds me of my sister, Ellie. Sometimes they're both like Babe. I've never figured out how exactly that works." He was attractive now and seemed to have an easy manner. She wondered how he stood being married to Amanda.

"So," he asked, "you escaped the party?"

"I had an errand. What about you?"

"I've been hunting for Edward. I just returned the boat I stole from the neighbors. My vehicle is still there, but Amanda has the keys."

Carleen supposed there were more details to that story, but she decided to forgo the question. "I take it you didn't find my wayward uncle?"

"No. I was hoping he'd shown up at the house by now."

"Not as far as I know." They walked together casually, as if they'd spent lots of time with each other all these years. "What's he like now?"

"Edward?" Jonathan laughed an unassuming laugh. "I like the old goat. I've never been sure if the feeling's mutual, though he's mellowed over the years."

"Mellowed? How so?"

"Well, he speaks to me now."

It was Carleen's turn to laugh. "Uncle Edward always was hard to read. Which also accounts for why he invited me this weekend."

"Have you been in touch with anyone in the family since . . . since you left?"

She shook her head. "Not really. I always knew Edward was keeping track of me, though. He sends a card every year on my birthday. I send him one on his. But no," she said, "I've had no contact with my sisters."

"Man," he said, "that's so stupid."

"It works both ways. I haven't called or written to them."

"Why would you want to? The way they treated you?"

Carleen smiled and did not know what to say. She'd never expected that someone might have felt compassion for her side of the story. Imagine that. *You've come a very long way, baby,* she thought to herself. First, she'd had the courage to find Ray, who hadn't booted her out on her ass. Now Amanda's husband was being kind to her. And to think neither of the men knew the whole truth.

As they turned into the driveway, Carleen felt a little lighter, a little happier for the first time since she'd arrived.

Amanda stood at the window in her bedroom looking down at the driveway, hoping to see the party guests depart, one by one, *sayonara* and good riddance. They would have plenty to talk about on their trip back to the city—forget the court jesters and dunking booths, they'd had a goddamn helicopter and goddamn paparazzi and a boatload of juice about one of Edward's nieces, not Carleen for a change.

Carleen, Amanda thought as she leaned against the drape. *How was it possible Carleen had turned out so normal?*

A ninth-grade algebra teacher, for God's sake.

A wife. A mother. A woman with a husband who probably did not cheat on her.

And a wardrobe that didn't speak to a quarter of a million in debt.

Amanda closed her eyes and knew she shouldn't have been surprised. Carleen, after all, had always managed to come out on top, like with men, and with the fact that Carleen's boyfriend, Earl, had been Amanda's boyfriend first.

"You?" Carleen had laughed. "With a guy on a motorcycle? Man, I have to check this out."

Earl had been Amanda's bad-boy. It was the summer of her first year of college and she'd met him at the traffic light in the center of Lake Kasteel. Yes, at a traffic light. She had taken Edward's Triumph Spitfire into town to pick up a few groceries. Instead, she picked up Earl, or Earl picked up her, after he pulled up alongside her on his rumbling Harley and they exchanged smiles and then conversation and by the time the light turned green he had her phone number.

They went out a few times; he took her virginity. A girl doesn't easily forget the guy who did that, especially when she'd wanted so badly for it to happen.

Amanda sighed and looked back to the driveway, to the place where Earl had arrived early one night and Carleen—who'd still been in high school—entertained him while Amanda finished dressing.

By the time she was ready, Earl had gone, Carleen on the back of his bike.

Amanda had never kissed him or touched him again.

The worst part had been Carleen's cavalier attitude, as if she was entitled and Amanda was not.

Amanda was thinking those things, remembering it all, just

as who came into view in the driveway below but her husband, walking with—*No!*—Carleen.

Amanda blinked. Surely this was a dream. Just one more scene in the recent nightmare her life had become.

But after the blink they were still there. What was worse, they were talking. And laughing. Goddamn laughing!

Panic.

Adrenaline.

Something took over.

Amanda flew from her room and down the stairs without sliding into her Cole Haan ballet flats. She ripped open the front door.

"Stop right there!" she screeched in a biting C-sharp.

They stopped.

They looked.

They smirked. Or maybe it was only Jonathan who smirked.

"Amanda, what are you doing?" he asked. "Why aren't you at the party?"

Her hands went to her hips where they squared off with her waist. "I might ask you both the same thing. But you seem to be having a party of your own. Really, Carleen, aren't you a little old to be stealing boyfriends? Oh, wait, that's not my boyfriend. That's my *husband.*"

"Amanda," Jonathan said, "don't embarrass yourself. I ran into Carleen on the road. She looks like Heather, doesn't she?"

"No," she said. "Where is the rental car?"

Jonathan sighed. "You have the keys. I returned the boat but couldn't drive back. That's when I met Carleen, who was out walking."

She huffed. She puffed.

"By the way," Jonathan added, "I rowed down as far as the falls. I didn't find Edward or the boat. Not that you asked."

"Of course you didn't find him. He's on the island. The boys saw him there. According to Chandler. And I tend to believe him."

"What?" Carleen interrupted. "Edward's back?"

Amanda waved her off, as if she were a distraction. "He's on that stupid island of his, being obstinate. Chandler claims Edward said if the boys told anyone they'd found him, he'd cut all of us out of his will. Which I'm fairly certain would be illegal."

"Maybe I should try and reason with him," Jonathan said.

"Don't be ridiculous. He doesn't want that. He thinks he's being funny, all this cloak-and-dagger nonsense. Well, I say let him have his way. At some point, he'll show up. Edward Dalton rarely missed a party in his life."

She took Jonathan by the arm and spoke directly to her sister. "Now if you'll excuse us, I'd like to return to the guests with my husband. Next time, if you want a man, I suggest you bring your own." Tugging him closer to her, Amanda padded across the driveway and onto the lawn, not caring that her shoes were still upstairs in her room.

Chapter Twenty-five

Ellie watched Myrna Goldsmith smiling and chatting with a group of ladies that included Nola, the former costume designer, and Harriet, a makeup artist who'd once lived with Toni Parker, a frequent guest at Lake Kasteel who had scandalously vanished in Paris years ago. Harriet now held the ladies' attention by declaring that today's actors lacked dignity when they appeared onstage *au natural,* which, Ellie knew, simply meant without face makeup. In the theater, clothes did not matter; makeup did.

Myrna seemed to be having a nice time.

Keeping her distance as she stood by the dessert table, which now held several blends and flavors of coffee, Ellie watched with interest. Myrna, after all, was the same age Mazie Dalton would have been. The two had gone to the same public school when they'd been girls, then had met again through Uncle Edward. "Isn't that a wonderful coincidence?" Mazie had remarked one night, and Father had grunted, then returned to his newspaper and pipe.

Ellie supposed Myrna Goldsmith had known Mazie Dalton better than Mazie's own daughters had. She probably remembered what kinds of sweaters Mazie had worn and the snacks she liked to eat and if she liked Elvis better than Buddy Holly.

Those were the kinds of questions Ellie pondered from time to time, not because they mattered but because she didn't know the answers. It was easier to think about her mother's likes and dislikes than to look at women like Myrna Goldsmith and wonder if Mazie would have resembled her now, if her hair would be silver, too, or if she would have kept it blonde; if she would have similar brown spots on the backs of translucent hands.

Ellie did, however, have a few things that once belonged to Mazie, things Mazie had left at Edward's when she and Father had stayed the night during holidays and special celebrations, or when they brought the girls at the beginning of the summer and picked them up on Labor Day.

They were simple things: a hairbrush, a can of Arrid spray deodorant, a box of Jean Naté dusting powder. A toothbrush and a tube of Pepsodent. And, of course, her mother's facial soap that had come from France, had been made of lavender and cream and was "hand-milled," her mother once explained.

When her parents were at Edward's, they slept in the room where Ellie slept (still slept), and Ellie bunked in with Babe. Amanda hadn't wanted Ellie (or any of them) in her room, and

Ellie didn't like Carleen very much, though she never told the others.

One night after the fire, when everything had been lost, Ellie left her husband and the city and went to Edward's to be with her family. That's when she found the things in the dresser drawer. It wasn't much, just a small pile of drugstore stuff, except for the soap. It wasn't much, but her mother had touched every single thing there, smelled the things, used them. And they had touched her. Her hair, her face, her mouth.

Edward had some pictures of Ellie's father when the two brothers had been boys, laughing, fighting, playing tennis. But Mazie had been an only child of an older couple who had both lived well into their seventies, then died. Any memorabilia they'd had of their daughter had been stored in the attic of the farmhouse in Poughkeepsie. Stored, then turned to ashes.

The night Ellie found the things, she gathered them and went to bed, cradling the only proof of Mazie's existence in her arms. In the morning, she placed them in the small brass box where she kept her honeymoon cash and the travel brochures about the places she'd once dreamed of going—Cairo, Luxor, Aswan; the temples, the pyramids, the Nile.

She set the box in the back of her wardrobe and never showed it to Carleen or to Amanda. The night before Babe left for California, Ellie took her into her room.

"I have a few things that were Mother's," she whispered to Babe, not that she had to whisper, because Amanda was out courting Jonathan and Carleen was, well, Carleen was gone. "Would you like her hairbrush?"

Babe touched the bristles, held the brush to her cheek, raised it up as if to pull it through her hair. Then she stopped and set it back in the box. "No," she said. "You should keep it here, Ellie. Keep it home, where it belongs."

Ellie supposed that was when she, too, had begun to think of Edward's house as home, as if it was too difficult to imagine their own home was gone forever, that nothing was left.

Nola laughed a bawdy laugh now, jarring Ellie from her memories. Edward had often said the woman belonged outside the theater, standing on the red-light district street corner, back before Broadway had been cleaned up.

Edward, Ellie thought again. *He would have enjoyed the party. He would have liked the energy of his former cronies.*

Then she thought about her mother again and wondered why she'd never talked to Edward about either of her parents, as if, like their belongings, they simply had never existed.

"The Randalls are leaving," Heather said to Ellie, who was still mesmerized by the nattering ("chin-wagging," Edward would have called it if he had graced them with his presence) women. "Shotgun forgot which car is theirs."

Ellie closed her eyes. "The Randalls. Let's see, they still live in Manhattan, so it's probably a rental. I don't think they own a car." She opened her eyes. "Tell him to look for a small black Mercedes. I think that's what the places in the city usually rent out for the day."

"Oh, no!" Heather replied. "Do you have any idea how many small black Mercedes are in the parking area and lined up and down the street?"

Ellie laughed and cupped her hand on Heather's shoulder. "It's okay, dear. I'll come with you, and we'll figure it out." She was relieved to have a break, even more relieved that at least one couple was finally going home. Soon the family would be the only ones left. The family and Henry, of course, who perhaps had been closer to her parents than she had imagined. Soon it would be just them, to figure out what, if anything, they should do next about Edward.

Babe and Ray were near Edward's boathouse, so that's where they went to talk. Except for a sleeping bag sprawled in the corner and a duffel that was capped with two motorcycle helmets, the place looked as she remembered.

Babe's stomach ached, as if a baby was still growing there.

She moved a dusty sheet from the rattan sofa and brushed off the striped canvas cushion. "It looks as if they don't use the boathouse anymore."

"Places are quiet when no kids are around."

She sat and folded her hands on her lap. She didn't think Ray had made the comment about kids because of the child—*their* child. Nonetheless, she started to cry.

"Babe." He sat down next to her and put his arm around her shoulder.

Slowly, she leaned into him. It was natural, instinctive, to settle into the place she once had known so well, though it now seemed bigger, more muscular. She could have stayed there weeping forever. . . .

Except that was childish.

Drying her eyes, she sat up straight. "I'm sorry. I had no right to do that. Good thing I'm not an actress or you might think I was playing a role."

He folded his hands, leaned forward, propped his elbows on his knees. "You have every right."

They sat quietly, listening to the music that spilled from the party down to the lake. The banjo had been replaced by stringed instruments that were playing medleys of show tunes. Babe thought about how she'd stranded Wes with the guests, and how much he detested musicals.

"I'm married now," she said.

"I know. I used to see your picture in the tabloids at the A&P in Katonah."

He didn't mention whether he'd bought the tabloids, whether he'd read the gossip about her, the misguided, often misquoted, moments of her life.

"Don't believe everything you read."

"I don't."

Outside, the music moved from Rodgers & Hammerstein to Andrew Lloyd Webber.

"You look great," he said. "But you must know that."

"It's part of my job. What's your excuse?"

"What?"

"For looking great. What's your excuse?" She'd been trying to lighten the mood, searching for humor to quell her butterflies. But it was true, Ray looked great. He looked as if he spent a lot of time outdoors. "What about you? I haven't seen your name in the tabloids."

"I've tried to keep a low profile."

"That's good," she said. "That's funny."

He smiled. "I was married, now I'm not. I have a son who's twelve and lives with me. His mother travels for her job. She doesn't see him much."

He had a nicer scent than Wes, who usually smelled like grapefruit from the aromatherapy his masseur incorporated into his wellness program. Ray smelled like the woods and the lake on a sunny day. Once autumn arrived, he probably wore denim and flannel shirts.

"I can't believe I never knew," he said.

"I thought you dumped me. Carleen said it was for the best."

"Was it?"

"I suppose. I mean, what would we have done? I was fifteen."

"Your folks could have had me arrested."

"They didn't know. Only my sisters knew."

"It must have been awful for you."

"It was. Sometimes it still is."

"You have no kids?"

"No." She did not tell him that in order to do that she would need a surrogate and that she did not have the courage to think about that. She had the eggs: what she lacked was a place for the seed to be nurtured and grow.

"I'm sorry, Babe."

"Me, too."

She wanted him to kiss her. She wanted to taste his lips again, to see if they were as sweet as she remembered. But then the door burst open and Carleen stood there.

"Oh," she said. "Excuse me. I'm so sorry."

"Don't be sorry," Babe said. "He wouldn't be here if it weren't for you." For once she didn't spit her words at Carleen.

"I came for the canoe. I'm going to get Edward."

Babe stood up. "You know where he is? Do you want me to come?"

Carleen shook her had. "Thanks, but I need to do this alone."

Chapter Twenty-six

*Ellie helped decipher which car-for-a-day be-*longed to the Randalls by process of Mercedes-elimination. It helped that the Montorinis and the Cashmans and Julius Fini and his mother were leaving at the same time and two of them had rented cars that had been cloned.

As delighted as Henry would be that people were starting to leave, Ellie realized she was not. The element of distraction had been welcome.

Standing in the driveway saying, "Thanks for coming," to Julius Fini and the rest, she nodded to Amanda's husband, who had come from the backyard and announced he would help with car retrieval duty.

Amanda's daughter looked pleased that her father seemed

to want to work alongside her boyfriend. She left the men and went over to Ellie.

"I didn't think we'd have a good time, but we really did," Heather said with a smile. "It was fun hearing stories about the *glorious days* of Broadway, as if Broadway no longer exists. I wanted to ask if any of them have tried getting tickets lately!"

"I'm glad you enjoyed the party," Ellie said. "Even though the guest of honor never showed up."

"It was nice to meet my other aunts, too. My mom's never said much about Carleen, except that, well, you know."

Yes, Ellie knew.

"And Babe! She is so gorgeous! Her husband still looks pretty good for his age. He told Shotgun—um, Jarred—that he might be able to find him a part in one of his movies."

Ellie suppressed a frown. "I didn't know your boyfriend wanted to be an actor."

"It's why we cleaned up for the party—to make a good impression, you know? I want to act, too. Hasn't Mother told you?"

Oh, dear, Ellie thought. *Amanda must detest this.* "Well, you look wonderful, and, no, I didn't know you wanted to be an actor. I don't talk with your mother very often."

Don and Suzie Lyons completed the first wave of departees. Except for Julius Fini they all were quite old and commented that they had to return to the city before heavy traffic. They must have forgotten that this was Saturday, and that many weekend visitors to the city now came by plane, taking advantage of special deals. Dinner, show, Sunday brunch, round-trip transportation.

"I'm thinking about taking a year off from college," Heather reported. "I want to go with Jarred to L.A. Anyway, thanks for being nice to him. My mother did her usual best to embarrass me."

Ellie smiled. "I think she might have been a little startled by his nickname." *Startled,* however, would be a mild word to describe how Amanda would react when she learned Heather's intention to leave Wellesley.

"He hates when I don't call him Jarred. But I think 'Shotgun' is cool. His friends named him that when he was sixteen. He had a brain tumor, and after the operation he couldn't get his driver's license as early as the other guys. So they always saved him the front seat. Shotgun. Get it? It's slang for the passenger seat."

"Your boyfriend had a brain tumor at sixteen?"

"Yeah, it was cancer and all that, but he's okay now. Anyway, thanks for being nice to him, Aunt Ellie." Heather kissed her cheek and darted off toward her boyfriend, shouting, "Give me keys! I'll help, too!"

Ellie watched her go, stunned by what the girl had just revealed. It certainly wasn't obvious what the young man had been through. *And his parents,* Ellie thought, then her mind drifted back to Amanda and the prima donna she was. It was amazing that, so far, her children were turning out fine, though Ellie believed Chandler still needed work.

But Heather, their look-alike Carleen . . . well, in all of Heather's nineteen years on the planet, she had not once kissed her Aunt Ellie on the cheek, had never, for that matter, called her *Aunt Ellie.* Ellie touched the place where Heather's kiss had landed and smiled to herself, wondering what Amanda would think about that.

* * *

Amanda had retreated back to the gazebo, from where she now surveyed the party's final act as the guests at last started to funnel from the backyard toward the front.

Many noted their annoyance that neither Edward nor his famous niece, Babe, had bothered to surface.

Some commented that they'd had a quick flash of Carleen scurrying from the driveway past the tent down to the boathouse. They remarked that her hair was still red and hard to miss, but they seemed disappointed that she wore it in a ponytail, which made her whole appearance tamer than that of the girl they remembered.

At least Jonathan had been polite to everyone once Amanda had pried him from Carleen and introduced him to a few people who might still matter: Stephen Barnes, one of the famed redevelopers of the Times Square district; Landry Smith, a former city councilor in District 7 who now was the mayor of a small town in the Adirondacks; Jason Banks, who was related to real Manhattan money by way of his philanthropist grandfather, who had backed many early Broadway productions. They were men with power and connections. If only Jonathan would stop being polite and start working what was left of the room. Start networking. All he had to do was reinforce the fact he was married to one of Edward's nieces. It wasn't as if he'd have to hand out his business cards or sleep with their wives.

Not that it would be beneath him.

Beneath him, ha, she thought, wondering if Bibiana preferred being on the bottom or the top.

Now that the party was reduced to remnants and hangers-on, she supposed she needed to deal with having the wretched "talk" with Jonathan: did he want a divorce?

She had no idea how it would bode with Edward. Would he loan her the money she'd need for a good attorney?

Not likely.

When she'd approached him after Christmas, he'd acted as if it were a game.

"If I gave you money, I would have to write a codicil to my will," Edward had said the day he'd come into Manhattan and they'd had lunch at a little Greek restaurant in the Village because he'd said uptown restaurants had grown costly and she might want to pay attention to that once in a while. "If I were to die before you paid me back, whatever you still owed me would have to be deducted from your share of my estate."

It had seemed he was ready to grant her the cash.

Then he'd added, "Plus interest, of course. You wouldn't want your sisters to be penalized for your irresponsibility." He nibbled at his roasted beet and goat cheese salad as if he were enjoying this course of humiliation.

She'd wanted to tell him to forget it. If she had been Carleen, she would have told him where to put his two hundred and fifty thousand dollars. She would have stalked from the restaurant, leaving the old man to find his own way back to the boondocks, while she went uptown, where she belonged. But she was not her sister, and she was not in a position to do anything but say, "I expect to pay interest." He then suggested fifteen percent, as if he were a member of the *Cosa Nostra*.

Still, she did not have much choice, other than to accept his money and his terms. She would be able to pay down most of her credit cards—Bergdorf, Saks, Citibank (if they still were in business)—though she would need to set aside enough for a few charity checks: a thousand here, a thousand there.

Amanda knew Edward might deem such action absurd, but what would it look like if she said no to those long-standing charities? In light of a potential divorce, it would be more necessary than ever to maintain her status.

Of course, she'd had no idea how she would pay him back. She'd never had a job and would be too embarrassed to ask anyone where to start. Lately she'd considered becoming one of those high-class hookers who led two distinctly different lives, but she wasn't really certain she'd be very good. Sex had always seemed like such a bother, though she'd heard it was good for the complexion.

In the end, when the crème brûlée had arrived, Edward had announced that on second thought, lending money to family was not a good idea. "I just wouldn't feel right, taking interest from you," he said with his leprechaun grin, as if he'd saved her from a fate worse than death.

Death. His or hers now seemed to be the only way out of this mess.

As Amanda pondered that option, her younger son, who'd been listlessly watching the carnie people dismember the games, ambled over to the gazebo. His cheeks were pink from not enough sunscreen: she supposed that was one more area of incompetence for which she could be rightfully slandered.

"Mom? Can I talk to you for a second?"

Chase was a good boy, her easy child (thank God she at least had one of those). She hated that Edward always called him Dewey, as if he were a cartoon character who did not deserve respect.

"Of course, honey. Sit down." She wasn't sure she always called him "honey." She probably should do more of that.

He sat on the bench and sighed, as if he were Edward, or at least Edward's age. "Mom, I can't believe Chandler said that about Uncle Edward. In front of everyone. What a jerk."

At least Chase had run before his brother had informed those in attendance about her grim financial state. "It's true? You found him?"

The boy nodded. "He's on the island. Wes was showing us a stunt and he capsized the canoe. We hung onto it and made it to the island, but we lost the paddles. That's when we saw Uncle Edward. He helped us get the pine boughs to paddle back. Chandler was right: he made us promise not to tell."

So, Edward, indeed, was alive and well and hiding out on the island.

"It was right for you to tell me," she said. "We've been worried about him."

"So will he cut you out of his will? How will you pay your bills?"

Oh. So he knew about those, too.

At least he didn't add, "What's going to happen to us?" He was a kid, though, so Amanda knew that must be foremost on his mind. Self-preservation had worried her every minute when she'd been a kid, though she'd never doubted that her plumbing supply salesman father could support his family. Then again, she hadn't known about the possibility of divorce.

She put her arm around her son. "Don't worry. I'll take care of everything. I always have, haven't I?" But in order to accomplish that, Amanda realized she needed to take drastic action. Especially since her sons now knew about her lack of cash.

She stood up abruptly. "I have to go now. Don't tell a soul what you've told me, okay?"

His eyes grew wide and looked frightened, but he nodded anyway.

"Is the canoe at the boathouse?"

"Yes. We brought it back."

"Are the oars with it?"

"They're paddles, Mom. A canoe has paddles."

"Are they there?"

"We lost two yesterday, but there are more hanging up in the boathouse."

Amanda sprinted away.

"Mom?" Chase called out. "I'm coming, too."

"No!" she shouted back. *"Absolutely not!"*

Chapter Twenty-seven

He asked about her movies; she asked about his life. Babe and Ray sat on the faded flower-cushioned chairs in the musty boathouse and shared "remember when's." For the first time in forever, she felt the sweet taste of his name and not the sting about the baby and the past.

"All I wanted was a sixty-eight Camaro," Ray said.

"But you had your mother's Rambler!" Then she laughed. "I can't believe I remembered the name of that car!"

"It was white."

"It had push buttons for drive and reverse and park."

"The seats went down."

"Oh, yes. I remember that."

They smiled gently at each other.

"Remember when we went to the Tarrytown fair?" She

still had the teddy bear he'd won by hitting a tall scale with a hammer. The stuffed animal had comforted her through many bad relationships and two lousy marriages, and lately she'd considered taking it out of mothballs to help her survive life with Wes.

"We went with Carleen and her boyfriend. What was his name?"

"Earl."

"Man, I didn't like that guy. He smoked."

"And drank wine that came in screw-top bottles."

"Your sister did, too."

"Oh," Babe said. "She was such an awful influence."

Ray smiled. "Do you still hate dandelions?" he asked, and she laughed because he remembered that.

"I didn't like the *pouff,* and they were gone, the fact that one second they are beautiful, feathery flowers, then the next second they're not!"

"They aren't flowers, Babe. They're weeds." He said it with a smile, the way he'd always said it whenever they'd seen one and she'd cried, "Don't touch!"

She laughed and touched his arm.

He quickly set his hand on top of hers and lowered his voice. "After that summer, after you had gone, I never looked at another dandelion without thinking of you."

She looked down at their hands, turned hers over and laced her fingers through his. "I wish I'd known."

"My parents never saw this place again. My dad got lung cancer and died six years ago. Nine months later my mother had a stroke and died. I was divorced by then and had custody of Kevin. I wanted him to grow up here, so I came back. By then, everything had changed. Your uncle didn't have parties anymore. I never realized how much the lake came alive when he had one of his parties. How the music and the laughter drifted over the water and made everyone—even my father, though he'd never admit it—be in a happy mood."

"They were wonderful times."

"It's never been the same."

Ray leaned down then and softly kissed her fingers. "Whenever I've thought about you, I picture you in your jeans and that pretty blue top that had all that elastic."

"It was called a tube top. It probably wasn't fair for a teenage girl to wear one when she was with her boyfriend. Carleen bought it for me."

"Ah. Carleen again. Thank God for her."

Babe laughed, but this time Ray's lips met hers and her laughter dissolved into a soft kiss that lingered longer than it should have, with its warmth and its memory and its sweet taste of home.

"Oh, God," he said, pulling away. "I am so sorry."

"No," she whispered. "No, please don't be sorry." With that one little kiss, Ray had reawakened every part of her, the way he always had, as if it truly were only yesterday and not all these years later. "Wow," she said. "You still have it, you know?"

"Have what?"

"The key to me," she said. She'd forgotten she'd once called the spark—Ray's spark—*the key to me.*

"Shit, Babe," he said.

"Shit, Ray," she said back, and then the door banged open and there was Amanda, with cheeks as red as Carleen's hair and a wild-eyed look that said she had an agenda.

* * *

"Amanda." Babe spoke first in case Amanda hadn't seen them when she'd stepped into the darkness from the bright sunshine.

"Well, well," Amanda said. "Fancy meeting you here. Looks like you found our long-lost neighbor. Hello, Ray."

Ray stood up. "Hello, Amanda. How are you?"

Babe was surprised they seemed to still know each other.

"Well, I'm sure we're all better now that the tree-topping problem has been resolved."

Ray looked down at Babe, who hadn't stood up because she did not want Amanda to think she had caught her doing anything wrong. "I'm president of the lake association," he said. "I've seen Amanda here a couple of times when I've stopped by with information for Edward."

It was another reminder that the world had kept revolving after Babe had left town. She wasn't sure she liked those reminders.

"How's the party going?" Ray asked.

"People are finally starting to leave."

"And you came down here because . . . ?" Babe asked.

"Because I'm going to find Edward and bring him home. No one else seems to want to be bothered." She marched to her right and opened the door to the boat bay just as Ray said, "If you're here for the canoe—"

"There's no boat!" Amanda shouted. "There's no goddamn boat! How can I get him if there's no goddamn boat?" The last sentence was a question fired at Ray.

"Carleen took it," he said.

Which, of course, was probably the last thing Amanda wanted to hear.

"Carleen? My *sister*, Carleen?"

Babe could have corrected her by saying "*Our* sister, Amanda," but instead she and Ray both said, "Yes," and Amanda stalked out the way she had come.

"It's funny," Ray said after Amanda was gone. "I don't remember much about Amanda when you were kids."

"She wasn't much fun," Babe replied.

"She wasn't much of anything," he said, "compared to you." Then he went back to the sofa and leaned down and kissed her again. This time Babe leaned back and he leaned forward, gently stretching his whole body against her so she could feel his heat and she hoped he could feel hers, and she knew if she stopped breathing right then it would be all right.

"Leave it to my stupid husband to be stupid enough to return the stupid boat back to the owners who aren't even here," Amanda muttered to no one as she stomped back through the yard and up to the street then down the road toward the Donnellys' house, where Jonathan had left the car and picked up the boat and apparently returned it to the same spot. It occurred to her that she could have, should have, asked Ray Williams to borrow his boat because, as she recalled, he lived much closer by way of the overgrown path. But Amanda was angry and her feet were on fire from walking without shoes and, besides, stomping was a good way to vent and, without question, she needed to vent.

The Donnellys' mailbox arrived soon enough.

She hurried past the vehicle Jonathan had rented, not looking down at her feet, which were surely blistered and probably bleeding. Like stomping, pain served as a motivator to carry out her mission:

Find Edward.

Make him tell her what was really going on.

Use the opportunity to cry about Jonathan's infidelity, prey on Edward's compassion *for the sake of her children,* allow him to grant her the funds that would absolve her of her debt.

Amanda was going to triumph.

Best of all, she would be back in control, economically equipped to contend with life again.

"Edward?" Carleen called out. "Edward? It's Carleen. I know you're here somewhere." She'd pulled the canoe up onto the shore, grateful she'd been a frequent volunteer at the summer camp her girls attended and that she was therefore pretty good at handling a paddle.

Tramping through the underbrush, she moved toward the scrub pines that lined the way up the hill. She remembered there was a clearing that was carpeted with pine needles and protected by oaks: she and Earl (and others before him) often had gone there for privacy, which had really meant they'd gone there to smoke and drink and have sex.

Uncle Edward was, hopefully, there for other reasons, but Carleen knew the clearing would provide a perfect hideout.

A squirrel skittered past her: she stumbled; she swore. "Damn you, Edward Dalton! I've come all this way, I've put up with my sisters, and now you subject me to this. What are you up to, you crazy man?" She trudged a little further, then noticed footprints on the sandy earth. "You *are* here," she said. "Come out, Uncle Edward. Game over!"

But Uncle Edward was not one of her kids or one of the kids in her ninth-grade algebra class, and she had no authority, absolutely none, over the man and his dubious whims. Consequently, he didn't come forward, and she kept trudging.

At the top of the hill, Carleen gulped at the sight before her: a tent had been erected, a small campfire had been neatly extinguished, a knapsack and a sleeping bag had been settled on the ground next to an open can of beans.

But it wasn't Edward's things that took her breath away; it was the fact that the terrain was so familiar. She stood at attention, as if waiting to be quizzed about which tree stood where, which spot of ground was more level than the other, where the best place was to pee without being seen, because, as bold as she had been, Carleen had always been private when it came to those matters.

Once, right after she and her husband had conceded connection to the Internet and her daughters were boasting they knew how to find anyone on the planet, Carleen had done a Yahoo! People Search for Earl.

She'd typed in *Earl J. Harkness,* not sure if the *J* had stood for *James* or *John.*

The search turned up eight in the United States: three in New York, one in Mississippi, another in Texas, one in Utah, two in California.

She'd checked each one in New York. Two were her age. Both were married. With children.

She'd stared at the screen as if it would offer more information, like which one had been *her* Earl, and had he ever wondered what had happened to her and had he ever sat in a dark room and Yahoo!'ed her name to see where she was and what she looked like today. And did he ever think about the things they had done and how hot she had been and how much he had craved her and how once they'd started having sex they hadn't been able to stop.

Right here, she thought now, staring at the hard-packed earth. *Right in this very spot we must have had sex.* She bent down and touched the ground, as if it would still be warm. She pictured Earl lying there, smiling, his thick blond hair askew, his forehead still damp.

"Oh," she moaned, then another squirrel darted past and she realized someone might have heard her, someone meaning Edward, wherever he was.

She stood up, disgusted with herself for fantasizing about Earl when she loved Brian so much. She turned her attention to the tent and shouted, "Edward! This isn't funny. You've upset a lot of people."

Stepping around the campfire ashes, she went toward the tent, thinking Edward must be there. But when she pulled back the flap and squinted in, it was as empty as the can of beans by the doused fire.

"Uncle Edward," she seethed, "you dastardly man."

Three more squirrels made their presence known. Carleen decided enough was enough. She was making her way back down the hill when her peripheral vision noticed a strange object in a tree that did not seem to belong there. But the object was too far away and was partially blocked by a large tree limb.

She wanted a closer look.

Moving to the edge of the clearing, she still couldn't make it out. So she crouched and began to duck-waddle through the underbrush, pushing pine boughs and scrub oak branches out of her way, her bare legs smarting from the twigs and dry leaves that jabbed at them, as if they were angry she had returned, as if they were saying, *Oh, no! Not Carleen again! What's she doing here? Didn't she move on with her life?*

Finally, she reached the shoreline. She looked out at the water: it looked peaceful, unthreatening. Then, from over her head, the strange object again caught her eye. Slowly, she moved her gaze upward to a tree limb that jutted over the lake. This time, she could tell that the object hanging from the limb, swaying ever so gently, was a sizable, well-fashioned noose.

Carleen screamed.

Chapter Twenty-eight

Her first thought was that Edward was dead, that he had hanged himself there in the noose on the island, his favorite refuge. Then Carleen realized that if he had done that, the noose would not be hanging empty, that, instead, he would be in it, or, at least, his head would be.

Unless his neck broke and his head somehow slipped out and he landed in the lake and sank to the bottom.

She scrambled down the embankment that led to the water as if she could rescue him if he was still there.

CPR! Carleen thought. She'd been trained several years ago after one of her students had an alarming seizure. No one had ever had another in her classroom, but she'd kept her certification current; it was a school department requirement now. She'd never dreamed that the place she might use it would be on Squirrel Island, where she'd lost her virginity and now where Uncle Edward might have lost his life.

"Edward!" she called out when she reached the water, her eyes scanning the surface for telltale debris.

Without stopping to take off her shoes, Carleen plunged into the water. It was thick with lily pads and cattails and other things she did not want to think about, like snakes.

Snakes!

Water snakes.

Shiny.

Black.

Slithering.

She'd seen one years ago. She had not forgotten.

"Edward!" she cried out again, her skirt soaking wet now, her feet trying to maneuver along the deep, treacherous mud on the bottom. "Damn you!"

She looked up at the noose and tried to judge where he might be: she looked into the dark water, but there was nothing there, no shadow, no image, nothing but a few pollywogs.

Then the water rippled.

Her heart skipped. She braced for a snake. But when Carleen looked up, she saw a small rowboat curve around the bend. Inside sat a lone woman in a cherry red halter dress.

"What have you done?" Amanda squealed. "What have you done to Uncle Edward!" She stood up in the boat, not caring that it rocked back and forth. She only knew Carleen was knee deep in water and a noose dangled above her head.

Carleen slogged through the water and lumbered onto the

embankment. "For God's sake, Amanda, I haven't done any-thing. I was looking for his body, if you must know."

"His *body?*" Amanda's eyes narrowed and she scoured her sister, who stood on land now, wringing out her schoolteach-er's dress. "You're looking for his *body? You hung Uncle Edward?*"

"Oh, Amanda, shut up. I didn't hang anyone. Why don't you row over here and check the water. If you poke around with the oars, maybe you can find him. Maybe he pinned a freaking note to his shirt."

Amanda couldn't tell if Carleen was being sarcastic. She looked back up at the noose, then stared down her sister again.

Carleen decided she was done taking Amanda's abuse. She'd taken too much from all of them, too long ago. She'd lost ev-eryone she had loved, and she didn't need them. Not anymore.

Without looking back at her mouthy sister, Carleen went up the hill, then crossed the land and headed toward the inlet where she'd left the canoe. *The hell with them,* she muttered to herself. *The hell with all of them.*

"I'm going to tell Ellie!" Amanda's shouts reverberated across the tiny strip of land. "Don't think you'll get away with this! Just because you stole Earl away from me, don't think you'll get away with this!"

Carleen climbed into the canoe, propped her elbows on her knees, and rested her face in her hands. Earl. Oh, God, did Amanda still hate her for that, too? It had been kid's stuff! Still, Amanda would be the last person to think Carleen had changed, the last one to give her—or anyone—the benefit of any kind of doubt. She was so much like their father had been, so much like the way no one ever had acknowledged: self-centered and harsh. It was no wonder their mother had taken a lover.

Carleen lifted her head, then undid the pink ribbon wrapped around her ponytail, the same pink ribbon she'd untied from the letters she had found in the attic, the writings of love, the witness of adultery.

What had Mother been thinking when she'd saved those letters? Why had she tucked them in the house where her husband and her daughters had lived? Had she hoped one day her girls would find them? Had she thought they might read them? Would she have ever dreamed Carleen would burn them?

She'd burned them in the fireplace. She'd set their mother's infidelity ablaze—then left it to smolder, hot and smoky, the way her forbidden love had been.

Carleen had been so upset that she'd forgotten to check the fireplace flue. She'd never meant for the house to burn down.

She'd never meant for her parents to turn to ashes. How could she have known they'd come home early from their childless vacation and were inside the house?

Their remains had been located in their bedroom—had they been making love in the middle of the day? No one had asked that out loud. And no one but Carleen had known enough to wonder whether they both had relinquished their lovers and returned to each other one last time.

The questions would forever be unanswered; the love letters were gone, unread by anyone but Carleen, after she'd untied the pink ribbon that had once bundled them neatly and now rested cool and smooth against her palm.

She looked at it a moment, so glad she had saved it, a memory of her mother that was hers alone.

Then, rewinding the strip of fabric around her ponytail, Carleen picked up the canoe paddle and began to stroke once, twice on the right; once, twice on the left. She'd go back to the house and get help to find Edward. Amanda would not accomplish what needed doing. Hysteria rarely did.

Chapter Twenty-nine

Ellie settled up with the musicians, the carnie folks, and the caterers, even though a handful of guests remained steadfast in their folding chairs with the quilted covers that they'd reassembled after the helicopter debacle. When the caterers politely, yet firmly, collected those chairs, the guests moved to the permanent benches inside the gazebo. Ellie supposed they would leave by dark, or when their silver flasks had been drained.

As for her, she was tired and felt no need to continue her role as Edward's host-by-proxy. Making her way around trash bags, she avoided Jonathan, who was asking if anyone had seen his wife. She went into the house, then realized she had no idea where any of her sisters were. She only knew that, once again, she'd been left alone, the sane one in charge.

Upstairs in her room, Ellie closed the door, took off Babe's scarf, and flopped onto the bed. She wondered if Chandler had told the truth (and Wes had lied) about seeing Edward on Squirrel Island. Even if he was there, it didn't mean her uncle planned to come back. Maybe he'd decided to take his own life instead of letting cancer take it for him. Unlike Jonathan, Ellie didn't think Edward could have "accidentally" gone over the falls: he knew the falls were there. There had been conflict among the neighbors when the castle owners had requested permission for the excavation. Edward had sided with the environmentalists, led by Ray Williams, though he'd refused to attend any of the meetings.

If Edward had committed suicide, Ellie supposed he would have left a note. The message would be humorous, in the spirit of his personality, an effort to entertain rather than be maudlin.

If Henry had done away with him, there would not be a note.

She turned onto her side. The amber light of sunset seeped into the room, softening the ache growing in her heart, a realization that, if not now, then someday, somehow, Edward would be gone.

Edward knew it, too. The signs were eerily visible: bringing the sisters back together; having his former friends gather to celebrate his name; using the party and its silliness to deflect his intent, to keep them all (well, mostly Ellie) busy.

However, if death had been on his mind, why had he taken the iPod, the binoculars, the Dickens? Had it been a perverse way of resting in peace?

She stared at the walls that had confined her for twenty

years, then was jolted by a sudden thought: what had she believed would ever happen? Had she thought Edward would outlive her? That she'd never have to return to the real world?

The air in the room grew silent and still; her forehead grew moist, her breathing, shallow. She had never considered the *what if's* or the *when's* but had pushed such thoughts away, along with memories of her mother and her father and dreams of Tutankhamen and Cleopatra. But though Ellie had worked to forget the past, she'd forgotten to leave room for the future.

She sat up. She wiped her brow. Was it too late? When Edward came home, *if* Edward came home, could she convince him to have chemotherapy? She could nurse him through that, then she could leave. She could return to the Met and work her way to Alexandria. She could have her own life and not be afraid.

Couldn't she?

Couldn't she?

A firm knock on her door interrupted her thoughts.

"Ellie?" The door opened. It was Carleen.

Ellie straightened her dress. She tried to relax her throat and ease her breath back to normal.

"Ellie, I'm sorry to bother you. Were you sleeping?" Carleen stepped two steps into the room, wringing her hands the way Amanda did.

Oh, no, Ellie thought. *Don't tell me he's dead. I'm not ready yet!*

"Ellie, I think something has happened."

Ellie could not inhale; her airway had a sudden sock in it.

Then Carleen told her about the tent and the campsite and the noose.

Somehow, Ellie managed to breathe again. She heaved herself up from the bed and hustled past Carleen. "Do you have the canoe? How fast can you paddle?"

Babe and Ray were in the boathouse in what might be called a compromising position, except everyone there knew that Babe had compromised and been compromised long ago.

"Ray," Ellie said, "get one of your boats. Meet us on the island. There's apparently been an accident and Edward is there." She would not yet let herself grasp any concept other than *accident*.

Ray straightened his hair, his T-shirt, and his pants and said, "I'll take the pontoon. The motor's small, but it's faster than rowing."

"Whatever," she said. "Just get there. And please be quick."

Ellie didn't wait to see if Babe would go with him. Instead, she rushed to the end of the dock where Carleen already sat in the canoe. Ellie jumped in and they started to paddle. "One can only imagine what Babe is up to," Ellie said to Carleen. "But I'm done trying to solve other people's problems. Let them figure out their own lives for a change." It was a statement to herself, as well as to Carleen.

"Ellie," Carleen said, "I didn't take any of your jewelry. I didn't for one second intend to. I hope you believe me."

"Look," Ellie said, "can't we just worry about Edward right now?"

"Amanda is going to tell you I did something to Edward. I was wading through the water, looking for his body, when she appeared out of nowhere, spotted the noose, and assumed I was to blame."

Ellie quietly paddled and wondered if tomorrow would

be too soon to return to New York. She could get a hotel room and stay overnight and go to the Met in the morning. She could use her honeymoon money for a studio apartment. Maybe she could volunteer at the museum until a position came up. She could find a part-time job until then. Waiting tables. Sweeping floors. Anything would be mentally healthier than spending one more day with this idiotic family. Panic attacks be damned.

"Ellie?" Carleen called. "Did you hear me?"

Ellie dug the paddle into the water and pulled it so hard that the canoe turned to the right. "I heard you."

"I had nothing to do with Edward or the noose. Any more than I was stealing your jewelry. You can believe me or not. I suppose it really doesn't matter."

When they got to the island, Ellie saw Amanda sitting on the beach, holding binoculars that no doubt were Edward's. Ellie landed the canoe, disembarked on the shore, and didn't care that Carleen had to step out in the water.

"You haven't found him?"

Amanda shook her head. "Perhaps someone tied cement shoes to his feet." She threw a hard stare at Carleen.

Ellie left her sisters to deal with each other. She was halfway up the hill when they caught up, God forbid they should leave her alone.

Ducking inside the tent, she checked it out. "Damn you, Edward," she whispered when she found nothing there.

Back outside, she kicked the burned campfire remnants, then picked up the knapsack and emptied the contents: two unopened cans of baked beans, an unopened bottle of wine, a folded piece of aluminum foil. She spread open the foil: there were several crumbs. She raised it to her nose: the scent of her rum cake wafted up.

"This was his," she said, not that she needed to confirm it to her sisters.

But on further examination, Ellie realized the foil was small. Half her cake had been missing from the kitchen—too big a hunk to have been wrapped in such a meager piece. Where was the rest? If Edward had eaten half a cake, there would be more trash. Edward was fastidious about picking up trash, especially when he was outdoors.

Which left only one explanation.

"Edward isn't dead," Ellie announced. "I expect he hung up the noose because he thought it would be funny. He's gone off somewhere and he's taken what was left of the rum cake. God forbid he should leave it behind for the rest of the squirrels."

Amanda stood rigid, hands on hips.

"But where can he be?" Carleen asked. "He didn't have a boat."

"I have no idea," Ellie replied as she stood up, "but he must have had help." She turned to Amanda. "Amanda-Belle, where are your boys?" Then Ellie remembered she'd seen the boys juggling the plastic champagne flutes, trying to emulate one of the carnival acts. She'd seen Wes and Jonathan, too, ambling around, surveying the terrain the way men sometimes did. And, of course, they hadn't arrived at Kamp Kasteel until after Edward had disappeared.

Heather and her boyfriend were accounted for, too, having been more help than Ellie's sisters combined.

Which left Henry.

"You might be wise to do a background check on Henry. You might

learn this isn't the first time one of his lovers has disappeared," David Goldsmith had said.

Ellie felt a slow roll of her stomach. Good Lord, had Henry really done something to Edward? Had Henry been acting concerned, excited, erratic, in order to throw suspicion off himself? Why had she pooh-poohed David Goldsmith? What else did David know about the little man?

"I should have asked for details," Ellie said out loud, and Carleen asked what she meant.

But just then, they heard a putt-putting motor. They turned and saw a silver pontoon head toward the shore. Ray's son, Kevin, stood at the controls; Ray sat on a bench, waving to the women. Next to him sat Edward, the wandering man.

Chapter Thirty

Ellie was so angry that she couldn't speak.

"Uncle Edward!" Amanda shouted, running toward the boat. "We thought you were dead! There's a noose in the tree! We thought it was you!"

Ellie watched Edward chuckle and haul himself from the boat and onto the shore, looking the same as he had at breakfast yesterday.

"You missed your party, you silly man!" Amanda continued prattling. "And why are you with them?" She poked a finger in the air toward Ray Williams and his son.

"Don't blame my captain here!" Edward said, nodding toward the boy. "I asked for his help—he's our *Times* paperboy, you know. I can be pretty convincing when it comes to doling out good tips!"

Ray stood up. "I found him when I went back to the house. Apparently Kevin brought him to the island yesterday. Today Edward called Kevin on a walkie-talkie, asking to be rescued. He said he'd been found out and he had to get away."

Of course, Ellie thought, Wes and Amanda's boys had "found him out." She wished she'd felt surprised that Wes McCall had lied.

Edward looked at Ellie with hangdog, please-forgive-me eyes. "I wanted you girls to get back together without me being in the way," he said. "Life is so short! It was time for forgiveness!"

"What about your two hundred guests?" Ellie seethed. "What was the point of inviting all of them?"

His eyes twinkled. They twinkled! He was really enjoying this!

"I thought my guests could be a buffer if the four of you tried to strangle one another. But how was the party? Damn, I hate missing a party! Did the acrobats show up on time?"

If Ellie had been home, she would have retreated to her bedroom and locked the door. Instead, she turned her gaze up to Carleen. "Carleen, I'm sure someone will give you a lift back to the house. If all of you will excuse me, I am going to leave." With that, she brushed past her uncle, who had started trundling up the hill.

"My dear girl, you came," she heard Edward say to her red-haired sister. "It's so nice to see you."

Ellie didn't wait to see if he kissed Carleen's cheek, if he continued to act as if he'd done nothing wrong. She got into the canoe, picked up a paddle, and took a long, long breath.

I will leave this place now, she promised herself as she calmly began to stroke. *I will leave Edward to his dysfunctional life and his untreated cancer and his questionable lover, and I will start my life again, all by myself.*

Amanda watched Edward fuss over her long-lost sister. It was disappointing that Edward was still alive; it was annoying that she would not be able to pin his demise on Carleen. That would have been so sweet.

"You look wonderful," Edward continued. "Was it a very long ride? Where is Belchertown, anyway?" He was acting as if they had all the time in the world and he hadn't just played the ultimate mean stunt.

"Uncle Edward," Amanda interrupted, "I am going to have Ray bring me back. Unless you want to row the boat I borrowed from the Donnellys, I suggest you come with us. Ray can tow the rowboat with the rope you fashioned into that ridiculous noose."

Edward laughed. "Oh, all right. We'll come with you. But only if you tell me what the dickens was going on with that helicopter. And if you promise all the guests have finally left. I really had no interest in seeing most of them. They always were bores. I expect that now they're simply *old* bores."

"Sort of like you?" Amanda asked.

"Amanda can be so unyielding," he said to Carleen. "Sometimes she's quite boring, too."

"She was worried about you, Uncle Edward. We all were. It wasn't very amusing, the way you disappeared."

"Oh, tit. I send you away and you come back like the rest of them." He put his arm around Carleen and gave her a fatherly hug that made Amanda want to puke, because what right did Carleen have to Edward's stingy affection?

She supposed, however, she should give credit to her sister for not agreeing with Edward's comment about her being un-yielding.

Then Edward looked around. "Where is Babe? Didn't she come to find me?"

Amanda stopped short of announcing that Babe had been screwing Ray Williams, or something close to that, and no doubt was freshening up. But that would have been crude, and Amanda wouldn't lower herself to that, so instead she said, "I'm sure she's with her *husband*," loudly enough for Ray to hear. "She's really *devoted* to him." She couldn't see Ray's reaction.

"Then, let's get a move on!" Edward said, as if, next to Carleen, Babe was the most important person in the world. He turned back to the boat and asked Ray and the boy to give him a hand with the tent and the rest of his crap.

Yes, Amanda thought again, it was very annoying that Edward wasn't dead.

They chugged across Lake Kasteel like an overweight barge on the Erie Canal. Carleen wished she'd hitched a ride in the canoe with Ellie: between Amanda, who clearly was angry with Edward, and Ray, who didn't seem to know quite what to say, and Edward, who could not stop firing questions like a five-year-old child about who had shown up at the party, had they been amused by the games, and had anyone brought him a gift, Carleen was ready to board the next bus home, if she could only find a ride to the station. The last twenty-four hours had been grueling, and they had certainly quashed any smidgen of hope that her sisters would forgive her, that they could reconnect, whether she told them about Mother's love letters or not.

Ray Williams, she suspected, might be more than glad to accommodate her transportation needs, given the remarks Amanda kept making now about how handsome Babe's husband was, and how terrific he'd been with her boys.

"So," Edward continued, "do you think there are any leftovers? I've had nothing except rum cake and beans since yesterday morning."

"Who's fault is that?" Amanda snarled.

Edward answered with a chuckle, and Carleen turned away, her gaze roaming toward the rowboat that the men, indeed, had attached to the pontoon (thanks to the nasty noose rope) and now bobbed in the tiny wake. She wondered if Amanda and Edward always sniped at each other, and, if so, why Amanda let it continue. Didn't she realize he was toying with her? Didn't she realize he was merely doing it because she was such easy bait?

"Carleen," Edward said, apparently having tired of teasing her sister, "I hope you brought your husband and children. For the family photograph I'm planning tomorrow."

The invitation had noted to bring something white but had not specified that the whole family would be in the photo. Even if it had, she wouldn't have brought Brian and the girls. Why would Edward think she would subject her husband and children to . . . them?

"I came alone," she replied. She didn't add that she had not intended to stay for the photo, anyway.

"Well, we can have their pictures taken later and Henry can Photoshop them in." Edward chuckled again, his jolly old self.

Carleen kept her eyes pitched on the rowboat and the water.

Then Ray said, "You're married, Carleen? You have kids?"

"Yes," she replied, grateful that Ray's son then bumped Edward's dock and the others became more engaged in securing the boat than in listening to details of Carleen's family life. She decided that when they disembarked, she might as well ask Ray for a ride to the bus station.

The four adults padded toward the boat's small metal ramp.

Then, Edward moved close to Carleen. He tugged the ribbon on her ponytail, undid the bow, and held it in front of her. "I hope you haven't worn this to taunt me," he said quietly. "I've often wondered how much you knew."

Without further comment, Edward returned the ribbon, tottered off the pontoon, and walked up the hill toward the house.

Babe tucked herself into the shadows of the big oak trees down by the boathouse. She hadn't wanted to go with Ray to find Uncle Edward—she was too confused in the moment, too unsure what to say, how to act, what to tell and not tell. Her heart was too happy to let reality sneak in. Especially if reality meant they'd found Edward's remains instead of him.

She sucked in a tiny breath, hoping that was not the case, hoping he had not died before she'd had a chance to see him one last time.

Finally, the pontoon boat thumped against the dock. Babe's heart skipped a beat when she saw who was at the controls: the boy looked so much like Ray had at that age. In a few years he, too, might steal the heart of a summer girl. Hopefully, their story would be happier.

From her place in the shadows, Babe watched Amanda and Carleen walk off the boat. Then came the white-haired man who looked vaguely like Uncle Edward, though he ambled more slowly and did not seem as tall as the fifty-something-year-old she'd left behind. Her eyes started to mist.

She supposed she should step out of the shadows and welcome him home. But since Ray had kissed her, had *touched* her again, Babe didn't want to think of anything but him. But *them*.

So she waited until her sisters and her uncle had gone by, until she heard Ray tell his son to wait there, until Ray jumped off the boat and walked up the dock before she moved into view.

"One uncle delivered unscathed, so to speak," he said.

"I noticed."

He nodded toward the group ascending the hill. "You don't want to see him?"

"Not yet." *Not while I'm still thinking about you. Not while I'm still feeling you pressed against me.*

He looked into her eyes. "Babe, I don't know what to do. This is crazy, you know that?"

"I do."

"I mean, it's absolutely nuts. What are we doing?"

"I can't speak for you, but I'm following my heart."

He looked at his watch. "We've seen each other all of three hours in the last twenty-five years. Why hasn't my heart stopped hammering?"

"If you're going into cardiac arrest, I must be, too."

"Shit."

"I know."

He moved his gaze up to the house. "You have a husband up there. A famous, rich, incredibly handsome husband, according to Amanda."

"She can have him." There. She'd said it out loud. She didn't want Wes anymore. Maybe she never had. He'd come into her life when it had been convenient and she'd been lonely, and that's where it had ended.

And even though they'd never had real sex, Babe had never understood why he'd insisted on separate bedrooms when they were home, why he never tried to satisfy his wife, who had needs in that department. It was as if he wanted no reminders that he couldn't complete the deed that came with man-and-wife roles.

Still, her issues with Wes weren't solely about sex.

"I only want you, Ray. That's never changed."

"Maybe you only felt that way because you didn't have me. Maybe because of the baby."

She flinched a little—it was hard to hear him refer to "*the baby*" and know it had been his. "No. I've always loved you. From the first day I saw you."

"By the water."

"Yes."

They stood in silence. He reached down, took her hand, held it to his cheek. "Shit," he said again, closing his eyes.

"You don't have to love me if you don't want to," Babe said, listening, at last, to her full heart. "But I'm going to tell my husband tonight. He will go back to the coast without me."

"Whoa," Ray said. "You're going to tell him what?"

"That I don't love him. I never really did."

Ray hesitated. "And then what, Babe? Are you planning to move here, to Lake Kasteel? Are you planning to live happily ever after out here with a guy who works in his house in a T-shirt and jeans? Who types newsletters for the lake association on his ten-year-old laptop because he doesn't want the land and the water to go to crap?"

"Yes," she said. "If he'll have me."

He dropped her hand. He stood perfectly still. Then he wrapped his arms tightly around her and said, "I can't believe you're finally home."

Chapter Thirty-one

Because Babe knew that few things were as easy as she might hope they were, she also knew that Ray had to leave, that she had to face her uncle, her sisters, and Wes alone.

She watched Ray get back onto the pontoon, watched the boat glide from the dock. Then she walked up to the house with long, determined strides: her head bent, her fists tight, her eyes riveted to the grass, which had been flattened by party footprints.

Was she being impulsive? Definitely. But she'd always pondered things over and over to exhausting death, so Babe couldn't be sure what was insane and what was not.

When she reached the top of the hill, she raised her eyes, and there were her relations, aligned like bowling pins. Uncle Edward stood in front.

"Naomi," he said, "I am so glad you're here." His old eyes filled with tears and he opened up his arms. Babe stepped into them as if she were a little girl again receiving Uncle Edward's hug. She was, indeed, taller than him now, but his hug still seemed as soft and safe as she remembered.

Like him, she cried.

Then she viewed the rest of them: Ellie, Amanda, Carleen. Amanda's husband was behind the sisters, and Amanda's boys and her daughter and her daughter's boyfriend and . . . Wes.

Oh, right. Wes.

"Uncle Edward," Babe managed to say, "it's good to see you. I'm so glad you're okay."

He grinned and nodded and pulled away, dabbing his eyes, then hers. "Fit as a fiddler on the roof," he said, dredging up a joke from his Broadway days. "Too bad the photographer won't be here until tomorrow! This would be a lovely shot right now!"

No! Babe wanted to scream. *No, no, not with Wes!* But, of course, she couldn't say it yet, not with everyone standing there.

"Let's go inside," Ellie said. "Henry has set up sherry in the drawing room."

They moved *en masse* into the living room, which Edward always insisted on calling the drawing room because he thought it made the house sound important. He said *drawing room* was the proper term because his bedroom—which, in its day, had been reserved for the king—was directly off the room, just as it had been in sixteenth-century England. When Babe was a little girl, Edward had told her the drawing room was a magical place where people went to draw, so she'd often dragged Mrs. Minerva there with crayons and a big pad from the table in her room. When Babe was eight or nine, Amanda had told her that wasn't what it meant, that *drawing* room meant it was a place for people to *withdraw* from other things like cocktails or dinner or relatives they didn't like. She might as well have said there was no Santa Claus or Easter Bunny. In fact, Amanda had told Babe those things, too, long before it had been necessary or even nice.

They filed into the drawing room now, Edward and Babe in the lead. Somewhere between the backyard and there, Wes had materialized on her other side, cupping her elbow, acting like her protector, because he didn't know the role had been recast.

The small man who Babe guessed was Henry stood next to the sideboard sporting a tiny grin. "It's nice to see everyone together."

"It's nice to be here," Wes said first, as if he belonged in Edward's house or perhaps intended to take over.

Edward plucked the first glass for himself. "I understand there was quite an aerial show at the party, my boy," he said to Babe's husband. "A bit of publicity?"

Wes removed his sunglasses, an act Babe knew he performed when trying to seem sincere. *An act,* she thought. *His whole life was an act!* Why hadn't she seen it before now?

"We were harassed at the airport," Wes said. He said *harassed* with the emphasis on *har-* and not on *-assed,* unlike the way most people in America pronounced it.

Babe took a glass and a hearty swallow.

"Sometimes the paparazzi are so inconvenient," Wes droned. "I'm sorry if it disrupted anyone." He turned toward the others, as if in apology.

Babe took another drink and looked around the room at the brocade-covered English sofas and the heavy dark wood chairs with faded burgundy cushions and thick arms. Nothing looked as large as it once had, as exciting, as magical. It merely looked worn out and tired. She decided she would tell Wes her decision after dinner.

"Well, my boy," Edward guffawed and patted Wes on the back, "of course it disrupted everyone! That was your intent, was it not?" Edward didn't have to explain how he knew Wes had orchestrated the show. Everyone knew Edward had been a master at manipulating the press. With a contented smile, Edward turned from him to Jonathan. "And how are things in the world of architecture?"

Babe suppressed a laugh; she'd never seen Wes speechless. She meandered toward the far end of the room as if suddenly captivated by the thick-framed portraits of men no one had known but whose coloring and style matched the wainscoting.

Amanda smirked. Even a moron would have picked up on Edward's mockery of Babe's once-pretty-boy husband, who, well, look at that, had finally graced them with the removal of his sunglasses. She had to admit, he did have gorgeous eyes. As for the rest, no matter what she wanted Babe or Ray to think, she wished Wes would stay the hell away from her boys. Something about him was too aggressive and too phony. Oh, God, she thought, I hope he's not a child molester, someone who looks for vulnerable boys and ... well ...

Could one tell by scrutinizing?

Her boys didn't look any different. Chandler sipped sherry as if he were of age, as if he enjoyed it, though Amanda detected a row of sweat beads shining on his upper lip. Chase was drinking ginger ale out of a sherry glass and was preoccupied with a spider that marched along the baseboard.

No, she thought, it didn't look as if either boy had been molested by the Hollywood-has-been.

Draining her glass, she moved back to Edward's man, who poured her another although she had not made eye contact. Perhaps in another life he had been not a chorus boy but a valet.

She wondered if Ellie was right, that he had something to hide.

Like the rest of us.

Sipping again, she strolled to a tall window whose tiny panes were framed by leaded glass. She wondered if Edward would choose this evening—tonight!—after dinner to tell them he was going to divvy up his fortune, or if he would wait until after the picture-taking tomorrow.

Could she hold out until then?

Could she survive one more night pretending everything was fine?

Staring out the window, past the arborvitae and the peonies and the rest of the damn flowers, Amanda wondered why she still clung to the hope that Edward was going to bail her out, when he'd already said he would not.

Ellie watched Uncle Edward, who was deep in conversation with her brother-in-law. Edward didn't look like a man with cancer who had refused treatment. His cheeks were rosy and his spirits were, well, spirited, and he didn't look as if he only had a short time—what . . . weeks? months?—to live.

He was exasperating, but that was nothing new. Had he really disappeared in order to get the girls back together without him in the way? Yes, she could believe that, now knowing that he was sick. The staging of the noose, however, had been worthy of reproach, yet, yet . . . for now, Edward was alive, so staying angry at him simply wasn't possible.

Turning away, Ellie moved to Babe, who was sitting in one of the massive chairs that Edward had refused to let Ellie discard when she'd tried sprucing up the place. She sat down next to Babe and smiled.

"You've seen Ray again."

Babe nodded in reply.

Ellie toyed with her glass. "He never asked about you. I always thought that was so sad. You both had been so young."

"He never knew about the baby. He thought I didn't want to see him anymore. Neither of us knew his parents kept us apart."

"I figured that. Once, I almost brought it up after a lake association meeting. But I decided there was no point in digging up the past. He'd been married and had a son by then. And your life had taken off in such a fabulous direction."

Babe smiled. "If you're going to try and talk me out of what I'm going to do, forget it. I appreciate the effort, but my mind's made up."

Ellie lifted her eyebrows.

"I'm going to be with Ray, Ellie. I'm going to divorce Wes. He's fine for Hollywood, but he's no good in the real world."

"Oh, honey, are you sure? You have your career; you've been in California so many years. You only saw Ray today—"

"I've never been more sure of anything."

Ellie had to give Babe credit for knowing what she wanted, that she did not hem and haw the way Ellie might have done. "Well," she said, patting her sister's knee. "I'll support your decision, no matter what." She stood again, having remembered that she'd resolved to stop giving advice.

Carleen declined both sherry and ginger ale, wishing she'd found enough composure to have asked Ray for that ride to the bus station. But even now, she was still trying to regain her bearings after Edward's remark about the ribbon: *"I hope you haven't worn this to taunt me. I've often wondered how much you knew."*

With those few words, he had confirmed the secret. Shouldn't that be enough? Did her sisters really need to know the rest?

Sometimes Carleen thought the fire had given them a good excuse to strip her from their lives. They'd never liked her: could she blame them? She'd done so little back then that was likable.

No matter what, Carleen knew she had, at least, accomplished a few things this weekend: she'd seen them all and they'd seen her; they'd seen that she had straightened out her life; they knew she had a family, a career, some respect. She supposed that was more than she could have hoped for.

As a bonus, thanks to her, Babe and Ray had met again. It looked as if they were getting more than closure.

She'd also stood up to Amanda and left her bemused (and disappointed?) when she realized Carleen hadn't hung Edward, after all.

Yes, Carleen had accomplished a few things, though she wasn't sure if Ellie still thought she'd been trying to steal her jewelry. Leaning against the ornate walnut sideboard, Carleen wondered what purpose it would serve to tell them the rest.

Edward knew that she knew. And that should be enough.

Chapter Thirty-two

At six o'clock Edward announced he would take supper in his room, that he'd see them at breakfast. He reminded his nieces to show up in white for the picture. Then he decided Amanda's children should be in the photo as well.

"Not the men, though," he said. "Spouses aren't allowed. They change so quickly in this day and age." He disappeared into the king's bedroom, and Henry quickly followed.

Amanda's hands went to her hips, where they often went these days. "For his information, my boys don't have anything white. And I doubt that Heather does. I thought this was only for the sisters."

"I have a white shirt, Mother," her daughter said.

"I'm sure it's not appropriate." She turned back to the others. "How dare he change the rules on a moment's notice?

How dare he make us jump through hoops just because it is his birthday . . . just because he thinks he *can*?"

"Mom," Chase pleaded, "Uncle Edward will hear you."

"I don't care if the pope can hear me," which made no sense, of course, but neither did Amanda when she was on a tear.

"Amanda-Belle," Ellie said, "why don't you come with me into the kitchen. I could use your help setting out leftovers for supper."

"Leftovers," Amanda groaned. "How fitting. I, for one, have never doubted that's how Edward has always treated us, as if we were doggie bags from our parents, his poor leftover nieces, who'd been shoved into his fridge."

The good news was that Amanda actually followed Ellie from the drawing room and left the rest of them in peace.

"Thanks for rescuing me," Amanda surprised Ellie by saying once they had closed the kitchen door behind them. "Between Edward's shenanigans, our lovely sister, Babe, and that other one—Carleen—I've had as much as I can stand."

Ellie opened the refrigerator and saw the foil-covered trays of meat stacked the way she had asked, the bowls of salad and beans neatly covered. Martina and her staff were certainly as efficient as their reputation indicated.

Amanda propped herself against the counter with no apparent intention of helping. "Honestly, Ellie, don't you find it absurd? The kissy-face about how happy Edward is to see the two of them? Where have they been all these years when we're the ones who put up with his eccentricities and watched him get cranky and despicable?"

"You're right, sometimes his antics are despicable. But

Edward hasn't changed. His hair is gray now and he walks a little more slowly, but he really hasn't changed."

"More's the pity," Amanda cackled, then yanked the silverware from the drawer and started lining up the knives as if each were a weapon. "Why are we *really* here, Ellie? I know something is going on that has little to do with a party and a photograph and Edward's fake suicide. Or to bring us back together because 'life is so short.'"

Instead of laughing at her sister's predictable agitation, Ellie realized that if she told Amanda about Edward's cancer, maybe Amanda would calm down. She'd been like an irate wasp since she'd arrived, which was understandable, given Jonathan's behavior and her financial predicament.

"Amanda-Belle," Ellie said as she set a tray of barbecue on the counter. "Uncle Edward is sick."

Amanda froze. "What do you mean, he's sick? Yesterday you said he was fine."

"I thought he was, but he's not."

"Well, he looks fine to me. He was fine enough to sleep on the *ground* last night, for God's sake. He was fine enough to climb a tree and hang that moronic rope."

"He has cancer."

Amanda tipped her head and scowled a tiny scowl. "Cancer? Oh, puh*leeeze*. What's he trying to pull off now?"

Ellie supposed she shouldn't have been surprised by her sister's reaction. "It's true, Amanda-Belle. Edward has colon cancer."

Amanda snorted. "Did you see the test results? Did you talk to his doctor?"

"No. Of course not."

"How long does he have? A minute? A day?"

"Amanda, stop. This isn't funny."

"Well, it *is* funny that he hasn't mentioned it before now. When did he tell you, anyway?"

"He didn't tell me. Henry did."

"I see. Well, that explains it. Didn't you say Henry can't be trusted?"

"No. I asked if you'd ever heard anything suspicious about him."

Amanda laughed. "Well, I have now. I think it's rather suspicious that Uncle Edward *suddenly* has cancer. So did he want to have the party before he starts chemo? Before he loses what's left of his hair, so his friends and family can remember him when he was still hale and hearty?" Her sarcasm was nearly palpable.

Ellie took the potato salad from the refrigerator and set it on the counter. "He isn't going to have treatment. Apparently he doesn't want any."

"That's absurd."

"It's his choice, Amanda-Belle."

Amanda folded her arms yet still made no gesture to help. "I can't believe you're buying this story."

"Henry seemed sincere." Ellie felt her lower back tense. She felt her neck tighten.

"Well," Amanda huffed, "it's bullshit. And it's all the more reason I am not going to sit around making small talk and eating stupid leftovers and pretending everything is fine." She waved at the food as if it were the enemy.

"Amanda, stop it. I only told you because I hoped it would explain why he'd invited everyone. I think what he really wanted was for the four of us to reunite before he dies. I think he wanted us to have a chance to correct some things in our past. Like Babe and Ray, like Carleen, like, well, like you and Martina."

Amanda's face scrunched up. "Who?"

"Martina. The caterer." Ellie dumped the baked beans in a pot and turned the stove burner to simmer. "She's the daughter of Edward's old housekeeper. You used to make fun of Martina."

Amanda laughed. "You're kidding."

"Not at all. When we were kids, you thought she wasn't as good as us because she was Spanish. You were mean to her, Amanda-Belle. Edward hated that."

Peeling back the foil from the top of the salad, Amanda looked inside, as if she might see something interesting. "I remember the day he made me apologize. It was ridiculous."

"No. He was trying to teach you a lesson."

"Is that why she was here this weekend? To teach me another one?"

"Martina is a successful woman with a fabulous business. Maybe Edward wanted to show you it never pays to be judgmental."

Amanda pulled off the foil and shoved a serving spoon into the salad. "And now the supposed cancer has incited him to once again screw with our heads?"

"I think he's trying to help."

"Help? *Help???* Didn't he think I might appreciate something other than settling an old score with a maid?"

"Please, Amanda-Belle. He's sick . . ."

"Is he? Do we really know that's true?" She leveled her eyes at her sister. "I'll tell you what I'm going to do. I'm going to get to the bottom of this! Straight from the horse's mouth!"

At least she hadn't called Edward a horse's ass. Still, Ellie backed up in case there was a chance Amanda threw something, like the bowl of salad, or worse, the barbecue.

"Amanda . . ."

"No! This is such utter bullshit!" She twirled like a mini tornado, then stormed out of the kitchen.

Ellie's heart plummeted to the terrazzo floor because she suspected where her sister was headed next.

"Mother, what are you doing?" Heather and the boyfriend were leaving the drawing room when Amanda had the misfortune of a head-on collision with her daughter.

"Out of my way."

"Your face is red. You're out of control."

Amanda should have known better than to issue an edict to a nineteen-year-old whose major in college was psychology, and who hadn't agreed with her mother since turning twelve.

"What's going on?" That came from Jonathan, who had suddenly materialized in a David Copperfield moment.

So now half of Amanda's immediate family stood in her path between nonsense and reason.

"Stay out of this," Amanda said, her voice stern and level though her blood pressure was rising. "I am going to talk with my uncle."

"He has retired for the evening," Jonathan said, as if she hadn't been there when Edward had departed from the table with his hovering man-friend.

"Well, he is about to un-retire himself. He and I are going

to have a conversation. And no one is going to interfere."

"Amanda," Jonathan said, taking her by the elbow. "Calm down."

It was sort of like telling a rabid raccoon to run along and bother someone else's trash can. "I said, *get—out—of—my—way*."

Well, of course, he didn't, because Jonathan didn't do anything she wanted anymore.

"Edward has gone to bed. Whatever you want can wait until morning."

"No. It can't."

Jonathan waved Heather away and moved closer to Amanda, diverting her into the hall, as if he hoped it put them out of earshot from the others.

With her shoulders hunched, Amanda knew this might be a good time to confront her husband, to tell him she knew what he'd been doing late at night in the Village and with whom he'd been doing it. It might be a good time in terms of her on-the-surface rancor, but she was too focused on Edward and the latest injustice he'd employed, pretending to have cancer so he could shake them up. Again.

"He claims he's dying," she hissed. "Now get out of my way."

Jonathan took a step back. "Wait a minute. You can't announce your uncle is dying, then blow me off. I am your husband."

Tempted though she was, she did not address the comment about him being blown off. Still, he'd offered an opening she couldn't resist. "Is that what you are, Jonathan? My husband? Perhaps another time we should discuss your definition of that word. I, for one, wouldn't think *husbands* engaged in back-waxing without first informing their wives. Or perhaps they'd rather inform their wives' attorneys."

He was so stunned that it was easy to push past him then, to march into the drawing room, past the remaining shards of family, and up to the entrance to the king's room, which, of course, was locked.

She banged on the door that she had never passed through, never been allowed to enter, even when she'd been a girl. Edward's domain had always been off limits, its secrets securely hidden from unauthorized eyes.

"Edward!" Amanda shouted. "Open the goddamn door!"

Edward did not come to the door, but Henry did, sneaking through the open slot like a mouse through a basement's foundation.

"He's sleeping," Henry said. "Go away."

She tried to insinuate herself around him, but he remained stalwart, which was pretty admirable because he was so thin and one good push would have sent him careening. "Henry," she said, "get out of my way."

He shook his head. His eyeballs bounced like the ping-pong sport he favored. "No admittance."

"He can't be asleep already."

The next thing she knew, someone was at her elbow again. This time it was Babe. "Amanda-Belle," Babe said, "let's go for a walk before the sun sets. We'll see Uncle Edward in the morning."

Babe rattled her—she always had, the spoiled, perfect baby of the lot. "Oh, for God's sake," Amanda wailed. "Can't you all just leave me alone?" She pulled her arm away from Babe and paraded from the drawing room, up the immense staircase, where she stomped down the hall to her bedroom and slammed the door with great affect in case anyone was listening.

"I don't know what's gotten into my wife," Jonathan told Carleen after Amanda fled the drawing room.

From where she'd been sitting, Carleen had had an unobstructed view of Amanda's tirade. "There's no need to apologize. For one thing, I know my being here has upset her terribly. That, and not knowing what was going on with Edward."

Jonathan put his face in his hands. "She wasn't like this when she was young. She wasn't so . . . angry."

Carleen didn't know how to tell Amanda's husband that, indeed, Amanda-Belle always had been angry—angry that Ellie was older and, ergo, had more authority; angry that Carleen got away with behavior that was so unruly; angry that Babe was sweet, and Amanda was not. Yes, Amanda had been angry.

"You have a nice family," Carleen said. "I'm sure she can't be angry about that."

"She's angry at me all the time. I have no idea why. A minute ago she lashed out about me having my back waxed or something. Did she say anything to you about it?"

Back-waxing? Good Lord. Her daughters would have cried, *Too much information.* "Sorry," Carleen said. "Amanda hasn't said much to me since I've been here."

"Right. I am ashamed of her for that."

"Don't be, Jonathan. I learned the hard way not to judge anyone else. I mean, we never really know what's going on in their worlds, or in their minds, do we?" She hadn't intended to criticize him or stick up for her sister. But Carleen had begun to realize how nice it was to have been sheltered from the family drama for so many years. She stood up. "I should see if Ellie can use my help with supper."

She tapped her pocket to be sure she had her cell phone. Before going to the kitchen, she'd step outside and make a call. She missed Brian and the girls more than she'd ever thought she would; their normalcy was now blissfully inviting. Besides, the time had come to leave. Carleen decided that if she waited around and told her sisters the truth, it would solve nothing. It would only heighten the family-in-chaos and end up hurting them more.

Chapter Thirty-three

Babe could not sit and eat supper with Wes and her family and pretend everything was the same as it had been last night.

After failing to calm Amanda down, she'd gone outside alone to sit on the dock. Sunset on the lake had always been a favorite time for her, when she would sit there and watch the salmon-colored ribbons cloak the water like a soft evening quilt. She'd spent a lot of time on that dock during the three years after the abortion and her parents' deaths, looking for comfort any way, anywhere she could find it. Maybe, too, she'd been looking for Ray, though his house had been rented and his family had not returned.

"Hey, sister," Carleen called quietly now. "I came to say good-bye."

Babe looked up at Carleen, who glowed in the rose-amber evening light. "Good-bye?"

"I've decided it's in everyone's best interest if I leave early in the morning. I don't want to cause a scene—I know, how unusual for me—but I thought I should at least tell one person I've gone. I wouldn't want anyone to think I'd pulled one of Uncle Edward's stunts and was cloistered on Squirrel Island, hoping for attention."

"Is that what he was doing? Hoping for attention?"

Carleen shrugged. "Aren't we all?"

Babe dangled her feet into the water and made wide ripple circles with her toes. "I don't want you to leave."

Carleen laughed. "I'm sure you'd be the only one. Except maybe Ellie."

"Ellie's such a good person."

"I know. She has all the admirable genetics." Carleen sat down next to Babe. "Are you going to leave your husband for Ray Williams?"

"No. I'm going to get out of my marriage. It was a ruse, anyway. Wes seems like a nice guy, but . . ."

"But he's too old for you?"

"For starters, yes. But did you know he found Edward and didn't tell anyone? That was so wrong."

"Yeah, that was kind of strange."

"He did it for himself. To get on Edward's good side."

"Well," Carleen said, "I'm sure you know what you're doing, kid."

"Do any of us ever know?"

"Ha! No, probably not."

Babe kicked her feet again. "You won't stay until after breakfast? For Edward's family picture?"

"I didn't bring anything white."

"You are a bad girl, aren't you?"

"Absolutely. Or maybe I somehow knew I still wouldn't fit in."

"Carleen, that's not true. You have as much right to be in the picture as I do. Go into town. I'm sure Uncle Edward would let you use his credit card."

"I don't want anything from him."

"Not your share of his fortune?"

"If that's what I wanted, I would have come a long time ago." She stood up, leaned down, kissed the top of Babe's head. "I called for a cab," she said. "The driver will pick me up just after dawn. I'd leave tonight, but there are no more buses from New York to Amherst until tomorrow. Do me a favor, before you tell anyone, give me a head start?"

Babe bit her lip; surprising tears rose in her eyes. She scrambled to her feet and hugged Carleen. "I wish you'd stay."

Carleen tightened the pink ribbon around her ponytail. She shook her head. "Sorry, kid. I'll se ya' at the movies." With that she moved lightly up the hill toward the house, toward the life that had nothing to do with them.

And Babe felt a hollow ache deep in her heart, the kind she felt when someone died.

Supper was disjointed, to say the least. Attendance at the table was comprised of Amanda's three children plus Shotgun-turned-Jarred, Amanda's husband, Babe's husband, and Henry, who'd emerged from the bedroom with the quiet announcement that Edward was *resting comfortably,* as if he'd had a complicated surgical procedure.

Amanda, Babe, and Carleen were in their respective rooms: Babe had claimed she was tired, Carleen had a headache, and Amanda was, well, Amanda.

Ellie passed the coleslaw. "So," she said with as much steadiness as she could muster, "Heather? Boys? Do you have something white you can wear tomorrow?"

"We didn't get the memo," Chandler said.

"I have white shorts and a shirt with a silver glitter star on the front." Heather cut off her brother. "I'm sure my mother's right, though. It's probably not appropriate."

"And *I'm* sure it will be fine," Ellie replied, not sure at all, but knowing that discussing clothing and pictures seemed easier than addressing the fact that her sisters were absent or wondering if Edward was pretending to have cancer or if Henry simply wanted them to think he did. "I have an idea, boys," she quickly said. "Why don't we go to the mall in Tarrytown? There must be at least one store where we can get you outfitted the way Uncle Edward wants."

Then Ellie put down her fork and realized going to the mall would require driving. When was the last time she had driven?

She stared at the potato salad on her plate. Her heart began to gallop, her palms started to sweat. Then Amanda's youngest was on his feet.

"Cool! Can we go now? Can we get fast food instead of this gross junk?"

Jonathan rubbed his neck. "Sorry, kids, but I didn't come prepared for shopping."

Ellie stood up. "Shopping's on me!" she shouted, much

more loudly than necessary. "White outfits coming up! My treat!" Her better judgment told her she was being crazy, that she couldn't leave the grounds, let alone behind a wheel. Her other judgment said, *What the hell, you're going to leave this place anyway, aren't you? Why not start right now?*

"Race you to the Range Rover!" Ellie shouted and launched herself from the table before she could change her mind.

"Have fun," Jonathan called after the mad dash of bodies from the drawing room. "I'll tell your mother you've gone AWOL."

Heather and Shotgun decided to go, too, which left the men, minus Edward, to discuss whatever men discussed when women and children weren't around. Ellie considered asking Heather or her boyfriend to drive, but then she thought, *No . . . this is your chance to begin starting over.*

Not that it was easy when she started the engine of the eighteen-year-old vehicle and engaged the transmission. *Here goes,* she thought, bracing herself as she backed down the driveway, wondering if her palpitations were visible to those whose lives she had taken into her unsteady hands, especially Chandler, who sat up front in the passenger seat gripping the dashboard as if he'd boarded a ride at Six Flags.

For some bizarre reason, his agitation calmed Ellie down.

"Something wrong?" she asked the boy as she shifted into first gear and turned onto the road that led to the center of Mount Kasteel. As she remembered, she could pick up the back road there and avoid the highway. No sense taking more chances than necessary.

"Mother once said you don't drive."

"Well, clearly *Mother* was incorrect." She tried to smile as she spoke, not that he'd notice, with her eyes fixed on the asphalt and her knuckles a whiter shade of pale. She hoped he didn't ask her to produce a driver's license: she hadn't had one since nineteen eighty-seven.

"Mother said you don't drive because you're a recluse. That you have issues." He said it with the degree of snootiness Ellie would have expected from his mother.

"Shut up, Chandler," Heather said from the backseat.

As much as Ellie wanted to *wipe that smirk off his face,* as Uncle Edward might have admonished, she tightened her grin and said, "It's all right, Heather, we all have issues. But Chandler, for the record, I am not a recluse."

He seemed to grapple with a response. Then, from the corner of her fixated eye, Ellie saw his smirk grow into a grin. "Really? When was the last time you came into Manhattan? Mother says you're afraid of people. That's why you won't leave Uncle Edward. That's why you stay at the lake. That you pretend it's because he needs your help, but it's really because you are scared."

Ellie pursed her lips. "So that's what she says about me. Well, that's very interesting, because you wouldn't believe the things I say about her." Without conscious intention, she punched her foot down on the gas pedal and thrust the gearshift into second. The vehicle lurched, seat belts tightened, and, for once in Ellie's life, she took real control.

"We're finished," Babe said to Wes when he finally went upstairs for the night. She had been lying on the bed without rehearsing her lines: she wanted them to come, unscripted, from her heart.

He laughed. "Very funny." He tugged off his black T-shirt, revealing a belly rimmed by puckery skin that looked like rolled-up plastic wrap. Tossing the shirt onto the floor, he sagged onto the bed. "You can't leave me now, darling. This will work. You'll see."

"No," she said, "it won't. You tried to exploit my family for the sake of publicity. You dragged me here under the ruse of getting to know my uncle and my sisters, when all you cared about was what was in it for you. And you took advantage of us by not telling us you'd found Edward, when you knew how worried everyone was."

"I tried to get your sister to call the police."

"She had reasons not to."

"Babe," he groaned. "Please. I'm tired from entertaining the masses today. And might I remind you that someone had to do it, seeing as how you disappeared? There is such an epidemic of that in this family."

"I did not disappear. I was with my former lover." She said that intentionally to hurt his feelings. She would not have done that before this afternoon, before his behavior had proved that his narcissism was greater than his compassion.

He turned onto his side and looked her straight in the eyes. He paused for a moment, as if assembling tears. "God knows, if I could make love to you, I would," he murmured. "Still, I want you to be happy."

She wondered if other women would believe the deliberate softening of Wes McCall's eyes or the fake sincerity that knitted his words. He reached out to touch her. She got up off the bed.

"I mean it," she said. "We're through. It's been fun, but it's over."

He closed his eyes. "Okay. Fine. You're a brat, anyway. Just like your whiney sisters."

She sucked in a deep breath and lifted her suitcase. Then she left the bedroom, descended the front staircase, and left *Kamp Kasteel,* heading toward the neighbor's by way of the path. The full moon was rising, so there would be plenty of light.

Chapter Thirty-four

"We're finished," *Amanda said to Jonathan as* soon as he entered her bedroom, a strong scent of cigars and Edward's favorite bourbon haloing his body.

"Excuse me?" he asked, because even in crisis, Jonathan was polite. Amanda had taught the boy from Vermont well.

"We're done," she said, swiveling in her chair, her gaze traveling out the window, where it was now growing dark and there was nothing to see. "*Kaput,*" she added, "as in divorce court."

She sensed he must be loosening his tie and examining her for signs of a breakdown.

"Amanda," he asked, "what are you talking about?"

Her eyes fell to her hands, which were perfectly folded in her lap, hardly creasing the Dior silk. "I know about your whore."

"My what?"

"Your whore, Jonathan." She kept her voice quiet, which surprised even her. It was almost as if now that she'd gotten this out, the rest of her problems—her damn debt and her place in society—no longer mattered. "I believe her name is Bibiana. Back-waxer to Broadway Stars."

It would have been nice if Jonathan answered. It would have been nice if he tried to lie, to defend both his honor and hers by saying she was mistaken, that he loved her deeply and for-ever, that there was no other woman, never had been, never would be.

It would have been nice, but he stood there, mute.

Amanda sighed. "I suppose you're going to say I brought it on myself, that I'd become so wrapped up in my charities and in the children that I no longer had time for you. I suppose you can think of a million ways to blame me, but you don't even know the truth about my life. You don't even know we are so far in debt that it is about to become very public and very humiliating. Not to mention that your little whore might be disappointed to learn her rich man is as dead broke as the men in her neighborhood in Queens."

"Amanda," he said, taking a step forward. "Are you all right?"

She nodded. "I am perfectly fine. Edward is telling people he's going to die, and who knows, maybe he is. I should be delighted. My share of the estate should pay off our debts. But even if that happens, I've realized I'll still have you, and you'll still have your whore, and if nothing changes, nothing changes. So chances are it won't be long before we're back in the same hole, with no one left to bail us out."

He didn't speak; she didn't speak. Then he cleared his throat. "You're right," he said.

An ache burned in her heart.

"I have been seeing someone," her husband continued. "She is a prostitute. I have been fucking a prostitute because I could not fuck my wife, who has not wanted me to fuck her for almost a year."

A year? Had it been that long since they'd made love? Since they'd *fucked*, as the Princeton man so indelicately put it? Then Amanda realized he'd said the back-waxer was a prostitute. A hooker—not a lover?

"Well," she said. "Shame on you."

His scent moved closer. His hand rested on her shoulder. She stiffened.

"Yes," he said. "Shame on me. The fact that I'd tried talking to you on more than one occasion isn't an excuse. It's merely an explanation."

"Oh, come on, Jonathan. When did you try talking to me?"

"At Christmas. Right here in this room. I gave you the sapphire necklace."

"We couldn't afford it. It maxed out our Cartier account."

"I didn't know that. I was trying to find a way to please you. You seem to like things that sparkle or have designer labels better than you like me. But you said, 'Take it back. It's gauche.'"

Outside, the shadow of a woman crossed the driveway, suitcase in hand. It must have been Babe, Amanda knew. She might not have seen her in nearly twenty years, but she'd seen all her movies. She'd gone at night when Jonathan was out of town, taking a yellow cab rather than using their in-town car service, because she hadn't wanted the world to know what she was doing. She was, after all, still immensely pissed that Babe had left them high and dry, had run off to "start anew," as if she'd been the only one left hurting. Amanda had never known what to say to Babe after the abortion. She'd always been so afraid that she would be judged by the things her sisters had done. Still, as time passed, Amanda was proud of what Babe had achieved. Of course, she hadn't told her. Any more than she'd ever conversed with her husband about things that really mattered. "The necklace wasn't gauche. It was beautiful. But we couldn't afford it."

He squatted beside her, turned her face toward his. "Amanda-Belle?" he asked, not knowing that her childhood nickname always reduced her to Jell-O, always made her feel vulnerable again, the second child not as smart as the first, not as clever as the third, not as beautiful or as talented as the fourth. "Can we talk about this? Can you forgive me? Can we be a family again?"

This time, she was the one without words.

He reached down, took her hand. "How bad is the debt?"

"Bad. A quarter of a million. How often have you seen Bibiana?"

"Three times. Including last night."

The burning moved down to her stomach. The nausea rose again, as it had after the trout. But Amanda was too numb to excuse herself. Then again, it would serve Jonathan right if she threw up on him.

"Amanda, I'm trying to be honest. I am so sorry I've hurt you. But you've hurt me, too, by shutting me out."

She supposed that was true. But she'd been so disappointed,

so angry at him for . . . for what? He'd been a good husband as husbands went. He'd been a great father. Why had it mattered that he hadn't made millions?

He moved in front of her, blocking her view. "We'll find a way to get out of debt. I hope Edward's not sick. But we can figure this out without his money. You and me, Amanda. Together. The way we got through it when your parents died."

She blinked. Two huge tears plopped onto her Dior. Two more followed. Then a whole freaking river.

Thank God Henry had snuck him a plate heaped with barbecue and potato salad and a huge hunk of cake, which Edward devoured first. It was his cake, after all. His birthday cake! He ate it first because he was seventy-five, loaded with cancer, for all he knew, so he could do as he pleased! No more pretending to count calories or watch his cholesterol or feel compelled to eat raw veggies and fruit. *Bleccch.* No more needing a brisk constitutional every morning in order to yield a good crop of healthy poop; no more abstaining from his favored bourbon for the sake of his naughty, swollen liver.

Oh, yes, Edward mused, as he swiped frosting from his chin and dove into the tender, sauce-saturated meat, having a diagnosis certainly made life more livable.

How he had enjoyed his alone time on Squirrel Island! He'd finally had a chance to see things from the perspective of his neighbors way back when, as he'd peered through his binoculars, trying to imagine the party-in-progress, playing the role of the uninvited. No matter the outcome, Edward felt certain he had done the right thing to let the girls be alone (surrounded by two hundred!) to finally sort through the past, to absolve one another, to rediscover themselves, before his cancer took over and he wasn't there—or wasn't able—to help them reconnect.

As for himself, he'd had a walloping good time with the beans and the Mozart and dear *Oliver Twist*! How he relished the memories of those solitary hours as he now plumped the down pillows that Henry had tucked around him before dashing to the kitchen because the hired help had finished and Ellie had escaped.

Ellie, Edward thought as he turned from the pillows and inserted another forkful of meat into his mouth. He couldn't believe that she'd gone out. *To the mall,* according to Henry. And she'd driven! So, this weekend had yielded some good after all.

It was unfortunate, however, that Henry had told her about the cancer. Edward had wanted to keep that a secret until long after he'd sold this mausoleum and moved to London, until Ellie had regained enough confidence to be content on her own, until his body was shriveled and his breath came in short pants. (*Short pants,* he thought—*Ha! That's funny! Perhaps they should be called Little Lord Fauntleroy Breaths!*) Anyway, he'd wanted to keep his cancer a secret until no one—not even Ellie—could change his mind about having treatment. He wasn't sure why he'd turned down the protocol. Maybe he'd simply grown tired of life and dying seemed much more exotic.

As for the other girls, Amanda, as usual, was angry about something that no doubt was connected to money. The poor thing still hadn't learned that the only difference between the haves and the have-nots was the kind of coffee they drank. Maxwell House? Starbucks? Gevalia? Who cared? No, she still hadn't learned that what truly mattered wasn't the brand but having someone who loved you sharing a cup. Even if the guy was Ivy League.

Babe had a husband, though he was washed up, a fossil of a man desperate for the days that had come and gone when he apparently hadn't been looking. Edward had seen Wes McCall's type a thousand or more times: flat, one-dimensional characters, trying to convince others—and themselves—that they were still young and virile, even while crawling into their beds at night, their bodies and spirits broken and withered, but too stubborn to let go.

He didn't like the man.

Hopefully, Babe would come to her senses this weekend. She was such a loving girl—the one most like her mother. The good news was that Ray Williams had come around. Maybe happiness was still achievable for Babe. Edward hoped he'd never have to tell them that he'd known about the baby, that he'd overheard the hullabaloo the day Babe had learned she was pregnant because when all four girls had hurriedly convened in Babe's tiny room, he had eavesdropped. They were in his charge, after all. He needed to know what was going on.

What he'd learned that afternoon, however, had nearly killed him. Had Mazie known, she would have gladly helped by pulling the trigger, if his brother didn't do it first.

Without hesitation, Edward had power-walked to the Williamses' place.

"My niece is in trouble because of your boy." He'd accosted Duke Williams on the back porch. "Make it right, Williams. The boy must take responsibility. Babe says she loves him, that they love each other. I know they're just kids, but you must make this right." The coward had responded by skipping town. Then Babe had had the abortion and the fire had happened and then . . .

He swallowed the last piece of barbecue now and pushed away his plate. Duke Williams had been a cad. But the man was dead and Edward wouldn't rattle his grave. His son, Ray, was too good a guy—who knew how that had happened.

Besides, Edward had other fish to fry. Most notably, Carleen.

After all, he now knew what he had feared throughout the years, the real reason he'd kept tabs on Carleen, and why he hadn't invited her home until now, until the Angel of Death was knock-knocking on his palace door. He'd been right all along: Carleen knew the truth. And Edward must decide what to do about that, now that his days on this crappy-ass planet were finally coming to a close.

He took a big swallow of tea and wished it wasn't so bitter.

Ellie was happy, but she was glad to be home, though not for reasons she might have expected. The boys had white shirts and pants that would please Edward; even Heather had found a more demure shirt that should not provoke a scene with her mother.

More than those things, Ellie was infused with a sense that she'd traversed the Himalayas, reached the Arctic Circle, gone to outer space and back. She had driven without incident, without panic attack, to Tarrytown and back again with a car full of teenagers who'd been counting on her. Well, all right, she admitted as she pranced into her room with a celebratory cup of hot chocolate and the *Oliver Twist* that she'd plucked from the kitchen counter where Edward had dropped it, maybe the kids hadn't been counting on her. It wasn't as if three of the four of them couldn't have driven if she'd stopped breathing, or had felt like she'd stop breathing, somewhere along Route 448.

But none of that had happened, because Ellie had done it! The oddest part was, she thought, as she set her cup on the bureau, slipped out of her dress, stepped into her night-gown, and headed into the bathroom to wash up for the night, it hadn't been hard! Aside from those first moments of angst with her unpersonable nephew, Ellie had had a great time!

How long had it been since she'd been into town? There were so many changes to the landscape! There were strip malls and boutiques and a couple of parks. Even a once-questionable neighborhood had been transformed into a trendy arts district with galleries and coffee shops and outdoor cafés!

She had been so mesmerized by the scenery that she'd for-gotten she was driving, which, in her case, had proved a good thing.

Cleansing her face, Ellie decided to tell Edward tomorrow. They'd never openly discussed her *issues,* as Amanda appar-ently called them, any more than they'd talked about his rela-tionship with Henry or, now, the cancer, if there indeed was cancer. But Ellie was certain that Edward knew (after all these years, how could he not?) that she'd become, yes, a recluse. She hoped he would be thrilled for her driving success and not resent this new independence.

She finished in the bathroom and returned to the bureau for her bedtime hot chocolate. That's when Ellie noticed the pink ribbon on top of her jewelry box. And the small note next to it.

The handwriting was filled with feminine loops and circles: it was Carleen's. Ellie had always admired her sister's bold script, always had seen it as a mark of self-assurance.

Slowly, she picked up the note. She drew in a breath and read:

You said you have nothing of Mother's. This was her pink ribbon. She'd used it to tie up old letters. I found it that day in the attic. C.

Ellie picked up the ribbon. She studied the grosgrain as if it held answers in its tight pink weave, as if it held memories, as if it held Mother. Then she closed her fingers tightly around it. She didn't dare start to cry. She knew she should go to Carleen. Thank her for the ribbon. Thank her for the gesture. But the ribbon felt cool and good in her hand. And her thanks could wait until morning.

Chapter Thirty-five

Morning sunlight swathed the water of Lake Kasteel like a finely crocheted blanket, the kind Edward's mother had labored over even after her fingers had been knotted by arthritis and her vision had been blurred by years.

He wandered down the lawn toward the dock, puffing a cigar he'd found on the hall table. He'd bet that his pal, Goldsmith, had left it for him. David had been a friend for many years, so many that he'd known Edward's crocheting mother and his plumbing supply-selling brother, and, of course, his plumbing supply-selling-brother's wife. They'd known a lot about each other way back when: David had also known about Edward's one and only love.

Sitting on the dock, swinging his feet into the water, he remembered London and remembered her.

He'd called her Pia, after the quirky little actress who'd been so enchanting on Broadway in the sixties but who had taken a peculiar turn or two after that. Edward's Pia had had that same playful energy, that same impish beauty, and she'd stolen his heart the first day they'd met. It was not until several years later that they ran off to London, unhindered by media mongers (it was the early seventies, so gossip still moved slowly) or by her husband, whom they'd left back home in the States. Pia had joined him ostensibly for the shopping; he supposedly was scouting new acting talent. But they'd really gone for something else: alone time at the Chesterfield Mayfair, private, secluded, discreet.

For five days and four nights they existed on raspberry jam and clotted cream, sweet English scones, strong tea. And love.

She never saw the inside of Harrods, and he didn't attend a single play, didn't view a single actor or conduct even one interview.

So be it!

After the Mayfair, came sadness.

She'd returned to her husband, as they'd known she would.

He'd returned to Broadway, his heart in tiny pieces. He tried to put his feelings into writing, but it was pointless, so he finally gave up and began taking young men as lovers, chalking up his deep love for a woman as a bad joke played on him by Mother Nature. Edward Dalton had, after all, sensed he was gay—a *homosexual*—from the time he'd inadvertently walked into a backstage dressing room when he'd been around nine and spotted the male and female leads *going at it*, as they called it back then. He'd been more intrigued—excited, actually—by the man and his large, glistening parts than by the woman and her . . . well, he hadn't really noticed much about her.

He'd once revealed that experience to David Goldsmith, though they'd stopped talking about that sort of thing once David married Myrna and Edward was finally able to relax with his gayness. Gay men were, after all, much less complicated and so adoring. It helped salve the ache for his Pia.

He'd always thought David was the only one who'd known the truth, but now there was Carleen.

And now the time had come to tell his nieces what really had happened the day the house burned down and what had happened years before.

It was time they knew. Before he was no longer around to tell them.

He puffed another puff, watched the smoke snake to the heavens, and thought about the people he'd loved who were waiting for him up there.

"She's gone," Amanda said to Ellie as they both left their rooms and were headed downstairs. "I found this under my door."

Ellie opened the small square of paper. The loops of the handwriting were once again familiar.

I'm sorry about Earl, it read. *I'm sorry about everything.* It was signed with a *C*, the way Ellie's note had been.

"Yes," Ellie said, "she's gone."

They stood quietly for a moment, then Amanda said, "Thank God," and Ellie did not have the strength to disagree. Besides, it was nine twenty-seven, and there were other issues to address.

Brunch at nine thirty. Family picture at eleven.

If Henry had told them once, he'd told them a dozen times. But, as Ellie left Amanda and went down to the kitchen to make sure Martina was ready to serve, she looked out the window and spotted her uncle sitting down by the water. He wore a white shirt and white walking shorts. A white beret was perched atop his head. He was very still.

Ellie went to the back steps and hollered. When Edward didn't answer, she gathered the hem of her requisite white skirt, kicked off her white canvas pumps, and trotted down the sloping yard.

He was so dormant she thought he was dead.

"Edward!" she shrieked from half annoyance, half fear. "Get up! You're getting dirty!"

It was another heart-stopping second before he turned to her and blinked.

She sighed. "What are you doing? Stop scaring me."

His impish smile skated across his time-lined face. "I was conferring with my muses. Seeing into the great beyond."

She could have mentioned it was nine thirty and there would be plenty of time for great-beyond-seeing after the rest of the family left. But that was the old Ellie, and this one was different. This one was in charge of herself and no one else. Not anymore!

So she simply said, "Well, get up. Like it or not, this still is your party and it's time for brunch." New Ellie or not, she was not in the mood for his twisted humor or his antics. "Of course," she added, "it will be different than we expected. Carleen left during the night, and apparently, Babe's husband did, too."

"Carleen's gone?"

"Yes. I'm sorry."

Edward stood up and brushed the seat of his pants. "It's me who's sorry, Ellie. I'm sorry that my absence upset you and the girls. Especially you. I honestly thought you'd get along better without me as a referee. And I'm really, really sorry about that stupid stunt with the noose. I did it because I didn't like the looks of Wes McCall. I'd been hoping he'd get in trouble for it. Questioned by the cops, or something humiliating that would get back at him for that baloney with the helicopter. I had a feeling he was behind that."

She could have asked about the cancer. She could have asked why he'd refused treatment. But he looked smaller, standing there in his white, his blue eyes *a-twinkle*, as Henry sometimes called it. "You upset Henry, too, by disappearing."

He nodded. "I couldn't tell him. He hates having to keep a secret. But Henry will forgive me. It's you girls I'm worried about."

"We're fine," she said. "We're all fine." Then she put her arm around him and realized, for the first time, how much smaller he'd become, how his once muscular back and arms had thinned with age. "I even think Carleen is fine in her own way." Then Ellie guided Edward up the dock and toward the lawn and the house where they'd lived for far too long.

Two people were missing from the table—Carleen and Wes.

Ellie wondered if the family had had a meal *in toto* since the weekend had started and decided, no, they hadn't. Still, it was nice to see everyone seated, dressed in virginal white except Jonathan and Heather's boyfriend. Babe was there—Amanda whispered to Ellie that she must have packed her white dress in her suitcase because she'd seen her leave the house before bedtime.

Henry also wore white, though he hadn't been invited to join in the picture.

So far, no one had noticed that Ellie had disobeyed instructions by tying her hair in a small ponytail and wrapping it in the pink ribbon Carleen had said had belonged to their mother. She would tell the others after the photograph was taken. Until then, it would remain her special secret. Hell, if Edward Dalton could have secrets, so could she.

She passed the platter of strawberry blintzes and silently hoped no one spilled fruit on their white.

Edward did most of the talking, directing his chatter toward the children, as if he was determined not to acknowledge that two people were missing or to admit the fact that, without Carleen, most of the tension had abated.

Amanda, good Lord, was actually smiling. Not huge, OhMyGod-I-am-so-happy smiles, but little lifts at the corners of her coral-lipsticked mouth that hinted at lighthearted amusement. She even aimed one or two smiles at her husband, which Ellie thought was puzzling, under the back-waxing circumstances.

Babe, too, seemed to exude an aura of well-being that even Edward apparently noticed, because halfway through his wedge of melon he turned his attention to her. "You look especially lovely this morning, my dear." He did not include Ellie or Amanda in his comment, and Amanda did not seem to care.

"I spent the night at Ray's," Babe explained without flinching. "As you can see, my husband isn't here. It was my idea for him to leave. But when I was returning from Ray's early this morning, I saw a cab out on the street. Wes got in. Along with Carleen." She sipped a mimosa, then added, "I must admit, that was a surprise. I thought Carleen had changed."

"I doubt they ran off together," Ellie interjected. "I think Wes simply saw a chance to hitch a ride."

Then Babe said yes, she supposed that was possible.

Amanda asked Babe if she and Wes were divorcing and Babe said yes, without a doubt.

Heather asked if she and Shotgun should still look him up when they went to California. "He promised Shotgun he'd introduce him around," she added, ignoring the quick, surprised movement of her mother's eyebrows.

"Do what you want," Babe said. "But the man is self-centered, so I doubt he'll remember. If you really want to go, I can give you names, and I can make some calls on your behalf. But I am staying here." It was the first time those assembled had heard such a notion. "Well," she continued. "Not here, in this house. I'll be at Ray's. Until we decide what to do next."

Ellie passed the four-cheese frittata and thought it was ironic that Babe was vying to live at Lake Kasteel, while Ellie had finally garnered the courage to get out.

Then a cell phone rang. Edward's eyes narrowed, because he detested what he referred to as satanic technology, cell phones, computers, anything that required a charger or a wireless card.

"It's mine," Babe said, standing up and pulling the phone from her pocket. "Sorry. It must be Ray." Then she looked at the caller ID and scowled. "Oh, no. It isn't Ray. It's my agent."

* * *

"Will she really stay here?" Heather asked once Babe had excused herself and left the room to take her call. "I mean, geez, what about her career?"

"When was the last time she starred in a film?" Chandler interrupted with his nose in the air the way Amanda had once promoted but suddenly detested. "I bet no one wants her for those romantic comedy things anymore. She's too old."

Amanda rubbed the irritation that tingled in her neck. She supposed her children were waiting for her to agree. Instead she said, "Chandler, for starters, you need to show some respect. Babe is your aunt. She is your elder."

Chandler gawked at his mother as if she were a stranger.

"Her career," Amanda continued, "or what she does with her life is none of your business. We should all be supportive and hope that she'll be happy. And I, for one, will be delighted to have her back on the East Coast."

Everyone else's eyes had shifted from Chandler to her.

"Besides," she added, "haven't you heard that money is the root of all evil?"

The feedback from the group was pretty funny, especially since no one spoke.

Amanda turned to her husband. "Jonathan? Would you please tell everyone the rest?"

Jonathan cleared his throat and slid his arm on the back of Amanda's chair. "We've decided to make some pretty major changes. As a family. We've decided to sell the brownstone and move to Vermont."

Chandler dropped his fork onto his blintz.

Heather was mute.

Chase said, "Cool."

Jonathan put his elbows on the table and tented his fingers. "We're going to get back to basics. Burlington is a wonderful town. It's where I grew up; I still have friends there. I think the town can use a decent architect."

Chandler laughed. "For what? Designing cow barns?"

"Chandler," Amanda scolded.

When the boy snorted he sounded just like his mother, which did not please her. "Right," he said. "Well, it won't really involve me, anyway. I have one year left at Choate. Then I'll be off to Princeton or somewhere. It's not as if I'll actually ever have to live in Vermont."

"Oh, but you will," Jonathan said. "Neither you nor your brother will be going back to Choate. You'll attend public school. As for college, you'd better start thinking about scholarships and financial aid."

The boy turned as white as his shirt. "Financial aid? Like a loan?"

Amanda felt sorry for him. She had trained him so thoroughly to be such a boor. It would take time to untangle the knots.

"Yes, Chandler," Jonathan said firmly. "You'll be amazed, but it won't kill you. We'll talk about the details later, but for now, we wanted everyone to know. The truth is, we've run into some financial difficulties, but we'll work them out. Frankly, we think we'll enjoy our new life." He reached into Amanda's lap and took her hand. She'd never felt more proud of him. He wasn't perfect, but as it turned out, neither was she.

Chandler leaped to his feet. "You're nuts! Financial difficulties? What the hell does that mean? Uncle Edward will help us!" He flipped his focus to Edward. "You'll help us, won't you? Before my parents do something crazy?"

Edward looked at Amanda, who shook her head. "No, my boy," he said, "I don't think your family needs my money."

Amanda smiled and squeezed Jonathan's hand. Gratefully, he squeezed back.

Then Babe returned to the dining room, her face flushed, her blue eyes glazed with tears.

Chapter Thirty-six

"*Well*," *Babe said,* "*we're all over the* Post."

Edward pummeled his napkin onto his plate. "Crap. I was hoping this could wait until after the photo."

So much for a peaceful family gathering.

Ellie closed her eyes, wondering what he'd been up to now. "You were hoping *what* could wait?"

He shook his head. "It doesn't matter. Nothing matters now. Carleen is gone and you know about the *Post* and Ellie, you're wearing that godforsaken ribbon. Everything is ruined. Henry, call the photographer and cancel the goddamn shoot."

Before Ellie could respond, Babe interrupted with an uncharacteristic snap. "Uncle Edward? What do you know about this?"

Edward sighed a long, slow sigh, as if he were releasing decades of anguish, a gusher of guilt. "For starters, Ray's son, Kevin, buzzed me again this morning on the walkie-talkie he gave me in case I needed anything when I was sequestered on Squirrel Island. He's a nice boy. Considerate." He leveled his eyes on Chandler. "A young man you might take a lesson from." Then Edward looked back to the group. "Kevin delivers the *Post* as well as the *Times*. He told me that the newspaper has pictures from yesterday. Pictures of the party, of Wes, of all you girls. Babe, they even have one of you down at the boathouse with Ray."

"Apparently it made page six," Babe said, more quietly now. "I was kissing a man who isn't my husband. It's generated three film offers already. My agent is ecstatic."

"And you?" Amanda asked.

Babe shook her head. "I told her to turn them down. I am finished with Hollywood. I honestly am."

Silence sprinkled like salt around the table.

"Unfortunately, it's more than pictures," Edward continued. "They rehashed our story. They couldn't stand to leave it alone. To leave *us* alone."

That's when Edward's eyes teared up.

Chandler and Chase squirmed in their chairs.

Ellie got up and went to Edward. She touched one shoulder; Babe joined her and touched the other.

"It's all my fault," Babe said. "That damn husband of mine . . . I knew this might be trouble, but I stupidly thought it would be okay. . . ."

Edward shook his head, shook them away. "Oh, sit down, both of you. Wait until you hear the whole bloody story before anyone takes credit for being at fault."

So Ellie and Babe returned to their seats, and Edward wiped his tears, and they waited for Henry to fetch more tea from the kitchen so they could hear the things they didn't know.

"First of all," Edward said, once new tea was poured and all had leaned forward, enrapt. "I need you to be quiet and listen. There will be no comments, no conversation, and, God help us, no crying. Everyone here is a grown-up, except maybe Chase, but he's close enough to being a man to handle adult things, aren't you, boy?"

Chase nodded vigorously, as if he'd just been handed a pass from the kids' table at Thanksgiving.

"Good, Edward said. "Then it won't scare you when I say that I have cancer."

Babe expelled a tiny moan, then silence fell again.

Ellie touched her heart. *So it was true.* She didn't dare look at Amanda.

"Are you going to die?" Chase asked.

"Well, my boy, I thought that was what I wanted. But now I realize that would be pretty selfish. I have to admit I've enjoyed this weekend, even though I know I haven't been around for most of it. Anyway, seeing all of you has helped me rearrange my thoughts."

Chase was enthralled; he nodded but didn't speak.

"They tell me if I have chemo I'll probably be fine," Edward continued. "At first I thought no, I was ready to die. I've carried a bucketload of manure around all these years, and it would be a damn comfort to finally be done with it. But now—let's say I've decided that rather than die, I might as well get it out in the open."

They watched.

They listened.

"I'm going to sell this place," Edward said. "It's time to come out of the closet, so to speak. Henry and I will move into the city for a year or so, while I'm having treatment. I'll take a suite at the Waldorf and live like a senile old man. When that's done, I'll move to London. I want to live where I was once happiest. I want to be surrounded by wonderful theater and memories that give me so much pleasure. Maybe I'll stay there until I croak, who knows. But it's something I really want to do, and not one of you is going to stop me."

He pushed back in his chair and folded his arms. "The house and the land will bring in a bundle. I'm going to divide it equally between my nieces, between those here at the table and the one who's missing. Before you go off on Carleen, there's more to the story. Give me a minute, because this is the hard part."

"Wait," Ellie said. "I have a question. Will Henry go with you to London?"

Edward blinked. "Why, yes. If he can still stand me. If he doesn't try forcing me into marriage. I'm just not the marrying kind."

She shifted in her chair. "If he is with you, you won't disappear?" She looked at Henry. "Forgive me. But I've recently learned that there might have been a problem with your past lovers."

Henry looked at Edward. Edward laughed. "Where'd you hear that? From old Goldsmith?"

Then Henry laughed, too.

"I made that story up years ago," Edward said. "I wanted

to stop the gossip about the 'great love of my life.' Henry was willing to become the patsy—pardon the expression. I ended up with the life I needed, plus a great companion who didn't care if I walked away from Broadway or ever threw another damn party. I'd grown so tired of it all."

So. Henry wasn't an assassin.

Then Edward stopped laughing. He stood up, wandered to the window, and looked pensively toward the lake. "Which actually brings up the next part of my story. The great love in my life. That wasn't gossip. It was true. She was my great love. And she was your mother."

Outside, a gentle breeze stirred the fat peonies. A whisper of a hummingbird paused at the window, as if he were an interested spirit. Ellie didn't look at either of her sisters, but she'd bet they were thinking the same thing: Uncle Edward's great love had been their mother?

It seemed preposterous.

"It was futile, of course," Edward continued. "She was married to my brother. How could I tell my brother I was in love with his wife? But Mazie and I had a wonderful romance, short-lived though it was. I was with her in London. She is the only one—man or woman—who completely, totally, ever stole my heart. Henry understands this."

He sighed again, then finally turned around. He knew his tears were visible, but he made no comment about them.

"She had to return to Robert. She already had Ellie and Amanda-Belle and Carleen to look after. We never dreamed our love would give us you, Babe. We never dreamed we would create such a beautiful child."

That time, Amanda gasped.

"I had my asinine career; she had her family. She traded our life to be a good mother. We never slept together after London. To my knowledge, Mazie only slept with my brother." His voice cracked as if the thought still caused him pain. "I do know I never slept with another woman. I am a gay man. Mazie was my only exception. At the time we didn't understand why."

"So," Ellie asked, "you're Babe's biological father?"

"I said no talking!"

Ellie bolted up. "That's not fair! Are you or aren't you Babe's father?"

He lowered his head. "I believe I am, yes."

All eyes rolled toward Babe, who sat with her lovely mouth hanging open.

"I have come to believe that God wanted the world to have Babe," he continued. "And so he created the deep love between Mazie and me."

The silence at the table rested quietly now. Then Ellie said, "One more thing, Uncle Edward. Did Henry stop Mother from getting a divorce?"

Henry stood up. "I tried talking to her, because I, too, loved Edward, and I, too, wanted him. But it didn't matter. Mazie didn't want a divorce. She didn't want to tear her family apart."

Ellie looked at Edward, who didn't refute the remark. She sat back down.

"I know this must be confusing," Edward said, "but there's more to the story. And it involves Carleen."

Henry, too, returned to his chair, and Edward's audience waited.

"She knew," Edward said. "She found the love letters I had

written to your mother. Dear Mazie told me she was going to tie them in a pink ribbon and keep them forever; she could be such a silly, wistful girl." He uttered a small, sad sound, then returned to the head of the table and sat down. "The day Carleen went looking for her birth certificate, she found the letters in the attic. Ellie, I believe you're wearing the ribbon that tied them up."

Ellie's hand flew up to her ponytail. The others stared at her.

"Carleen didn't burn old school records in the fireplace," Edward said. "She burned the stack of letters. She was trying to save your mother from disgrace. She was trying to keep the family together. She never told anyone that those letters were what caused the fire and your parents' deaths."

Both Ellie and Amanda moved their hands to their mouths. Babe started to cry.

"Holy shit," Chase said, "this is unreal."

"No," Edward added, "it's very real. When Carleen wore the pink ribbon on the witness stand, I was suspicious. I was never sure, though, until I saw her today. When I asked, all she would say was that she knew everything. I guess she decided not to tell any of you. She's still protecting your mother—and all of you—after the lousy way we've treated her."

They puzzled over his words, then Amanda stood up. "Come on, girls," she said with sober conviction. "We have to find our sister. Before she gets away."

She was in Port Authority, buying a bagel with a schmear at Einstein's.

"We know what happened," Amanda said. "We know about Mother and Uncle Edward."

The four women moved quietly through the thin Sunday crowd, up to a bookstore, where they sat—three women in virginal white, the other one, Carleen.

By the time they were finished talking, they all were crying, especially Babe.

"Does this mean I'm not really your sister?" Babe asked. "I mean, I'm really your half sister. What does that mean?"

Before they could tell her to stop being a goof, a young woman approached with a long-lensed Nikon. "Babe!" she shouted. "Can you turn this way?"

Amanda bolted up and blocked the camera with her hand. The others fled as if they'd shoplifted a pile of Nora Roberts's latest books. Safely outside on the street, they laughed and laughed like mischievous conspirators.

As they headed for the parking garage where they'd left Edward's clunky Range Rover, Ellie said, "Hey, remember that summer when Mrs. McGuire arrived without a boyfriend and drank too much champagne and peed in the hydrangeas?" And they laughed again because at the time they'd just left their hiding place in the hydrangeas and had averted near disaster.

Then Amanda remembered a funny tale, then Carleen did, then Babe, and they reached the garage still chattering and laughing, a family, once again.

Epilogue

Ellie found a white dress in her wardrobe that suited Carleen. Then the photograph was taken and—click, click—they were gone.

Babe went to Ray's with true love in her heart, corny as it sounded. She said it was the one role she'd been meant to play. She also said she planned to look into finding a surrogate; she and Ray had decided to try and have a baby together, after all.

Amanda headed back to the city with her family, knowing she'd soon have the money to pay off her debtors, but feeling more enthusiastic about the new life that lay ahead. One son was excited, the other one was grumbling. Her daughter seemed happy just to tuck her wild red hair under a helmet and wrap her arms around her boyfriend's waist as they boarded his motorcycle. Amanda said that before they left for Vermont, she would look up Martina and offer a real apology.

Carleen rode with Amanda and Jonathan back to Port Authority, where she would catch a bus to Belchertown. She promised to bring her husband and girls to the family party they would hold before final sale of *Kamp Kasteel*.

Ellie briefly thought she could use her share of the proceeds as a down payment, then get a mortgage, buy the house from Edward, and renovate it as a bed-and-breakfast. The people who owned the castle at the far end of the lake had done that, and business apparently was booming. Then she realized she truly was done being a recluse. She would cruise Museum Mile in the morning and see if she could find a real job, with real people, in the real world.

Before going to bed that Sunday night, she took out the brass box that held her travel dreams—and the things that had belonged to her mother. Slowly, Ellie removed the pink ribbon from her hair and placed it inside.

"That's lovely," Edward said from where he stood in the doorway. She hadn't heard him approach; it was so rare that he ventured upstairs.

"They were Mother's things. She left them here in a drawer."

He stepped closer, looked into the box. "Deodorant? You saved her deodorant?" He smiled. "Oh, my, we've all been in pain for a long, long time." Then he poked around in the box and noticed the brochures. "Egypt?" he asked. "Do you still want to go?"

"Oh, I don't know, Edward. It was only a dream."

"I never dreamed I'd be having chemo, but look at me now."

"That doesn't make sense."

"Nor does it make sense for you to put off your dreams any longer."

She picked up a brochure, studied the pictures on the cover, the golden image of King Tut, the Valley of the Kings, the desert in mystic repose. "Well," she said. "Well." Then she noticed the travel agency's address and wondered if they were still in business.

Edward kissed the top of her head and left the room. He tottered back toward the stairs and toward his own memories. He had, after all, a few things of his own—pictures from London, a lock of Mazie's hair, the fork she'd used to nibble on her favorite English scones. But he would keep these for himself. He would put a note with them and ask the girls' forgiveness. But when he was gone—in a year or twenty-five—they would find his meager treasures and know how very deeply their mother had been loved.

A+
AUTHOR
INSIGHTS,
EXTRAS &
MORE...

FROM

**ABBY
DRAKE**

AND

AVON A

On Writing *The Secrets Sisters Keep*

I've heard it said that inspiration often comes at the oddest times in the oddest ways. For me, that's true. I've had that clichéd lightbulb go off over my head at a party, in the supermarket, in the middle of the night–even once while driving down the MassPike. Such situations, of course, are not always convenient for making notes.

The idea, however, for *The Secrets Sisters Keep* came from a phone call. Or rather, from the lack of a phone call.

Do you have one of *those* friends who never answers the phone? Someone who is always busy doing something more productive or entertaining? You *know* she's home, or at least in cell phone range. So what's she doing that's more important?

Watching *Dancing with the Stars*?

Updating her Facebook page?

Changing the baby's diaper? (Well, okay, that one is acceptable.)

Or . . . maybe *you're* the one who leaves the phone jangling in dead air.

The truth is, I think, many of us don't pick up today. Caller ID is just so darned handy.

"It's Betty Ann! Well, I can call her later."

Or . . ." Oh, it's Bob. He'll want to know about Saturday, and I haven't decided yet."

Or . . ." It's Sally. Ugh. Not *her* again."

But I digress.

I have a friend—let's call him *Edward*—who is often otherwise occupied when you call. I have no idea what he is doing. (Actually I have a few ideas, but I won't get into them now.) He lives out west, far from me, and I don't see him very often.

One day, I returned a call from Edward that I had missed. (I suspect a day will come when no one answers a telephone anymore. Oh, wait. I think they call that e-mailing. Or texting.) Anyway, Edward didn't pick up. I left a message.

Three days later, he hadn't called me back. Where the heck was he? Herding cattle across Wyoming? Rappelling in the Rocky Mountains? Perhaps he'd been abducted by alien space beings somewhere outside of Reno.

I called again. He didn't answer. He did not return the call.

You get the picture. No matter. I was working on my last book, *Perfect Little Ladies*, so I really was too busy to talk to him, anyway.

I went back to my keyboard.

But then, the strangest thing happened. A few words floated into my mind that had nothing to do with Elinor, Alice, Poppy, and CJ (the ladies from the aforementioned *PLL*).

Uncle Edward had wandered off.

The sentence was crystal clear. I tried and tried but couldn't shake it. Quite simply, it beckoned.

That's when I knew the next book was knocking on my brain looking for attention.

Uncle Edward had wandered off.

I wrote it on a Post-it. I stuck it to my bookcase. I went back to *PLL*.

A day, a week, who knows how much later, I stared at the Post-it. I guess because *PLL* takes place in the fictitious town of Mount Kasteel, New York, I thought it would be fun to set Edward's book there, too. After all, I'd been living there in my mind for several months by then and knew the area quite well.

There was a lake. *Lake* Kasteel. As with the town, it had been named by the original Dutch settlers because of the castle someone had built on the south side of the water. In my mind, of course.

Always having been a sucker for Fitzgerald's *The Great Gatsby*, I suddenly envisioned a Gatsbyish house not on Long Island's North Shore but on my imagined lake, where music and laughter—party sounds—drifted across the water to curious onlookers who were not unlike Nick Carraway. Like Nick, I've often wondered what happens in the grand homes where privileged folks live. Surely those people have delicious lives, fabulous friends, and quirky, yet lovable, families.

Of course, there must be at least one eccentric in the bunch. There must be one Uncle Edward . . . who now has wandered off.

So that's how *The Secrets Sisters Keep* began: an unanswered phone call. A fantasy lake. And a little Gatsby inspiration.

As for Edward . . . well, he finally called. You would not believe what he'd been doing.

But wait—there goes my cell. Oh. It's just the dentist's office. I'll get back to them later.

Reading Group Questions

1. Which of Edward Dalton's nieces would you like to have for your sister?

2. Which of the sisters' lives would you most like to have . . . knowing you could make it better?

3. Why do you think Carleen really stayed away from her sisters for so long? Why did Babe?

4. Have you ever "forgotten" to show a trinket, a bauble—something decadent you purchased—to your husband? If you showed him, were you honest about the price?

5. Like Ellie, have you ever tucked a dream away in a small box in a closet?

6. If you were Edward, would you have wandered off?

7. Name one secret you never told your sister, brother, mother, or father. Surely there is at least *one*!

James A. Langone

A graduate of Skidmore College in Saratoga Springs, New York, **ABBY DRAKE** is a Mayflower descendant (with papers to prove it!). She has one sister, Joan Elizabeth, with whom she loved keeping secrets from the very proper, guarded world in which they grew up. She lives in Amherst, Massachusetts, but enjoys wandering off from time to time. To learn a few of the secrets she shared with her sister—and for more about Abby Drake—visit her Web site www.abbydrake.com.

Abby Drake

ALSO BY **ABBY DRAKE**

GOOD LITTLE WIVES

ISBN 978-0-06-123221-3 (paperback)

Meet the women of New Falls, New York: four former trophy wives sliding into middle age, worrying about their weight, wealth, and whether they're about to be replaced. When the banker husband of one of the wives runs off with a younger, sexier hairdresser, he winds up dead— with his ex-wife standing over him with the smoking gun.

PERFECT LITTLE LADIES
A Novel

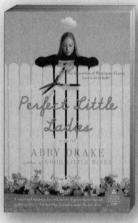

ISBN 978-0-06-164836-6 (paperback)

With her perfect husband, gorgeous grown-up children, and a house with more rooms than she can count, Elinor has it all—including her own personal blackmailer who's ready to expose her affair with a married politician. When Elinor and friends set out to track down the extortionist, none of them expect other secrets to be revealed.

THE SECRETS SISTERS KEEP
A Novel

ISBN 978-0-06-187832-9 (paperback)

Amanda, Babe, and Ellie attend their Uncle Edward's seventy-fifth birthday to celebrate—and to find out exactly who is included in the rich old man's will. When Edward disappears, however, the sisters have far more to worry about than just money. It may not be the first time he's gone missing, but they all fear it might be the last.

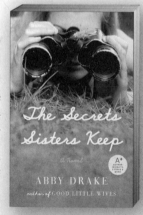